They dropped like a stone through the night, plummeting back to earth.

Tumbling end over end, Kelley felt Sonny's arms and legs twisting about her and she realized that Sonny—mortal, human Sonny—was trying to turn them around in the air so that when they hit the ground, he would bear the brunt of the impact.

"You dumb-ass," she muttered through clenched teeth. "You can't break my fall."

Her shoulder blades burned with sudden, dark fire, and Kelley's cry of triumph ripped through the sky.

"Not when I can fly!"

The ground beneath them—mere inches away—blazed with sudden purple fire as Kelley's wings unfurled, delicate as gossamer, yet strong enough to catch at the air and sweep her and Sonny back up into the sky.

Kelley kissed him quickly before he had time to say anything. She felt his arms tighten around her as they spiraled up, borne aloft on wings that were dark as the night, bright as a new star.

LESLEY LIVINGSTON

Wondrous
Strange

a novel

HARPER TEEN
An Imprint of HarperCollinsPublishers

For my Dad

HarperTeen is an imprint of HarperCollins Publishers.

Wondrous Strange
Copyright © 2009 by Lesley Livingston
www.harperteen.com

Library of Congress Cataloging-in-Publication Data
Library of Congress Cataloging-in-Publication Data
Livingston, Lesley.
Wondrous strange : a novel / by Lesley Livingston. — 1st ed.
    p.   cm.
    Summary: When seventeen-year-old actress Kelley Winslow meets
Sonny Flannery, she discovers he is a changeling and guardian of the gate
between the faerie Otherworld and the mortal realm. She also learns that
her mother had otherworldly powers that she has passed on to Kelley.
    ISBN 978-0-06-157539-6
    [1. Fairies—Juvenile fiction. 2. Actresses—Juvenile fiction.
3. Fairies—Fiction. 4. Actresses—Fiction. 5. Fantasy.] I. Title.
PZ7.L7613 Won 2009   2009275886
[Fic]—dc22   CIP
                                                    AC

Typography by Andrea Vandergrift
09 10 11 12 13   CG/RRDH   10 9 8 7 6 5 4 3 2 1
❖
First paperback edition, 2009

Rehearsals @ Avalon Grande on 52nd
Mon-Thurs- 10:00 AM
Sat- 11:00 AM

Kelley's Script— Please Return
(This means YOU, Bob!)

UNDERSTUDY

A MIDSUMMER NIGHT'S DREAM ~ BY WILLIAM SHAKESPEARE
~DRAMATIS PERSONAE~

THE FAIRIES

OBERON- King of Fairies: Oberon quarrels with his Queen, Titania, over the matter of a changeling child in her care, whom the King wishes to make his page and servant.

TITANIA- Queen of Fairies; she is the guardian of a mortal child—a changeling—whom she refuses to surrender to Oberon. This argument between the two fairy monarchs has caused much upheaval in the natural world, causing the seasons to alter.

PUCK- Sometimes called **Robin Goodfellow**; this mischievous fairy is Oberon's chief henchman. Puck turns Bottom, a rough-mannered workman of Athens, into a ass-headed monstrosity and—at Oberon's malicious bidding—slips Titania a love potion, which causes the Queen to fall in love with the temporarily freakish Bottom.

too much glitter cheek w/ Mindi

Puck is also responsible for creating chaos amongst the Athenian lovers when he accidentally administers the same love potion to the wrong suitor.

also **PEASEBLOSSOM, COBWEB, MOTH, MUSTARDSEED,** and others, *fairy attendants on* Queen Titania.

shorten skirt

THE ATHENIANS

THESEUS- Duke of Athens: betrothed to the mighty Amazon Queen, Hippolyta.
HIPPOLYTA- Queen of the Amazons: betrothed to the mighty war duke, Theseus.
LYSANDER- beloved of Hermia.
HERMIA- Beloved of Lysander.
HELENA- in love with Demetrius.
DEMETRIUS- in love with Hermia: but later falls in love with Helena (thanks to Puck's meddling).
EGEUS- father of Hermia: wants to force Hermia to wed Demetrius.
PHILOSTRATE- Master of the Revels.

find sandals

THE "RUDE" MECHANICALS

rough craftsmen of Athens,
in the forest rehearsing the play **Pyramus and Thisbe** *to present to*
Theseus and Hippolyta at their Wedding Revels.

Fix ear on Ass Head

NICK BOTTOM- performing the role of Pyramus in 'Pyramus and Thisbe': Bottom is a blithely egotistical fellow, who simply has no idea that his head has been transformed into that of an ass!

also **PETER QUINCE, FRANCIS FLUTE, ROBIN STARVELING, TOM SNOUT, SNUG,** craftsmen all, who find themselves terrorized in the forest by prankster fairies and an ass-headed monster!

Opening Night Nov 1st!!

"Lord, what fools these mortals be!"

SAMHAIN

October 31

Up and down, up and down,
I will lead them up and down.
I am feared in field and town.
Goblin, lead them up and down.

Puck's tortured words rang in Kelley's ears as she lifted her head, struggling against the darkness that threatened to descend upon her. She stared in horror as the Central Park Carousel shuddered in the cloud-shattered moonlight. Though no one was there to operate the machinery, the platform lurched into motion and the painted horses began to bob up and down. The gilt and jeweled trappings of saddles and bridles glimmered, winking at Kelley like hundreds of wicked, malevolent eyes.

In the sky above the merry-go-round, amid clouds bruised purple and black by the violent winds, a figure appeared, hovering in the air astride a fiery roan horse. Kelley felt the hot sting of tears on her cheeks as she looked up and met the eyes of the Rider. He stared down at her—cold, pitiless, with no hint of recognition in his beautiful, haunted face.

Beneath him, driven to madness by the presence of the Rider on his back, the Roan Horse screamed defiance. Bucking and rearing, it lashed out with hooves of flame.

The carousel began to turn.

In the distance, Kelley heard the sound of the hunting hounds.

The Rider drew his sword, the blade flaring like a firebrand. Kelley's breath strangled in her throat as the carousel began to spin faster and faster.

Smoky, glittering figures coalesced out of the air to ride the painted mounts. Bloodthirsty and red-eyed, brandishing swords of flame, their joy was a terrible thing to behold. Beneath them the wooden horses transformed, snorting furiously and stamping hooves on the spinning carousel platform.

Then they burst forth. Legs churning, they galloped madly into the night, climbing an unseen path into the heart of the roiling storm.

After centuries spent imprisoned, locked in the chains of uneasy, enchanted sleep, the Wild Hunt was awake.

It was Samhain. Tonight they would ride out. Tonight

they would kill. Nothing in the world could stop the Faerie war band—not with the Rider and the Roan Horse at their head. . . .

I am feared in field and town.
Goblin, lead them up and down.

I

"What do you mean, 'promoted'?" Kelley Winslow felt her pulse quicken.

It was the fifth week of rehearsals for the Avalon Grande's production of Shakespeare's *A Midsummer Night's Dream.* Never mind that the Avalon Players—a third-tier repertory company so far off Broadway it might as well have been in Hoboken—had only hired Kelley as an understudy, which really meant glorified stagehand. It was her first real job as an actress after a disastrous stint in theater school, and, at only seventeen, Kelley had been grateful for the résumé builder. But today, three steps into the theater,

Mindi the stage manager had waylaid her.

Kelley was carrying a box of props she'd gone to fetch from the company van parked outside, and she had a pair of fairy wings strapped to her shoulders—the only way she could carry them without crushing the wire frames. "Mindi?" she asked again. "What do you mean?"

"I mean, don't bother taking off the wings, kid." Mindi took the box of props from her hands. "Our darling Diva deWinter just busted her ankle. She is out of commission, and that means you, little understudy, will be stepping into the lead role of Titania, the fairy queen, for the run of this show."

Kelley was speechless. She'd dreamed of this—although however many times she'd sat through rehearsals, watching Barbara deWinter overact and undercharm her way through her scenes, she'd never wished anything *bad* upon her. But Kelley guiltily felt a rising sense of glee. *This is it. This is my big break!*

"Hey!" Mindi gave her a friendly shove. "Enough daydreaming. We open in ten days and Quentin is—well, to put it mildly, our esteemed director is now freaking out. So I suggest you go slip into a rehearsal skirt and haul your understudy butt onstage so that the Mighty Q can run you through your scenes. Good luck."

My scenes. My scenes . . .

Thoughts in a whirl, Kelley almost ran down the actor playing Puck as he swung himself gracefully off the set scaffolding, singing "Am I blue?" Funny, because he was actually green, a pale iridescent shade head to toe—hair, skin, eyes—right down to his leafy tunic. Kelley had been told by one of the other actors that his name was Bob but that he was something of an extreme Method actor and had demanded he be referred to only by his character name while in costume and makeup—on threat of quitting the production otherwise.

Lunatic actors.

Between him and the equally demanding and very English director Quentin St. John Smyth, Kelley was beginning to think she'd fallen in with a real asylumful at the Avalon Grande. She threw open the doors to the wardrobe storage and fumbled with the rack of rehearsal skirts, slipping one over her jeans and buttoning it as best she could with trembling fingers. "'Fairies, skip hence,'" she muttered aloud. "No— that's wrong. . . ."

Oh, God—what's my first line? Kelley thought frantically.

"'These are the forgeries of jealousy.' Aw, crap!" She was blanking. "That's not even the right *speech*!" Her heart pounded in her chest, and she leaned her head on the door frame.

This is what you've wanted your whole life, she told herself sternly. All those years of putting on one-woman shows for the household pets, and all the months of begging Aunt Emma to let her move to Manhattan to try to make a go of it. *This is it. Get out there and show them what you've got!*

6

Feeling marginally more confident, Kelley took a deep breath and dashed down the hallway and through the backstage area—at the exact moment that "Puck" launched a handful of glitter into the air. Kelley gasped, startled, as the cloud of sparkles settled on her hair, face, and shoulders.

"Oh—thanks a lot, *Bob*," Kelley muttered, brushing at the shimmering dust as the eccentric actor laughed wickedly and darted toward the stage-left wings. It was futile—she was coated in glitter. "That's just super. I look like a disco ball." At least it matched her vintage My Little Pony Princess glitter T-shirt.

"Is she coming sometime *today*?" Kelley heard Quentin's irate tones echo through the theater and felt her nervousness come flooding back as she picked up her skirt and ran toward the stage.

Once there, Kelley discovered that under the lights the fairy dust was shiny to the point of blinding. Distracted, she found herself tripping over both the hem of her skirt and her lines. Her heart began to flutter in her chest as she heard the exaggerated groans and sighs of frustration coming from the darkened rows of seats, where the director sat watching her stumble around like an idiot.

After forty-five minutes they'd progressed only a little over a page into Titania's first appearance. Kelley had already managed to butcher half her lines, trip over a bench, and step on Oberon's foot. When she almost toppled off the stage and into the orchestra pit, Quentin called a merciful halt to the proceedings.

"Kelley. Your name is Kelley, isn't it?" He didn't wait for her confirmation. "Yes. Well. Tell me . . . that bit just now . . . was that from Dante's *Inferno*?"

"Uh . . . no," Kelley stammered. Her face felt hot.

"Really?"

I'm in for it.

"Are you *sure*?" he continued. "Because it most *certainly* wasn't from *this* play. And it *bloody* well sounded like *hell*."

"I—"

"You know . . . as—well, let's *face* it, shall we?—as *completely* incompetent as our former diva may have been in this part"—Quentin sauntered up onto the stage, where he circled Kelley like a shark—"she did *still* have one *tiny* advantage over *you*, luv."

"She . . . she did?"

"Of *course* she did. She *knew* the *bloody* lines!"

The entire cast took a step back to avoid the leading edge of Quentin's immediate blast radius.

"And, while I *obviously* appreciate *all* the effort you've put into making yourself *sparkly* . . ." Kelley shot a glance at Bob, who'd found something particularly fascinating to look at under one of his fingernails. Probably a sparkle. "What kind of *crap*-arse UN-DER-STUDY *doesn't* know the *bloody* LINES?"

"But I do know them!" she protested. "I mean, I did. A second ago. Backstage . . . "

The Mighty Q's sneer grew. "Well, that's *marvelous*. Perhaps we'll just invite the audience into your *dressing* room in *twos* and *threes*, and you can deliver your performance from *there*."

"I . . . " *Oh, God*, Kelley thought, *it's just like theater school all over again.* The blood roared in her ears, and she thought for a moment that she was going to faint. Or maybe barf. Right there in front of the whole cast. Her cheeks burned with embarrassment.

"*Assuming* your delightful predecessor doesn't miraculously heal, then *you* have *less* than two weeks to *learn* the part. Less than *two* weeks. *This* production opens on the *first* of November come *hell* or *high water*. At *this* point, *I'm* betting on *both*." He turned sharply on his heel and waved one hand in dismissal. "Right. We're broken for lunch, minions. I can't see the point of belaboring this any further. Be back here at two for ensemble work. *You*"—he aimed a pointed glare at Kelley—"look at your damned script."

The theater cleared out quickly. No one seemed to want to hang around much after that, and certainly not around her. Kelley stumbled blindly to the courtyard and collapsed onto the steps.

"Kelley?"

She turned at the sound of her name, spoken by Gentleman Jack Savage, the actor playing the fairy king, Oberon, in the show. He was a veteran of the boards—in his early fifties, with a solid presence and a voice that could melt ice

9

or peel paint, depending on how he chose to employ it.

"Hi, Jack," she said, wiping her eyes in embarrassment.

"Gadzooks, my dear," he chided her gently. "I know the Mighty Q howls like a banshee, but really, you mustn't let the old fart get to you." He sat down beside her on the steps and unscrewed the top of his battered old thermos, pouring himself a cup of coffee. The scent of dark-roast Colombian was comforting.

Kelley gave him a watery smile. "Jack . . . you know that people—*most* people—don't actually use the word *gadzooks* in everyday conversation anymore, right?"

"I'm on a one-man crusade to bring it back into fashion. Along with *odds my bodkins*, *'sblood*, and, let us not forget, *yoicks*." He took a sip of his coffee and patted her knee with fatherly affection. "Everyone has to have a purpose in life, my dear. That is mine—quixotic as it may be."

"What if *I* don't?" Kelley stared fiercely at her sneakers, willing away the prick of tears from behind her eyes. She felt—she *knew*—she'd just blown her big chance. "Have a purpose, I mean? A destiny."

"Impossible."

"Why do you say that?" She looked up at him, desperate for his honest opinion.

Jack raised an elegant gray eyebrow. "I'm the king of Fairyland, my dear," he said, and winked at her. "All of that pixie dust has given me extremely potent powers of observation."

"Jack, I'm not kidding."

"Neither am I." Jack held her gaze, his face serious. "Kelley . . . you are seventeen. You are on your own in New York City. And you are chasing a dream that most reasonable people consider either unattainable or a damned-fool waste of time. *Believe* me, I know. All of which tells me that you are either fearless or just a little bit foolish. I suspect both. I also suspect that you are one of those precious few with enough natural talent to make a go of it."

Kelley scoffed in disbelief. "You *saw* what I just did in there, right?"

"And heard, yes." Jack chuckled. "You mangled just over fifty percent of your lines. I don't care what Quentin says, for a first timer that's not half bad. Well—it *was* half bad. But that's the point. It was also half *good*."

"You . . . really think so?" Kelley asked, trying to gauge whether Jack was being sincere.

"I really do." Jack shrugged and drained his coffee. "You've got a voice. You've got a presence. More importantly, you have the heart and the passion and the sheer mule-headed stubbornness that could very well take you to places most of us scarcely dare to imagine." He screwed the cup-lid back onto his thermos. "Now, call that destiny, call it purpose—whatever 'it' is, my dear girl, you have it in good supply."

Kelley was not entirely convinced, but she smiled, grateful for the kindness. "Has anyone ever told you that you've got a silver tongue, Jack?"

"Many times. Unfortunately, never the reviewers."

"Thank you."

"No need for that, my dear." Standing, Jack tipped an imaginary hat to her as he went back inside the theater.

The second half of rehearsal also ended early, but this time it wasn't Kelley's fault—it would have been hard to screw up her lines when she'd been ordered to rehearse script in hand. Although it was humiliating for Kelley to still be "on book" so close to opening, the company whipped through the large ensemble scenes at a pace and with a level of competency that even Quentin could only manage a few halfhearted mutters over.

After a couple of hours he released most of the cast, holding back the two girls playing Hermia and Helena so he could work on their monologues—because, he remarked pointedly and well within Kelley's earshot, "they already know their lines."

Lucky them, Kelley thought, as she changed back into her street clothes. She gathered up her stuff and hotfooted it out of there before the Mighty Q could change his mind.

Outside the day was glorious, the October sky deep blue and the air mild. The sun was shining brightly, and it reminded Kelley of fall days at home in the Catskills. She felt a wave of sudden homesickness.

Why am I doing this? she wondered.

In her six months in New York, Kelley had never once

questioned her life choices: graduating high school early, dropping out of theater training to move to the city—leaving behind what few friends she'd had, not to mention her aunt, who'd raised her single-handedly since her parents' death twelve years earlier. Kelley was all Emma had and they adored each other but, instead of continuing on with her studies at a nearby state university, visiting Emma on weekends, here she was. Living in the toughest city in America, chasing a selfish dream that—*Let's face it*, she told herself morosely—apparently, she really wasn't any good at. No matter what Jack said.

She scuffed her feet as she wandered up Eighth Avenue, reluctant to make her way uptown to the fourth-floor walk-up that she now called home. Except that home was something else. It was sky and grass and the trees of the woods outside her old window, and peace.

Kelley came to a stop at the corner of Fifty-fifth Street. Central Park was only a few blocks away. There would be trees and grass, and benches where she could sit quietly, looking over her lines away from the city crowds. Turning right to veer east, she broke into a jog.

II

Sonny Flannery opened the French doors and stepped out onto the stone terrace of his penthouse apartment. With cat-footed lightness, he leaped up to perch on the smooth, wide granite of the railing. Heedless of the nineteen-story drop to the pavement far below, he crouched there like a gargoyle, elbows resting on knees and his long, slender hands hanging in front of him, watching as the afternoon shadows of New York's countless high-rises began to grow long over Central Park.

It was too early for him to be so keyed up—the Gate wouldn't open for another several hours. Still . . . even the thought of what was to come made the adrenaline thrum through Sonny's veins like siren song. He'd heard actual siren song once, and it had not been a pretty thing. Beguiling, yes. Pretty . . . no. Beneath the heartbreakingly lovely surface of the Sirens' melodies, all Sonny had heard were discordant notes of hunger and rage. Need. Madness and nightmares. Compulsion.

The same kind of compulsion that had driven him down into the park every night for almost a year in preparation for what was to come when the Samhain Gate opened and all that would stand between the Otherworld and the mortal realm were thirteen Janus Guards. Including Sonny Flannery, the newest member of that elite rank.

This was his first year of service as a Janus and would be his first time guarding the Gate. He could hardly wait.

The October breeze was brisk that high up but, even shirtless and barefoot, wearing only a pair of jeans, Sonny was unaffected by the chill. Still, when the temperature plummeted in the apartment at his back, he couldn't help but notice.

"My lord," Sonny called, not turning to look. "Welcome."

"Sonny." The greeting floated out to him.

From his perch on the balustrade, Sonny turned to see Auberon, king of the Unseelie Court of Faerie, lounging against the door frame. A mane of charcoal-gray hair, shot through with silver, flowed down his back, and a mantle stitched from the furs of timber wolves fell from his shoulders in rich platinum layers.

"Your door," Auberon said. His voice was low and melodious, with hints of the slow crack and boom of a frozen lake breaking open on a midwinter night. "It was unlocked."

"I know. Most unwanted visitors never make it past the front-desk security in this place. Either that, or they're not the kind who come up in the elevator, so I don't usually bother." Sonny knew perfectly well that Auberon had not come over the threshold. The Winter King, Lord of the Unseelie, had no need of such trivial things as doors. He was simply being polite—in his own inimitable way.

The Faerie king's pale lips twitched. "Unwanted visitors?"

"Not you, lord. Of course." Sonny grinned and jumped down onto the flagstones. His bare feet made no noise as he crossed the terrace.

"Of course not."

"I only meant that I'll have enough doors to worry about keeping locked soon enough."

"Aye. You will." Auberon's cold eyes glittered.

"And, at any rate, this is *your* apartment." Sonny waved a hand at the expanse of polished floors and sleek furnishings. "I only live here."

It was true. Auberon's decrees had forbade the Faerie from having any interaction with the mortal realm, and his enchantments had made it virtually impossible to do so. But as king of Winter, the most powerful of the Four Courts of Faerie, Auberon could come and go as he wished. He'd done so through the years, and in the course of dealing with humans, Auberon had—among other things—amassed an impressive portfolio of priceless real estate, including Sonny's corner penthouse apartment on Central Park West. Lavish couldn't even begin to describe the young Janus's accommodations to most people; New Yorkers would sell body parts to get their hands on a place like it. But Sonny had grown up in the unimaginable splendor of Auberon's palaces.

Sonny was a changeling—a human, stolen as a child from the mortal realm by godlike beings who did not often produce children of their own. Growing to adulthood over the course of a century or more rather than years (for time in the Otherworld moved differently than in the mortal realm), the changelings served as surrogate offspring for the Faerie, walking in the shining halls of bright palaces, resting and feasting in canopied bowers. Mortals made almost immortal, they lived in that timeless, dreaming place, doted on or ignored by their capricious masters, sometimes treasured, sometimes tormented. But always in the thrall of the Faerie.

"I trust you find these accommodations adequate?" The king's voice shook Sonny from his reverie.

"It's not home, if that's what you're asking."

"It was not."

"Of course, lord." Sonny ducked his head, remembering himself. And who it was he spoke to. "The apartment is fine. Thank you."

"How fortunate that your predecessor vacated in time for your tenure."

"He had his throat ripped out by a glaistig last year."

"Aye." The king's mouth quirked in a mirthless grin. "But the timing was fortuitous."

Sonny cast about for a change of subject. "May I offer you a refreshment?"

"The occasion warrants that *I* do the offering." As Auberon drifted farther into the room, a gathering chill rolled through the air in his wake. He held up a dark bottle sealed with a silver stopper, and Sonny's mouth watered in instant, automatic response. Faerie wine. Mortal libations weren't even a shadowy taste of the perfection that was contained in that bottle. The king seemed amused by the expression on Sonny's face. "We must celebrate your first year as a Janus Guard."

"That's very kind, lord. But I haven't yet proven myself."

"If I had any doubts that you would, boy, I wouldn't be here. Of course . . . neither would you."

Sonny wasn't sure if the Faerie king meant that in a more or less ominous way. He watched as Auberon plucked two wine goblets from the hanging rack in the kitchen. With a deft twist of the silver bottle top, he poured out the sparkling liquid in generous measure.

"I have no qualms." Auberon shrugged elegantly, handing

a glass to Sonny. "You are the finest Janus I have ever chosen. Better even than Maddox, or the Fennrys Wolf."

Sonny fought against the urge to defend his friend Maddox, knowing it would be unwise to disagree with the king's praise.

"Joy to you," the king saluted. "And good hunting."

Sonny raised his own glass in return and took a sip, suppressing a groan of pleasure at the taste. The Faerie wine sparkled so brightly it seemed made of tiny stars.

"Titania sends her regards."

The delight Sonny took in the wine evaporated, and he shivered involuntarily at the thought of the queen of the Seelie Court. *Titania.* All the elemental charm and beauty of a summer thunderstorm . . . and just as dangerous.

"She wishes you luck."

I'll wager she didn't specify whether it was good luck or bad, Sonny thought. He was careful to keep the thought quiet, though. "Does that mean that you and the Summer Queen are on cordial terms, then, my lord?"

"For the moment."

Of course, in the Otherworld—the Faerie realm— time had no meaning. And so that "moment" could last for years . . . or vanish in an instant. At least, thought Sonny, if Auberon and Titania were on civil terms, it meant there would be no interference from her for the duration of the coming Nine–Night, and that was a relief—Summer and Winter were so rarely in accord. Sonny wondered fleetingly about the other two—the so-called shadow courts—with their unpredictable monarchs: Queen Mabh, capricious ruler of the malevolent Autumn Court; and Gwyn ap Nudd, the strange and secretive Lord of the Spring. Alliances among the monarchs were treacherous, constantly shifting, and Sonny marveled at his lord's ability to navigate those stormy seas.

Auberon moved across the floor, beckoning with a gesture for Sonny to follow him out onto the balcony. For a long while they stood in silence, leaning on the balustrade. Far below, pastoral and at peace, lay the green expanse of Central Park.

"Do not fail me, Sonny."

"My lord. I will not."

"This year of all years . . . I must not fail."

A weighty silence stretched out between them, and Sonny cast a sideways glance at Auberon. The pale, perfect skin around the Faerie king's eyes seemed tight, his features drawn. "You seem . . . weary, my lord. Ill at ease . . . "

Auberon turned away, murmuring to himself as though the young Janus had suddenly vanished and he stood alone. "My subjects tear at the chains across the Samhain Gate with teeth and claws. Batter at doors—doors that *I* have closed— with maul and sword. They would cleave each other limb from limb and die howling, if only to risk the chance to force their way through that infernal crack between the Faerie and mortal worlds. To escape from *there* to *here*. To this . . . sickly . . . tainted realm. How then should I seem?" the Unseelie king demanded. "When there are those who would flee my kingdom—all for the sake of cavorting with mortals." He spat the word from his lips.

"I . . . am mortal, my lord," Sonny said quietly.

"You are a Janus. I made you. Mortality has nothing to do with you." Auberon threw back his head and swallowed the rest of his wine in one mouthful. "Unless, of course, you die."

The Faerie king leaped up onto the balustrade. Spreading his cloak wide, he stepped into nothingness, the thin air blurring around him like smoke.

In his place, a charcoal-winged falcon soared off over the park, shrieking fury.

Less than half an hour later, Sonny was stalking the twisting paths of the Ramble in Central Park like a hunting cat, reaching out with his mind to touch all four corners of the Samhain Gate.

He often wondered what New Yorkers would think if they ever discovered the truth about their beloved Central Park: that the 843 acres of rolling, verdant sanctuary in the middle of the city was nothing more than a disguise, a carefully constructed façade cloaking a gateway between the mortal world and the Faerie Otherworld.

Only a century and a half earlier there had been four such Gates: Samhain, Beltane, Imbolc, and Lúnasa, scattered throughout the Old World—passageways by which the Fair Folk could come and go, interacting with the mortal realm.

But once the Faerie had begun to drift to the New World in the wake of large-scale human immigration from across the sea, the Courts of Faerie had decided to relocate one of the four Great Gates to this new land, where so many mortals—the kind who still believed in the Faerie—had settled.

As Central Park was being built at the end of the nineteenth century, the Samhain Gate had grown within its confines. Hidden from the populace of the city, it meshed seamlessly and unseen with the growing urban oasis, providing a perfect playground for those who crossed over, a place of nature and thus a natural habitat for the Fae, right in the middle of bustling human habitation.

The Samhain Gate had provided endless diversion for the dwellers of the Faerie Otherworld, but it wouldn't last long.

A few decades after the park's completion, around the turn of the twentieth century, Auberon had taken it upon himself to shut all four Gates. Angered by a mortal transgression, the king cast an enchantment that would seal them forever so that the Faerie realm and the world of mortals would remain separate.

But Auberon's enchantment had been flawed.

A crack remained in one of the Gates.

The Gate that stood in the center of the teeming New World metropolis would open for one night every year, from sundown on October 31 to sunrise on the first of November. What was more, every nine years the Gate would swing wide for nine full nights, of which Samhain was the last.

And so Auberon had decided that if he could not keep the Gate shut, he would bring together the most promising of all the mortal changelings from across the Faerie realms. Gathering thirteen of them, Auberon trained them and gifted them with abilities that would enable them to guard the Gate on his behalf.

The irony was not lost on the newly made Janus Guards. But they were a fairly pragmatic lot and understood the realities of the situation: They could serve the Faerie king or they could die. So they served.

They served so well, in fact, that most of them could never return home—never go back to their lives in the Otherworld. Auberon's Janus Guard had developed such a fearsome reputation that they found themselves unwelcome, reviled and shunned as murderers, called monsters by the same Faerie who'd treated them as pets and playthings in the times before. It was a lonely vocation.

Sonny pushed the thought away and focused on the Gate. As a Janus, Sonny could sense not only the park; he could sense every living soul *in* the park. They flickered in his mind like candle flames: clear, pale yellow fire—if they were human. There were fewer of them than usual. Mortals, he'd been told, tended to instinctively avoid the park around the time when the Gate opened.

Scattered here and there about the perimeter of the park, he could sense other flames: blue and green, a few red ones. These were the Lost Fae, the ones who'd successfully evaded the Janus in years past and, once through the Gate, now lived in secret in the mortal realm. They did not concern him, and they would be gone soon enough—well before sundown, in order to avoid crossing paths with the Janus.

But there was something else.

Something—someone—*different* had entered the park.

Concentrating, Sonny reached out with his mind to touch a presence . . . one distinctly unlike all the other candle flames in Sonny's mind's eye. This one did not burn with a steady glow.

It sparked erratically, like the lit fuse of a firecracker.

His Janus sensibilities alerted and his curiosity piqued, Sonny decided to investigate. The anomaly was moving, slowly. Drifting in a meandering fashion that Sonny recognized as following one of the paths of the part of the park known as the Shakespeare Garden. He looked at the sky. It was just over an hour before twilight and the opening of the Gate; but, intrigued by the prospect of a bit of preshow mystery, he took off at a run, following the spark.

When he reached the grove where his "firecracker" had come to a stop, Sonny slowed and approached warily. Drawing upon the magic that Auberon had gifted him, he called up a subtle veil to shield himself in case his quarry had the ability to sense him. He did not yet know what he was dealing with.

He crept close enough to catch a glimpse and still he wasn't sure he knew. It was a girl. That much he could tell.

Even from a distance, he could see that she was fairly young—seventeen, maybe. His age—his *mortal* age—eighteen, at the most . . .

He could also see that she was beautiful. Her hair had the sheen of antique, burnished copper, and her wide-set eyes were green. Intrigued, Sonny moved soundlessly through the dry leaves to crouch in the deep shadows of a yew tree. He watched through the branches of his hiding place as the girl moved restlessly, pacing to and fro in the little grassy square, one fingernail tapping on her front teeth.

Then she began to mutter to herself and gesture to the empty air.

Oh. Sonny sighed. *Just another Central Park crazy.*

The off-kilter mortals—the ones not quite right in the head—sometimes showed up differently on Sonny's radar. That's what must have happened with this girl, he thought. Still . . . he found himself surprisingly disappointed as he turned to leave.

The girl's voice rang out suddenly. "Out of this wood do not desire to go!"

Startled, Sonny looked back to see her pointing in his direction. He froze, his breath stopped in his throat. There should have been *no* way that the girl could have known he was there. He was too well hidden—both by the foliage and by the veil he'd conjured.

"Thou shalt remain here, whether thou wilt or no," she said clearly, her voice compelling.

Looking at her, Sonny noticed that she shimmered. Hair; skin; those long, graceful hands—every inch of her seemed to sparkle.

"I am a spirit of no common rate," the shining girl continued, the corners of her mouth turning up in a playful, gently superior smile.

Spirit? Sonny thought, suddenly alarmed.

"The summer still doth tend upon my state," she said, and took a step toward him, her expression dreamy, eyes unfocused.

Summer . . . Sonny felt creeping panic inching up his throat. *Please, no—not one of Titania's creatures* . . . He stood, prepared to bolt.

"And I do love thee."

What?

"Therefore go with me."

Without realizing what he was doing, Sonny had begun to reach out a hand through the yew branches in response to the summoning. He drew his hand back sharply. What exactly had he stumbled upon here? He noticed suddenly the shirt she wore beneath her open jacket with its sparkling pony and rainbow . . . and the word *Princess*. . . . Sonny could feel his heart beating faster than it had any right to.

"I'll give thee fairies to attend on thee." Her voice, honey-sweet, tempted him with its music, holding him captive in a moment of thrall. "And they shall fetch thee jewels from the deep . . . and sing while thou on pressèd flowers dost sleep. . . . "

The rhyming finally tipped him off.

Her words had started to sound terribly familiar, and understanding descended upon Sonny like a hammer blow.

Oh, seven hells! He cursed himself, grinding his teeth. His friend Maddox would laugh himself sick if Sonny were to tell him about this. Which, of course, he wouldn't! He glowered angrily at the girl, even though he now knew that she couldn't see him.

Smiling her enchanting smile, she said, "And I will purge thy mortal grossness so that thou shalt like an airy spirit go!" Then she turned away, glancing coquettishly over her shoulder, seeming to beckon with her eyes.

Except it wasn't really *him* she beckoned. Sonny felt a strange twinge of regret.

Then, quite abruptly, the girl stopped in her tracks, and her entire mood shifted. Clenching her fists, she whirled in a frustrated little dance. Sonny watched silently as the girl snatched up a sheaf of paper that had lain on the bench next to her bag. She slapped the words on the page, cursing. "Dammit dammit dammit! See? You *see*? You *know* the lines, idiot! Now why on earth couldn't you do *that* at rehearsal? Why? Dammit!" She kicked angrily at the ground, stubbing her toe on a moss-covered rock. "Ow!"

Sonny let his breath out slowly, grimly amused.

A script. An actress.

The fact that this slightly ridiculous girl had actually made him think that perhaps she was— Sonny stopped short before even pursuing that avenue of thought. He was a Janus. He, more than anyone, should be able to tell the difference. Poised to leave, he turned back for one last second to watch the girl.

She hobbled over to a bench and sat down heavily. Without warning, she crumpled forward, her face buried in her hands. Her shoulders shook with silent sobs.

Sonny felt his jaw drop.

He should go. He should leave the pathetic creature to indulge her sorrow in private. Definitely, he should go. . . .

Instead, Sonny glanced around, looking for something in the weathered remnants of the garden that he could make use of. He spotted a rosebush with one last, withered bloom. The petals clung to the flower head in a desiccated clump, and the leaves on the stem were brittle almost to the point of dust.

It would do nicely, he thought, plucking the flower. As he touched the blown rose, it quivered and shimmered beneath his fingertips, slowly regaining its color; the petals unfurled in a deep, creamy shade of peach, and the leaves turned a vibrant green once more. Sonny took a deep breath and stepped into the clearing.

"Excuse me . . . miss?"

The girl's head snapped up, and a little cloud of glitter burst from her hair. Her hand flew toward her enormous shoulder bag, her arm disappearing up to the elbow into its depths.

Fool, Sonny thought silently, although he carefully kept it from showing on his face. *If I'd wanted to hurt you, I could have done so easily by now.*

There was a hint of fear in her eyes. But just a hint. That impressed him.

"I'm sorry. I didn't mean to startle you." He glanced at her purse. "Please. If you're looking for mace, you don't need to. I . . . I only wanted to give you this." He held out the rose. "You looked as though you could use something . . . nice."

The girl's face changed from wariness to wonder.

"Wow," she said softly. She reached for the flower, hesitantly, looking up at him. He took another careful step forward and placed the rose gently in her hand.

"It's beautiful," she murmured, gazing down at the perfect rose in her palm. The heady scent of the flower filled the little clearing with its perfume, and the girl inhaled deeply, her face softening into a smile. "Thank you," she whispered.

But by the time she looked back up, he was already gone.

III

Kelley looked around the clearing, astonished, but the mysterious—and good-looking—guy had vanished without a sound. She sat on the bench awhile longer, holding the rose and listening.

Nothing.

At last, gathering her stuff, she picked up one of the footpaths that would lead her out of the garden and toward Bethesda Terrace. It was time she headed home.

Maybe he's still around here somewhere, she thought as she strolled leisurely. *I should at least make an effort to find him.*

Thank him properly for trying to cheer me up. Kelley toyed with the tempting idea, playing with the green-amber pendant that hung from a silver chain around her neck. It was a gift from Aunt Emma—a four-leaf clover, for luck.

Unfortunately, though she kept her eyes peeled, it seemed that she was *out* of luck, at least where Handsome Stranger was concerned.

She sighed, remembering the way he had looked at her with those extraordinary silver-gray eyes. His face was regal. High cheekbones. Straight, firm mouth. Unsmiling, but not harsh—although Kelley had a sense that his expression could turn that way, easily.

"Oh, come on!" Kelley said aloud. "How ridiculous can you get? You saw the guy for all of twelve seconds!" Walking south, she skirted the edge of the Ramble until she got to the northern shore of the Lake, opposite the rocky outcropping of Hernshead.

Somehow, it had become dusk. Kelley had never really felt unsafe in Central Park—but on the other hand, she'd never gone traipsing about in it after dark. Nervously, she squinted up into a sky that had gone from deep blue to indigo with startling swiftness. It was eerily still in the park, she realized. Utterly silent. A thin veil of ground mist swirled, sweeping across the path in front of her. Kelley quickened her pace almost to a jog.

The surface of the Lake on her right was like a vast black

pool of oil and so still that it reflected everything like a perfect mirror. She planned to skirt along the shore until she came to the eastern edge, near to where she could cross over and exit the park around Seventy-second Street. Then it was only about a ten-minute walk to home.

She hadn't gotten very far when the sounds of screaming split the night air.

The raw noise shattered the stillness, chilling and horrific. Kelley froze, listening to the high-pitched cries. They sounded as if they were coming from the middle of the Lake.

"Hey!" Kelley called, frightened. "Hey! Do you need help?"

A cacophony of frantic splashing reached her ears as if in answer. Kelley started running toward the source of the sound. Mingling with the horrid screams that had first caught her attention was a deeper huffing sound, punctuated by the frenzied splashing—as though someone was flailing around in a panic. Drowning.

Make that some*thing*. Kelley stopped at the edge of the Lake, realizing with a start that there was a distinctly non-human quality to the noise. She squinted and could only just make out where the water in the middle of the Lake frothed white. Suddenly something rose from the center of the disturbance, bucking and rearing violently. Heart pounding, Kelley saw a *horse's* head thrashing in the darkness.

The animal's front hooves churned at the water, as though it was trying to climb the air. Then it sank deeper. The water closed over the drowning creature's head again, choking off the sounds of its panicked whinnying. Kelley glanced around frantically.

"Help!" she called, but her voice sounded flat and small in the night. There wasn't anyone around to hear her.

She turned back to the Lake desperately and saw the horse breach the surface again, floundering, losing strength.

The thought of an animal drowning while she stood there watching was more than Kelley could bear. She dropped her bag, shrugged out of her jacket, and kicked off her shoes. Then she dove into the Lake in a shallow arc.

The chill in the October air was nothing compared to the temperature of the pond. As she hit the water, Kelley thought for a brief, horrible moment that her heart would stop beating in shock. When she surfaced seconds later, she gasped painfully and faltered.

The horse whinnied again, sounding much weaker. Kelley pushed the needle-sharp cold from her thoughts and began swimming with strong, purposeful strokes. Six feet from the panicked creature, she treaded water, wary of the flailing, deadly hammers of its hooves.

"Shh, shhh." Kelley tried to keep her teeth from chattering as she gentled it with her voice. "Nice horsie . . . good horse . . . easy there, fella."

The animal bobbed its head wildly, its dark eyes rolling white at the edges and its nostrils flaring wide.

"It's okay. It's okay." Kelley reached out a hand as she moved a little closer, treading water that was so cold it almost felt slushy. If she couldn't succeed in helping the poor creature out of the Lake soon, Kelley knew that she would have to abandon the attempt. Her toes were already numb. "You're okay. I'm here. I'll help."

She stretched her hand out farther, the tips of her fingers just barely touching the velvety skin of the horse's muzzle.

Please don't bite me, she thought desperately.

But instead, the animal pushed its nose into her hand, butting gently at her fingers and blowing out warm air.

"Okay. *Good* horsie. Okay." Kelley swam closer, still careful to avoid the horse's churning front legs. "Let's get you out of here."

She ran her hands along the animal's flank below the waterline to see if she could determine what was wrong. The horse seemed uninjured, from the little she could tell, but its powerful hindquarters weren't moving in the way they should to keep the creature afloat. She reached farther around under the surface of the water toward the horse's rump, and for a second she thought that she could feel something cold and rough . . . almost *slimy*—like fish scales.

Kelley jerked her hand back.

You're not a horse! she thought wildly.

Of course, that was ridiculous. *The cold is affecting your brain, stupid. You're imagining things.*

She reached out again and, feeling with her hands, realized there was a tangled net of slippery lake weed that had become wound around the back end of the animal—what

34

she must have mistaken for fishiness.

Kelley tugged at the strands of ropy vegetation, but the fibrous stuff was strong and she couldn't get much of a grip. It kept slipping through her fingers, which were already stiff from the cold. Groaning in frustration, Kelley looked back to see that the horse wasn't even struggling anymore. It just stared at her with one mournful eye. Its flaring nostrils were barely above the waterline.

It was going to drown.

Determination took hold. Kelley kicked herself back a little way from the horse's flank to gather what strength she had left. She took three deep breaths, filling her lungs to capacity with biting cold air, and then dove beneath the surface of the water.

Swimming down as far as she could, she grasped at the massed strands of weedy vegetation where they were rooted into the mud of the lake bed. Kelley swung her legs underneath her, planted bare feet in the mud, and wrapped the strands around her hands. Then she hauled on them for all she was worth.

The slimy weeds went taut, but refused to break or uproot.

Pull . . . once more.

Pull, damn it. Lungs aching, she heaved again.

Pull!

As her strength began to fade, Kelley tugged weakly on the waterweeds one last time. Starbursts bloomed in front of her eyes as her brain began to starve for oxygen. Kelley shook her head. A cloud of bubbles escaped her mouth and nose—the last of her air. She heard music, faint and far off, and thought she could see a weird, glowing light dancing through the water, swirling and coalescing all around her. She felt warm. One very last, feeble try . . . and Kelley felt the ropy stems give just a bit. Suddenly a sharp tug on the weeds jerked her painfully forward, wrenching her arms and shoulders.

And then everything around her went completely black.

IV

"Sonny!"

He turned at the sound of his name to see a fellow Janus emerging from the trees.

"Maddox." He held out a hand and they clasped forearms, smiling.

"How goes the day, Sonn?" Maddox asked, a slight warm lilt to his voice.

Sonny shrugged. "Does it feel different to you yet?"

"Nah." Maddox shook his head. "Feels just like every other year. Calm, serene, peaceful . . . well. That'll soon change. In less than an hour's time, the cracks will start to show in the

Gate. And every night after this one, for the next eight, there will be more cracks. Bigger ones. Until Samhain, when all hell breaks loose. Face it, Sonn." Maddox lowered his voice, even though there was no one who could possibly overhear them. "Nine nights of the Gate opening wider and wider, and only a handful of Janus to guard it. There's a lot of Folk—mostly the nastier ones—who are willing to take that risk."

Sonny grimaced. He didn't understand why any of the Fair Folk would want to live in this world. *He* certainly didn't. The noise alone was almost enough to drive him mad.

"Do you ever get used to it, Maddox?" Sonny asked, a bit hesitantly. "This place, I mean."

"I'm the wrong lad to ask," Maddox grunted. "For one thing, I don't think I've been here long enough. Even just the *concept* of electricity still gives me the willies."

"After three years?" Sonny asked, surprised.

"Aye, well. We may have both been, you know . . . *taken* . . . when gaslight was still in vogue, Sonn, but *I* was old enough when I was—when it happened that I actually remember that world. That time. I just try not to think about it now."

Sonny thought about that for a moment. He had been a baby when he'd been taken. The only life he'd ever known had been the one that the Fair Folk had given him. It must have been difficult for those like Maddox . . . to have known right from the start that the shining, glorious people who raised you were not your own. That you weren't one of theirs. And worse, knowing that your own world was no longer—could never again be—yours . . . Sonny felt uncomfortable. It wasn't something he had ever liked giving deep thought to, though he couldn't have explained why.

They stopped near the park's Bow Bridge, which spanned the Lake just west of Bethesda Terrace, linking the relative wilderness of the Ramble to the more formal, manicured gardens of Cherry Hill. The bridge struck Sonny as an apt metaphor for the Gate itself. They stood silently, gazing out over the water for a long moment.

"And after all"—Maddox shrugged off the suddenly somber mood and waved a hand at the beauty before them—"this place *does* have its charms." He clapped Sonny on the back. "Come on, then. We don't want to be late for the opening."

All around Sonny and Maddox, the air thrummed with tense anticipation as they reached the summit of the Great Hill and were welcomed into a loose circle of their Janus brethren. There were thirteen of them, changelings all.

There was the Fennrys Wolf, legendary for his berserker-like rages and sullen temperament. According to Maddox, the cradle Fenn had been stolen from sometime in the ninth century had been that of a Viking prince. War craft was in his blood—or so he declared almost every time Sonny saw him.

Camina and Bellamy were twins, sister and brother. Slender, graceful, and quiet, they'd been Janus Guards since almost the beginning and were notoriously efficient.

There was Godwyn, genial, handsome . . . ruthless.

Bryan and Beni—one light, one dark, different as night and day. Insanely competitive, and utterly inseparable, "the lads" could usually be found engaged in some sort of contest, be it darts or pool or just punching each other in the arm to see who could take it the longest.

There was Ghost. Thin and silent, with dark eyes in a pale face—more haunted than haunting, Sonny had always thought. He didn't know Ghost's real name, or even what part of the world he'd been taken from. An odd young man, but then . . . he'd been taken by Queen Mabh.

Beside Ghost stood Aaneel—the oldest, who had ages since left his home in India and was one of only a handful of changelings to have lived long enough in the Otherworld to have aged well into adulthood. His black hair had begun to silver at the temples, contrasting with his deep coppery complexion.

Next to Aaneel was Perry—Percival—the youngest, save for Sonny. Perry had been taken in 1719 from a tiny hamlet in the north of France that had suffered failed crops year after year. In exchange for Perry, Titania had granted the place mild weather and fertile soil, and so a town that had almost died didn't.

Finally, Selene, pale and pretty, with fox-brown hair and a smattering of freckles, and absolutely lethal aim with a longbow; and Cait, skilled in more forms of hand-to-hand combat than anyone else in the group, she much preferred to cast spells and warding enchantments instead.

Together they watched as the sun finally dipped completely below the horizon and Central Park slipped into darkness. The first night of the Nine had begun. With a singular purpose, the Janus moved, spreading out to cover the four corners of the park.

Splitting off from the others to travel south, Sonny ran along the treacherously rocky terrain of the Ravine, reaching deep into his mind, feeling past the delicate, obscuring mists of Auberon's flawed enchantment to where the walls between the worlds were so thin they became doors. He felt for which of those doors might just open that night. . . .

There.

Thirty yards east—maybe thirty-five. Sonny crept up the path and stood, loose limbed and ready, his blood warmed from running and anticipation of the coming fight. Some of the Faerie that tried to cross would retreat back to the Other-world at the very first hint of a Janus in the vicinity. But the timid among the Fair Folk were also less likely to try and cross in the first place.

Sonny reached into the leather messenger bag slung across his body and drew forth a bundle of three short, straight sticks, tied with a red leather cord: a branch each of oak, ash, and thorn. Sonny murmured an ancient secret incantation, and a silver-bladed sword appeared in his hand in their place. He held it ready at his side.

Suddenly the granite wall in front of Sonny began to waver

like a mirage, and then cracked. A ghostly, iridescent light seeped through the split in the stone, and Sonny could see diminutive figures silhouetted in the glow. A tiny, wizened face peered out at him. When the creature saw the Janus standing there, it did not turn and run back to the Faerie lands. Instead it gave a nasty, high-pitched giggle.

A piskie-fae.

Sonny tried not to roll his eyes as he reached back into his satchel and withdrew a handful of rock salt. He threw the salt into the piskie's leering face. The thing squealed and disappeared back into the rift.

That was far too easy! he thought, grinning. He might not even need to use his blade at all.

His reflection was interrupted by an angry buzzing. It was as though Sonny had just thrown a stone at a nest of hornets. Scrabbling at one another and the edges of the rift, a swarm of tiny, blood-lusting piskies came rushing at him, pale thin bodies glimmering like knives in the darkness.

It took Sonny the better part of an hour, and the carnage, even on a piskie-sized scale, was considerable.

As he cleaned the green, glowing piskie blood from the blade of his sword and veiled it once more, Sonny felt no remorse. The piskie-fae that had attacked him had got what they'd deserved. Piskie weren't all nasty. Some, back home, were even occasionally useful, although their malicious pranks made them annoying as hell.

But these had been positively homicidal, and in far greater numbers than Sonny had ever been warned about.

Maddox would give him a very hard time about how long it had taken Sonny to defeat such minor fae. Sonny wondered how Maddox himself was doing. Or any of the others, for that matter. Because there were only thirteen Janus, it was unlikely that their paths would cross much over the next nine nights. They had the entire park to cover.

The ground at Sonny's feet was littered with rock-salt crystals and flattened by his own boot prints in a rough circle that spread about three yards wide all around him. He hadn't, in the frenzy, realized just how big the swarm had been. He paced the diameter of the circle. *Really* big. Especially for creatures with an outside height of only six or seven inches.

Sonny stared at the trampled earth and frowned. It didn't make a ton of sense.

Piskie weren't necessarily the smartest fae, but they were usually pretty crafty. He would have expected them to have spread out. Come at him in staggered waves. Find more than just that one rift. Instead it looked as if they had launched a massed assault at this spot to keep him busy and anchored to one position.

Sonny swore explosively and spun in a circle on his heel, casting out with his Janus perception, so heavily preoccupied until now. A sudden, blinding crimson light shot through his mind. His insides went cold. Something was terribly wrong somewhere south. He struggled to focus, to pinpoint the blazing light on the map in his mind. . . .

There it was. Or, rather, there it *had been*.

Sonny started to run.

But he knew, in his heart, that he was already much too late.

Crouching near the edge of the Lake, Sonny put his cheek to the cold ground and peered along the surface of the water, still swirling with iridescence—evidence of recent passage through the Samhain Gate to this realm from the Otherworld.

Something other than piskies had come through the Gate, very recently. Maybe half an hour earlier. Sonny lay with his cheek to the ground for a better view and stared eye-level out over the obsidian surface of the Lake.

There.

There was a faintly glowing trail leading out of the water. Sonny sprang to his feet and ran over to investigate.

The soft ground at the edge of the Lake was churned to mud. It looked as if there had been some kind of struggle, or as if something had been dragged out of the water and onto the path. Here and there Sonny saw the elongated circular impressions of what could only have been hoofprints. He crouched on the path for a closer look.

It was Central Park, after all. Horses pulled carriages through the park, and wealthy equestrians rode their mounts along the bridle paths. But these prints had come from unshod hooves. And the water that pooled in the impressions had the same telltale iridescent sheen.

A kelpie? Sonny turned over the clues in his mind.

In one of the prints, Sonny found strands of coarse red horsehair and three glittering black onyx beads carved in the shapes of tiny stags' heads.

He pocketed the hair and beads and stood, looking around. From the corner of his eye, Sonny saw something pale hidden in the reeds. He retrieved the object, brushing damp vegetation from its surface. It was a script, held together with brass fasteners through the punch holes. The front cover was gone, but the *Dramatis Personae* page was mostly intact, although marred by a hoofprint that looked as though its edges were very slightly scorched. Handwritten notes were scribbled in the margins, and at the top of the page a note in marker said *Kelley's Script*. Sonny frowned, fanning through the play, until a smattering of dialogue caught his eye.

"Out of this wood do not desire to go," began the speech, and Sonny almost dropped the pages in surprise.

He'd heard those very words not long before.

Sonny scanned the lakeshore one last time and knelt at the edge of the path.

Buried almost completely in the mud lay the trampled

remains of a single peach-colored rose. Sonny plucked a bruised petal and held it up before his eyes. The script. The girl from the Shakespeare Garden.

His firecracker.

Kelley . . .

Exhausted, muddy, and soaked to the skin, Kelley kicked the apartment door closed behind her and yelled out for her roommate. There was no answer—*Tyff must be out,* she thought. Just as well. At that moment she didn't really feel like launching into a recap of her strange adventure in the park. The cold of the Lake still gripped her bones, even though she'd jogged the last few blocks home. It made her thought processes slow and sluggish.

Shivering hard enough that her teeth rattled, Kelley shed clothing in a trailing heap on the floor, tugged the afghan off the back of the couch, and wrapped it around herself as she stumbled to the bathroom and turned the shower taps on, setting the temperature as hot as it would go. She knew that the only thing that was going to drive away impending hypothermia was the longest, hottest shower she'd ever taken, followed by a large mug of even hotter cocoa.

The shower was about as close to heaven as she could imagine. Steam billowed in clouds around her, and eventually the chattering of her teeth stopped and her muscles unclenched enough to let her stand upright. Once the heat had restored her mental faculties sufficiently, Kelley allowed herself to mull over the evening's bizarre turn of events.

She'd come to her senses lying facedown on the lakeside path, retching out murky water, with the horse nuzzling at her shoulder. By the time she'd regained her bearings and struggled to her feet, the creature had vanished into the darkness, and Kelley was left with nothing but a few strands of long, reddish horsehair clutched in her fist. Sodden and shivering, she had gathered up shoes and coat and all the stuff that had spilled from her bag and headed for home.

That was what she remembered.

Only . . .

There was confusion in Kelley's mind. She could recall, from the moments before she'd blacked out, a jumble of images. Fleeting impressions of lights and sound—strange, beautiful music . . .

Or, to use the technical term, oxygen deprivation.

Kelley leaned her head against the tiled wall. At least she

hadn't actually drowned. What was that old cliché? Right: "Fortune favors the foolish." Stupid horse. She hoped it had found its way home. With the water starting to run lukewarm, Kelley reluctantly turned off the taps and slid aside the shower curtain.

And screamed.

The "stupid horse" was standing right in front of her, filling almost every available inch of her tiny bathroom with its big, lanky frame. The horse's back feet—in fact its entire back half—was still outside, as it stood half in her bathroom, half out on the landing of the fire escape. Kelley could see steam rising up from the horse, dissipating into the cold night air. It whickered softly and pushed at her shoulder with its velvet muzzle.

Kelley scrambled for something to cover herself and tried not to panic.

When she'd hoped that the creature had found its way home, Kelley hadn't meant *her* home! She wrapped herself in a towel and edged around the horse, out of the little room. As soon as she could, she shut the door with a bang and leaned against it, her heart pounding.

This is impossible, she thought. *This is* not *happening*.

She was imagining things. She had brain freeze. *Über* brain freeze—not just the kind you got from drinking a Slurpee too fast. No. The kind that you got from jumping into a lake in late October. The kind that made you hallucinate wildly.

The horse whinnied softly.

"Stop that!" Kelley clapped her hands over her ears. "You're not real! I can't hear you because you're *not* real!"

There was another little burble of equine noise from behind the door, followed by shuffling and thumping sounds. Then nothing. Kelley sank down to the floor and sat with her back to the door. This really wasn't happening. Because if it *was* happening, Kelley was in for a world of trouble.

Her roommate was going to kill her. Or kick her out.

Oh, God—if Tyff kicked her out, she might have to move back home! It wasn't as if her aunt Emma had wanted Kelley to move to New York in the first place, and it was only the fact that Kelley'd found such a great place to stay that made her agree. Tyff Meyers was a model—more than a little high-strung—and Kelley could recall the wording of her craigslist ad with absolute clarity:

> *Available to Rent: outrageously expensive, ridiculously*
> *tiny room with no view, in Upper East Side walk-up,*
> *w/ shared kitchen/bath/living. Must be single female.*
> *Nonsmoker, nondrinker, nonannoying. No late nights,*
> *loud friends, parties, or general weirdness. You must*
> *be neat, you must be civilized, and you must not*
> *touch my stuff—food and bath products, underlined especially.*
> *Interview required. Must answer skill-testing question.*
> *Serious inquiries only to: dragonfodder@hotmail.com.*
> NO CRAZIES. NO PETS.
> * * *

A horse in the bathroom would pretty much violate both the NO CRAZIES and NO PETS, Kelley thought, still trying desperately not to panic.

She stayed crouched against the door for a long time, her mind racing like a runaway train. This couldn't possibly be happening. After a long few minutes of silence, she dared to hope her fit of hallucination had run its course.

Then she heard the sound of water running.

Kneeling, she put an eye to the antique keyhole in the door and, feeling dazed, noted that the horse had climbed entirely—impossibly—through the small casement window and was now standing in the tub.

It also seemed to be running itself a bath.

"No, ma'am, I'm not drunk," Kelley said for the third time.

This, after the eighty-five minutes she had spent trying to get a real person to talk to at NYC Animal Control. "Like I said, he must've come up the fire escape—"

The receiver clicked in her ear.

"Hello? Hel*lo*?"

Exasperated almost to the point of tears, Kelley hung up the phone and began to pace. Maybe the Animal Control lady was right. Maybe she *was* drunk. Okay, so she hadn't had anything *to* drink, but that made about as much sense as a full-grown horse following her home from Central Park like a lost puppy, climbing up the fire escape, and squeezing itself through a tiny window into her bathroom, didn't it? She stopped pacing and went to check on it. Still hoping beyond hope that she *had*, in fact, been hallucinating, she cracked open the door. The horse rolled a big, brown eye at her inquiringly.

Kelley sighed in weary frustration and decided to attempt to physically remove the creature from the tub herself. She tried pushing from behind, pulling from in front, poking, prodding, enticing with a withered carrot she'd found in the back of the refrigerator vegetable drawer. . . .

The horse remained sweet-tempered throughout—and stubborn as a mule.

It—*he*, she noticed—affectionately snuffled her shoulder, nuzzled at her fingers, and remained entirely disinclined to budge from the half-full tub. Kelley leaned on the edge of the sink and dropped her head into her hands, still dully disbelieving that any of this could actually be happening.

Then she caught a whiff of lavender and jerked her head up to see a glistening white froth swirling around the horse's legs.

It was only *then* that Kelley's state of shock evaporated, and the panic set in for real.

Never mind the fact that there was a horse in her bathtub. The only thing that mattered to Kelley in that particular moment was that the horse had tipped over a bottle of her roommate's *insanely* expensive bath oil, emptying its shiny purple contents into the water. The bottle with its elegant gold-lettered label bobbed on the surface.

Tyff was definitely going to kill her.

At around four in the morning, Kelley resigned herself to her fate and went out into the living room to wait for Tyff to come home from her date. At the very least, maybe she could try and get some script work done. But, to top it all off, she couldn't find her damned script.

The only thing on TV at that time of night was infomercials, so she finally drifted off to sleep on the couch during a sales pitch for "Eighties HIT-SPLOSIONS." Deep within her sleepy brain, the bubblegum refrains of Wham! twisted and spiraled into minor keys, flowing seamlessly into the darkly alluring music that Kelley had heard as the world had disappeared around her under the waters of the Lake. The music enthralled her, leading her through a series of fantastic, strange dreamscapes.

But when she woke up late the next morning, she couldn't remember the tune.

VI

Out of this wood do not desire to go . . .

And I do love thee. . . .

Green eyes sparkled at him from the shadows beneath the branches of a nightmare forest. Laughter rang in his ears. The drumming of hoofbeats made it seem to him as if his heart would burst.

Love thee . . .

Long white hands reached out from the darkness, beckoning, and he wanted with all his soul to follow.

Love . . .

Sonny startled awake as the tree branches, dripping venom, reached out for him.

He sat up in bed in the darkened room and clutched at the ache in the middle of his chest. His head pounded as he got up and threw open the heavy curtains of his bedroom window, wincing at the late-morning light. It was a beautiful day outside. Groaning, he pulled the curtains shut again, plunging the room back into blessed darkness.

A knock on the door startled him. Sonny sensed it was Maddox; he called, "Come in," and pulled on a pair of jeans and a long-sleeved T-shirt.

"Afternoon, Sonn-shine," Maddox greeted him as he stepped over the threshold, his usual easy grin brightening up the room. "Pretty gloomy in here. You just get up?"

"Yeah."

"I thought I'd hit the Ramble with you tonight," Maddox said. "Any objections?"

"No. Company would be nice." Sonny ran his hands through his dark hair and pulled it back into a tail, securing it with a leather thong.

"Good. The Gate around midpark was a bloody bore last night."

"Anything get through?" Sonny asked, trying to shake his nightmare and figure out how to tell Maddox about his own discovery.

"Nah, don't think so. A whole pack of pissed-off nyxxies

gave us a bit of fun for the first hour or so, but after that it was quiet as a grave."

Sonny frowned, thinking about his similar encounter with the piskie-fae. And the fact that the diversion had prevented him from being in time to catch whatever had come through at the Lake. He wondered if all the other Janus had been similarly occupied for that first hour. "Where was the Wolf?" he asked.

"Aw, Fennrys doesn't like crowds—you know that. He's claimed the upper fourth of the park like he owns it. Might as well have gone around and peed on all the bushes up there. He'll fight anything—even other Janus, if they get in his way." Maddox looked at Sonny quizzically. "Been meaning to ask—how was *your* night?"

"It was . . . interesting."

Maddox's eyes gleamed with curiosity. "Something nasty?"

Sonny went to a closet and grabbed a pair of boots and a jacket. "Maybe. Look, I'm starving. Let's get something to eat, and I'll tell you about it."

Sitting in the booth at the back of a diner, the two Janus were far enough away from the other patrons that they didn't necessarily have to keep their voices down, but the subject matter dictated that they do so anyway. As Sonny had predicted, Maddox was deeply amused by the tale of his piskie brawl.

"Don't take it so hard, Sonn," he said in between shoveling

up mouthfuls of a western omelet the size of his head. "At least it wasn't hinkypunks!"

"The day I get my arse kicked by a hinkypunk is the day I hang up this," Sonny growled, tapping the iron medallion hanging from a braided leather cord around his neck—his Janus badge of office. "With my neck still in it."

"Especially since they only have one leg to kick with!" Maddox laughed, and, pushing back a plate that had been pillaged clean, sighed contentedly. "Now. Leaving aside nyxxies and pixies and all that small change, why don't you tell me what it is that's really got your knickers in a twist, hey?"

"What do you mean?"

"I mean, old Sonn, that something about last night has parked a thundercloud on your doorstep, and it wasn't a piskie drubbing that did it. You've got more of a sense of humor than to let something like that bug you."

Sonny picked up a coffee spoon and toyed with it for a moment. Then he sat back and told Maddox what had happened during the time he'd been fending off the piskie attack. Or, at least, what he thought had happened—his theory was based on circumstantial evidence, after all.

Maddox remained silent throughout, chewing thoughtfully on his bottom lip. "A kelpie, huh?" he asked finally.

"I think so," Sonny said. "Horsehair and hoofprints would seem to indicate that."

"You know, I've never seen one?"

"I did once—from a great distance—when I accompanied

Auberon on a visit to Queen Mabh's Borderlands. They mostly lurk in the swamps thereabouts. Vicious things." Back in the days when the Gates had all stood open, kelpie were known to appear near sources of water. They'd take on the guise of beautiful horses to lure unwary mortals. Once a person was mounted, the kelpie would plunge below the surface of the lake or river, dragging its hapless victim away to the Otherworld, or down to a watery death. Some kelpie even ate their victims.

"When I was a kid," Maddox said, "you know, before I was taken, I used to hear stories. The old village wives would screech something fierce if any of us kids went too close to the riverbanks. Said the kelpie'd come for us and take us away to drown."

"Well, this one was gone by the time I got there, and there wasn't a whole lot of forensic evidence left behind."

"In other words, no blood or body parts strewn about."

"Right. None of that. Just trampled rushes and these." Sonny pulled the black stone beads out of his satchel and put them on the table. Strands of horsehair, bright as copper filaments, remained knotted on the beads.

Maddox reached for one and examined it minutely. "Hmm. Strange . . . What are they?"

"I don't know."

He handed the bead back to Sonny. "Of course, no body parts strewn about does not necessarily preclude abduction. . . ."

Sonny nodded mutely. He thought uneasily of the trampled script he'd found and the notion that something terrible might have happened to the girl he'd gotten used to thinking of as Firecracker. After a moment he decided to solicit Maddox's help in a little detective work. "There was something else in the park yesterday too, Madd. Or, maybe, some*one* else."

Maddox settled back, crossing his arms over his chest, and waited.

Sonny pulled the tattered copy of the script out of his messenger bag and pushed it across the table. He told Maddox of the "anomaly" he'd sensed in the Shakespeare Garden—the girl—and about finding her script later on the lakeside. As Janus, neither of them was terribly prone to believing in coincidence, and Maddox was intrigued.

"You did have a busy day yesterday," he said.

"Not bad for the new kid on the job, right? Listen, we've got plenty of time before sundown—d'you want to come do a bit of nosing around with me? See if we can't track down my little stray."

"What, the kelpie? Or the girl?"

"The way I see it is this: Find the one . . . and we just might find the other."

"And how do you propose we do that?"

Sonny pointed to a note scrawled on the script: *Rehearsals @ Avalon Grande on 52ⁿᵈ*. "We start by paying this place a visit"—Sonny pointed again, at the letters indicating it was <u>Kelley's Script</u>—"and asking this girl some questions."

VII

"Don't go in there!" Tyff screeched at Kelley as she shuffled groggily in the direction of the bathroom.

Hand on the doorknob, Kelley turned to peer blearily at her roommate standing in the far corner of the living room—as far away from the bathroom as one could get in their apartment.

"Step away from the door, Kelley!" Tyff was just this side of wild-eyed.

Kelley did as she was told, trying as she did so to kickstart her brain into gear.

Tyff must have gotten in really late—or really early—and Kelley hadn't heard her, having fallen into a deep, exhausted sleep on the couch. The remnants of tumbled dreams swam through her brain—weird music that she couldn't quite remember and dancing lights, the pale perfect face of a woman with golden eyes and hair spread out behind her like seaweed floating in a watery current. And something else. Something about a . . .

"Horse! There's a *horse* in the bathtub!"

Oh, right. A horse.

Kelley squeezed her eyes shut. It *hadn't* been a bad dream after all. "Uh . . . Tyff—"

"In the bathtub!" Tyff pointed sharply with one manicured finger, her model's features drawn tight with anxiety.

"About that . . . " Kelley rubbed at the back of her neck. "I was going to tell you. I guess I fell asleep. . . . " She stared warily at her roommate who, in turn, glared at the bathroom door.

"Tyff—believe me—if I'd known he was going to follow me home from the park, I never would have rescued him. I mean—no, I probably would have, but I mean—"

"Wait a minute." Tyff's head swung toward her. "You mean to tell me this is *your* fault?"

"I guess so. I didn't mean for it to happen, but . . . " Kelley stopped, confused. "Who else's fault could it have possibly been?"

"Never mind. Go on." Tyff gestured Kelley to continue,

her eyes still on the bathroom door.

Kelley sank down onto the couch and told Tyff the whole story.

By the time she finished, Tyff seemed to have calmed down—slightly. "Can you at least get it out of the bathtub?" she asked.

"That's the thing—he won't move. I tried last night. Maybe . . . " Kelley hesitated at the suggestion, then said, "maybe we should call the police."

"No! What, are you crazy? If our landlord finds out about this, we are *both* out on the street!"

"I know, I know . . . that's what I thought."

Uncharacteristically, Tyff tore at the corner of one polished fingernail with her teeth. She was a "parts" model and got paid huge amounts of money to have her hands and feet and legs photographed for advertisements in glossy magazines. Chewing on a fingernail, therefore, was—for Tyff—a sign of *major* stress. "What the hell are we—no, wait. What the hell are *you* going to do with it?"

"I don't know!" Kelley groaned. She got up stiffly and limped to her bedroom to find something to wear. She had no idea what time it was, but judging from the light streaming through the window, it was a lot later than it should have been. Pulling on jeans and a hoodie, she continued, "Look, I called the city's Animal Control, but they wouldn't believe me." Kelley went to the bathroom door and opened it. The horse stood there, fetlock-deep in scented water, chewing placidly on the corner of a bath towel. "I think the lady who took my call thought I might be smoking something."

"If you *are*"—Tyff glowered—"considering the circumstances, you'd better share." She moved to peer nervously over Kelley's shoulder. "Why does it have beads in its hair?"

"What?" Kelley hadn't noticed that. "Where?"

"There." Tyff pointed. "And there. Shiny little black gems—they're knotted all through its hair. Its mane."

Kelley edged farther into the tiny room to get a better look. The light of the bathroom bulbs reflected the glitter of dozens of onyx gems.

"I have no idea." Kelley was mystified. "They're tied all through its tail, too. Hey—maybe it's a circus horse! That might explain how it got up the fire escape." Kelley reached out a tentative hand to pat the horse's gleaming red flank, and he whickered with pleasure. "You know, if we *both* push, we might be able to move him into the living room at least."

Tyff raised an eyebrow in silent censure at that idea.

The alarm on Kelley's cell phone chirped, and she went into the kitchen and picked it up off the counter, glancing down at the time display. She wasn't called for rehearsal until the afternoon that day, so she should be all right . . . except her phone said 12:35 p.m. "Oh no!" Kelly couldn't believe how long she'd slept. "I'm gonna be late for rehearsal—I gotta run!"

"Kelley . . . " Tyff's voice took on a threatening tone as

Kelley edged toward the door.

"Listen, Tyff. There's a bag of rolled oats with your baking stuff in the back of the cupboard—"

"*Winslow* . . ."

Kelley winced. Tyff only called her by her last name when she was genuinely pissed. "Could you maybe feed him some? Maybe you could entice him out of the tub!"

"You are a craptastic roommate."

"I'll be back as soon as rehearsal is over."

"Crap*tas*tic."

"I'll owe you forever, Tyff—I promise!"

"Do *not* say that. I didn't *hear* that. La-la-la . . . " Tyff stuck her fingers in her ears and was still la-la-laing as Kelley crept out the front door and took off down the hall as fast as her sneakered feet would carry her.

The last thing she heard as she reached the relative safety of the stairwell was Tyff's outraged cry. "Is that my French bubble bath?!"

By the time Kelley got to the theater, she wasn't sure which was making her feel worse: her guilt over leaving Tyff in the lurch, or the restless sleep she'd gotten the night before. As the fairy dancers warmed up onstage, she sat in her dressing room with her head in her hands, fighting off a major headache.

"Hey, kiddo."

Kelley looked up to see Mindi standing in the doorway

with the corset for Titania's costume in her hands. It'd had to be taken in rather drastically, and most of the lacing grommets had been replaced.

"I had Wardrobe do the work on this last night—you should get used to wearing it. See? They added some lace trim to hide the alteration seams. What do you think?"

"Oh, Mindi, it's gorgeous!" Kelley ran a finger along the handiwork appreciatively. "It looks brand-new." She glanced up into the older woman's face, feeling suddenly guilty. "I guess this means Barbara's really not coming back, huh?"

"Frankly, hon, I think it's better this way. You're doing a bang-up job—well, at least, you will. You know. I mean it was only your first rehearsal, right?" Mindi shrugged. "And this role needed some new blood, if you ask me. Now let me see how this fits."

Mindi turned Kelley to face the mirror and wrapped the stiff, sparkling garment around her rib cage, holding the two ends together at the back.

"Perfect."

Kelley smiled for the first time that day. Getting into costume was always one of the best parts of the whole process for her. She looked at her reflection in the mirror and could almost see a fairy queen lurking in there somewhere. Light glinted off the rhinestone detailing along the top hem and the embroidered front panel of the corset.

"Hey, Mindi?" Kelley touched her necklace, which also sparkled in the mirrored reflection. "Do you think I can keep this on for the show?"

"What is that?" Mindi peered through the half-glasses perched on her nose. "Like a four-leaf clover or something?"

"Yeah. The stones are green amber. My aunt gave it to me when I was a baby." Kelley rolled her eyes a little, admitting, "It's sort of a good-luck charm."

"Sure, hon," Mindi said. "It's pretty—the green goes with your costume. And as far as I'm concerned, this production can use all the luck it can beg, borrow, or steal!"

"Thanks, Mindi."

"Don't mention it. Now get your butt out there—you're due onstage for your bower scene in five."

Grabbing her wings from the hook on the door, Kelley ran down the hallway, the exhaustion that had weighed her down all morning left behind in the dressing room.

VIII

The Avalon Grande turned out to be an old church converted into a theater, and it held more than one surprise for Sonny and Maddox. Aside from the fact that it was disconcerting to watch a bunch of mortals wandering around pretending they were nobles of the Faerie courts, it was substantially *more* disconcerting to discover that not all of the actors were, in fact, mortal. It was Maddox who noticed it.

"Well now," he murmured in a tone of voice that made Sonny turn and look. "There's interesting for you."

"What? Where?" Sonny craned his neck to see what it was that Maddox had seen.

"There."

"Maddox, if you're pointing at something, I can't see it. We're invisible," Sonny hissed. They had secreted themselves in a dim alcove backstage and had called up strong veils just for good measure.

"That one way over there—in the green tunic. The one playing Puck."

"What about him?"

"Let's just say he's not exactly 'acting' the part."

"He's a *boucca*?" Sonny's eyes went wide.

"Sh!" The veils might have hidden them from the sight of humans—even other Janus—and all but the most powerful Faerie, but they didn't mask the sounds of their voices, and the acoustics in the old building were surprisingly good.

"Sorry." Sonny stared at the actor in green cartwheeling around on the stage. "Are you serious, Madd?"

"The real deal." Maddox's tone was tinged with wariness. Boucca were a rare breed of Fae that were almost as powerful as High Fae royalty. Characteristically mysterious and notoriously changeable in their moods and allegiances, they had been known to serve the various Faerie courts, but mostly preferred to serve themselves. Wherever they went, stories of mischief and mayhem abounded. They were a colorful lot, flamboyant, but they also had a reputation for being dangerous if provoked.

Sonny was dubious. The figure cavorting clownishly around the stage, hanging upside down by his knees from the set scaffolding as he said his lines, didn't seem so very threatening. "Gods. No wonder he's slumming at a theater. Pooks and their bloody theatrics."

"Yeah, see . . . *I* wouldn't call him a 'pook' to his face if I were you."

"Ooh, I'm scared." Sonny snorted, but he cast his Janus awareness in that direction, to get a sense of whatever it was about the boucca that had managed to impress Maddox so very much. After a moment he frowned. "I'm not reading him."

"No—and you won't." There was a great deal of respect in Maddox's voice. "That there isn't just any garden-variety boucca. He's *old* magic. Powerful. A boucca like that can fly under your Janus radar without so much as breaking a sweat."

"How can you know for sure?"

"I recognize him. I used to see him coming and going from the Unseelie Court in the days before Auberon shut the Gates. Before your time, Sonn."

Sonny blinked. "You don't mean to tell me he's *the* original Puck?"

"Dunno," Maddox mused. "I heard a rumor that the *actual* Puck has been stuck in the mortal realm for the last hundred years or so—trapped in a jar of honey buried under a rock somewhere in Ireland. Ever since he did something that royally pissed off a leprechaun."

"Wow." Sonny whistled low. "I wonder what he did to deserve that."

"Who knows? Consider it a cautionary tale." Maddox chuckled. "Leprechauns have their own fair share of ancient power and *no* discernible sense of humor."

From a seat in the audience, one of the mortals—the director, it seemed—had called a stop to the boucca's scene, apparently satisfied with the work done on it (or perhaps just tired of telling Puck to "quit bouncing around the bloody set"). At any rate, they moved on to a scene with Sonny's girl from the park.

"C'mon, let's get closer," Sonny whispered to Maddox as he stepped farther into the wings, nearer to the stage proper.

"Why?"

"We might be able to find out something about her. You know—get a clue."

"You suit yourself. I'm not getting any closer to that boucca than I have to."

"Fine. Go have a look around outside then. See if you can find a kelpie tied up anywhere."

"I don't even see why you think there's any connection. That girl could have dropped her script anytime," Maddox muttered as he turned to leave. "It could have been sitting there for days. Weeks."

Sonny had considered that, but he had also seen the girl—Kelley—with the very same script only an hour or two before he'd found it beside the Lake. He'd found the crushed rose. It was hers, all right. He knew it. Now he just needed to find out what she'd been doing there. And what, if anything, she knew about a dangerous Faerie horse.

"Come, now a roundel and a fairy song. . . . "

The girl made her entrance through the center stage arch, lifting the trailing edge of her skirt and stepping gracefully up a set of stairs and onto the floating platform suspended by cables that represented Titania's bower. Garlands of silk flowers hung from the tops of ivy-wound poles, and gauze and organza draperies hung in filmy panels around the sides and back. The whole thing was lit in shades of green, gold, and blue to mimic a dappled forest.

It was sort of pretty, Sonny supposed, but nothing the least bit like any of the places where Titania and her Seelie Court were likely to spend time.

Gauze wings sprouted from the girl's shoulders, held there by elastic ribbon. Somehow, despite the ridiculous contraption, "Titania" managed to impart a kind of Faelike elegance to the lines as she went about assigning various duties to her fairy attendants.

"Some keep back the clamorous owl that nightly hoots and wonders at our quaint spirits." The girl finished her commands, reclining among the cushions. "Sing me now asleep, then to your offices, and let me rest."

A few members of the fairy dance corps flitted away into

the wings to do her queenly bidding while the rest gathered about, kneeling or perching on the set rigging. They began to sing:

"You spotted snakes with double tongue,
Thorny hedgehogs, be not seen;
Newts and blindworms, do no wrong,
Come not near our Fairy Queen."

The quaint Shakespearean lyrics wound through the air.

"Philomel with melody,
Sing in our sweet lullaby;
Lulla, lulla, lullaby, lulla, lulla, lullaby. . . . "

The song was like an enchantment.
The stage lights seemed to flicker and dim.
And the girl in the bower began to glow.

IX

Kelley sighed a fairy queen sigh, and her head sank to rest on her forearm. She loved this part of the play. The chorus of fairy singers had wonderful voices, and the tune for the "Philomel" song was an authentic Elizabethan roundel. It was strange, though. Even though Kelley had found herself humming the melody almost constantly for the past few weeks, today it was as if she'd never really heard it before.

I guess that's what happens when you're onstage instead of backstage, she thought, smiling to herself. Kelley felt her eyelids begin to droop as the murmuring refrain flowed over her like a babbling brook.

"Never harm
Nor spell nor charm
Come our lovely lady nigh.
So good night, with lullaby."

Dimly, as if from a great distance, she heard the actress playing the fairy named Cobweb say her line: "Hence, away! Now all is well. One aloof stand sentinel."

That was Jack's cue to enter as Oberon, sneaking near to anoint Titania's eyes with a magic potion as part of his trickery. Kelley lay still, waiting to hear Jack's mellifluous voice. Behind closed eyelids, she sensed the lights growing warmer. They must have turned a spotlight on her.

Part of her wanted to open her eyes to see how the lights looked, but she was just too comfortable. And anyway, they were running this scene straight through without the intervening "lovers" scenes, so she'd see soon enough—just as soon as Jack said his lines.

"What thou seest when thou dost wake, do it for thy true love take."

Jack's voice sounded *way* different from normal—the words hissing like a snake, sibilant and sinuous in her ears. The sound guy was definitely playing around. It was a cool effect. Creepy.

"Love and languish for his sake."

The rest of the line fell away into silence, and Kelley opened her eyes to find herself on a mossy bank. On all sides, the forest loomed, a soaring black battlement of gnarled and knotted branches, but in the tiny, moon-strewn jewel of her grove, all was pristine and beautiful.

She turned and saw someone standing in the shadows. Long hair hung in a loose sable wave to his shoulders, framing the sharp angle of cheek and jaw. A face she knew. Kelley felt the blood rush from her head as her heart thumped wildly. Moonlight glowed in his eyes, turning his gaze to silver fire, and the stark white branches of birch trees arched above his head as though he wore the antlers of a king stag. He was clothed only in leggings made of supple, dark-brown leather and belted with silver; his feet and torso were bare. Around his neck was a thin braided cord from which hung an iron-gray medallion. A dark line of glossy blood seeped from beneath the charm to trickle halfway down his chest.

What thou seest when thou dost wake . . .

He smiled. It was the saddest expression she had ever seen, full of unspeakable longing and heartache. Kelley felt her own heart tear in two.

Far off in the distance, she heard the harsh, keening cry of a hunting hawk.

Kelley's eyes snapped open and she sat up with a start, glancing wildly around.

She was in the theater, on the bower set. Frantically, she

twisted to look over her left shoulder. For an instant, she *saw* him. He stood in the shadowed corridor of the stage-left wings. Instead of heartsick longing, however, his expression was one of shocked surprise. Her green eyes met his gray ones for the briefest instant, and then he was gone.

"Much as I do not advocate the use of artificial stimulants, could somebody *please* provide our fairy queen with some bloody *No-Doz* before the next rehearsal?" Quentin shouted from the audience.

Dreaming. She'd been asleep and dreaming. . . .

Kelley felt the heat creeping up her neck into her face as she realized that, aside from her director's basilisk stare, there were about a dozen other pairs of eyes on her, all expressing various degrees of annoyance or amusement.

"Right. That's *it* for today, then, children." Quentin got up and strode toward the direction of his office. "Either get some *sleep*, Miss Winslow, or dial down the *Method* acting, hmm?"

Kelley glanced around apologetically at the rest of the cast, her cheeks burning with embarrassment. Her gaze fell on Alec Oakland, the actor playing Bottom, sitting off to the side of the bower platform with his fake ass's head tucked under one arm. Fortunately, he was smiling.

"Jeez, Winslow," he said. "Did I bore you?"

"Oh, God, Alec—I'm sorry! I didn't get much sleep last night and . . . "

"Don't worry about it." Alec waved a hand in dismissal. "I

don't think the Q was really going to do much with our scene today anyway—it's almost quittin' time."

He stood and hefted the prop mule head. Kelley stared at it, chagrined, abruptly reminded of the horse in her bathtub. Alec held out a hand to help her to her feet.

"You know," he said as she stood, "I've been meaning to ask . . . do you want to grab a coffee together sometime?"

Pain flashed in Kelley's head, accompanied by the dream image of the shadowy figure in the forest.

"Kelley? Are you okay?"

"Yeah . . . "

Alec was looking at her, concerned.

"Yes, thanks. Just the sleep deprivation, I think. Um—coffee. Coffee would be nice. Sometime."

"You look like you could use some," he joked, a hopeful expression on his handsome, freckled face. "Wanna go find a Starbucks?"

Kelley laughed and held up a hand. "Maybe not so much today. I think I'm just going to head home and try and get some rest . . . you know?"

"Sure. Right." Alec nodded and backed off a step.

Kelley felt vaguely guilty and more than a little confused by her own reaction. A week earlier, she would have jumped at the chance to go out with Alec. Now? Now she couldn't see past the twisting branches of her dream forest—and the dark-haired young man who stood beneath them, his eyes full of anguish. A moment of awkward silence ensued. Kelley reached out a hand to scratch the mule-head prop behind one fake, fuzzy ear.

"Rain check?" she said, and tried to inject some enthusiasm into her voice.

"Absolutely!" Alec nodded, and his smile halfway returned. "See you tomorrow," he said before loping off toward the dressing rooms.

After a minute she followed in his wake, walking a deliberate path through the darkened wings where she'd seen—where she'd *thought* she'd seen—someone. But, of course, there was no one there.

X

The boucca had Sonny by the throat.

Sonny was furious with himself for allowing his guard to drop—Maddox had warned him about the boucca and not getting too close. But he'd been distracted by the boy with the ridiculous donkey head under his arm, and the uncomfortable surge of emotion that had washed over him when he saw him take the girl by the hand.

The boucca wrinkled his nose, an expression of grim delight on his pale-green face. "I smell a Faerie killer."

"And I smell a pook," Sonny ground out between clenched teeth. "Which of us is more pungent, I wonder?"

A long, tense silence passed between them, and then the boucca threw back his head and laughed, releasing his punishing grip on Sonny's larynx. "What's a Janus doing down in Hell's Kitchen on a day o' the Nine?"

Sonny rubbed at his neck, wincing. Sizing the boucca up, he dug into his messenger bag and tossed one of the onyx beads at him. "Where is it? *What* is it?"

The boucca caught the bead out of the air, stared at it flatly for a long moment, and then tossed it back. "Not a clue."

"All right, then." If Sonny was going to get any answers at all, he thought, he was going to have to play rough. A Faerie could be compelled to obey commands if one knew the secret of its true name. Sonny stared the boucca in the eyes and said gravely, "I do compel thee—"

The boucca covered his pointed ears and began keening.

Sonny pushed on, relentless. "By thy truest of names, I do compel thee, and thou shalt obey my commands, for I do call thee *Robin Goodfellow*."

The boucca's shrieks suddenly turned to peals of laughter. "Oh, please!" he said finally, gasping in mirth. "That name's not exactly the earth-shattering secret it once was, you know." He wiped a tear from his eye, chortling. "You stupid great yob—you should get out to see more theater!"

Sonny stood there, chagrined, the heat of embarrassment creeping up his cheeks.

"Shakespeare spilled those beans quite some time ago.

How do you expect me to go onstage night after night if every time someone chirps 'Robin Goodfellow' I fall to the ground in mindless submission?" The boucca shook his head in amused disgust. "I warned old Willie—gave him a scorching case of fleas, even. Bah—writers! Stubborn lot. Well, after that, the name sort of lost its potency, you know? Same with 'Puck,' so don't bother trying. I can no more be compelled by those names than if you had just hallooed 'Hey, buddy!' at me." He snorted and gave a parting shot. "Auberon's breeding 'em up stupid these days, I see."

Sonny's hands clenched into fists at the insult. Then he remembered the script he'd found, with the scribbled words: *Kelley's Script—Please Return (this means YOU, Bob!)*

Bouccas were notorious thieves.

"Let's try this, then," he said. "I do compel thee by the name of . . . Bob."

The boucca stiffened and stopped in his tracks. He turned and pegged Sonny with a shrewd gaze.

"Will you help me?" Sonny implored.

Relenting, Bob the boucca said, "I've not a clue as to where it is. But . . . I do know *what* it is."

"It's a kelpie, isn't it?"

"If you already know what it is, then why do you need me?"

That seemed to confirm Sonny's suspicions. He could press the boucca further on the matter of the kelpie, but there were other things he needed to understand now, and he didn't

81

know how far he could push his luck. "All right," he said. "Another question, then."

Bob waited.

"That girl. The actress playing Titania." He nodded in the direction of the dressing rooms where she'd gone. "She saw me just now."

"I noticed that."

Sonny was beginning to lose patience. "I was veiled and she *saw* me."

Bob tilted his head, his expression maddeningly inscrutable, and said, "How is that possible for a mortal?"

"That is my question to you. How is it possible for a mortal to have seen through my veil?"

"It isn't."

"What are you saying?" Sonny's wariness of the ancient, powerful boucca warred with his absolute need to know.

"You ask a lot of questions."

Sonny took a deep breath. If he angered Bob, the boucca was likely to just vanish without another word. "Please. It is . . . important to me."

Bob cocked his head to one side, considering that. He seemed to shift and change in size and proportion ever so slightly as Sonny spoke to him. It was subtle, hard to notice unless you were only looking at him sideways—as if his appearance mirrored the slipperiness of what he said.

"Do you know *why* Auberon shut the Gates, young Sonny

Flannery?" the boucca asked.

"Of course I do." Sonny barely contained his frustration. "I'm a bloody Janus."

"You're a Janus, certainly. And I'm sure you're a fine one, at that," Bob said, almost without sarcasm. He put up a hand to forestall any interruption. "And you're a changeling—cradle-took from a mortal home to the Otherworld, just like the rest of your kind. But, *un*like the rest of them . . . I happen to know that you're also the only Janus that Auberon handpicked to raise under his own roof, at the very center of the Unseelie Court, almost as if you were a son."

"Do you have a point to make?"

"Aye. I do." Bob nodded slowly, returning Sonny's steady gaze. "But not about you. About *him*."

Sonny knew well how Auberon was regarded by the majority of changelings and also by a good portion of the Faerie Folk: with suspicion and with fear.

But the king *had* treated Sonny like family and, despite an arrogance that could border on casual cruelty, he had never given the young mortal a reason not to trust him. If Sonny was to be honest, Auberon had his loyalty and respect.

"What tale did the mighty Auberon spin by the fire for his panting Janus pup about the closing of the Gates?" Bob asked, his voice thick with mockery.

Sonny glared at him. "He closed the Gates to protect us."

"Which 'us,' little changeling boy?" Bob cocked his head,

his tone quizzical. "The mortal us or the Faerie us?"

"Both. He did it to protect both worlds—each from the other."

"What you call 'protection,' a goodly portion of the Fair Folk call 'imprisonment.' What else did good king Auberon tell you? What dire threat from the mortal world was our benevolent lord and master keeping his loyal subjects safe and sound from?"

Sonny frowned. He failed to see what this had to do with him or the kelpie or the girl or anything he actually *wanted* to learn from the boucca. But he obviously had no choice but to play along with Bob's game of questions. "He told me that, around the turn of the last century, as the mortal world measures time, a human woman found a way through one of the Gates to the Otherworld. And that she stole a Faerie child right from out of the cradle and escaped back to the mortal realm. So the king closed the Gates to keep it from happening again."

"And there's thundering great hypocrisy for you!" Bob did a little jig and swung himself effortlessly up onto the landing of a set of escape stairs. His eyes glowed fiercely. "Putting aside for the moment the fact that stealing children in the *other* direction was—up until that time—a sort of national pastime for the Fair Folk . . . don't you think that whole story is a bit odd? Pretty drastic measures for one wee bairn gone missing, wouldn't you say?"

"It wasn't just *any* Faerie child that mortal stole!" Sonny protested. "Granted it may have been a harsh decision at the time, but Auberon was well within his rights to make it. The child was his heir!"

Bob was relentless. "And the fact that *you* were, what, the son of a poor crofter? Or that your friend who waits outside the door—whatsisname? Maddox—that he was a mere blacksmith's child . . . did that then make it all right for the Faerie to cross thresholds and steal *you* from *your* folk?"

"I . . ."

"Do you not think that your own mother wept bitter tears at the loss? Tear at her pretty, dark hair and fall to the ground in an agony of mourning for her stolen child?"

"What do you know of my mother?" Sonny demanded, suddenly furious.

"Pretty thing, strong-willed, and a wild heart. Blue eyes. Lovely face . . . when it wasn't all twisted up with grieving, that is." The boucca spoke in low, thrumming tones. The glint of mischief was gone from his eyes. "The theft of you tore her apart. Tore her family apart. They all thought she'd gone mad. Husband up and left because he couldn't stand the pain in her."

"Stop it."

"Do you not think a woman like that might have sworn revenge?" The Fae's eyes glowed green as his stare bored into Sonny. "A child for a child?"

"My mother—"

"Could *never* have crossed into the Otherworld. No matter

how strong, nor wild, nor willful. Not without help."

"But you just said—"

"Yes. I did."

Sonny could only stand there staring at the boucca, mystified.

"Now. There's something to *think* about, eh?" Bob fell silent then. He crouched on the landing, utterly still, watching Sonny with his unblinking eyes.

Riddles. Why is he giving me riddles? Questions with no answers, all obscured by the emotional impact of thoughts of his mother. His mortal life that could have been . . . He clamped down hard on the urge to ask anything further and turned to leave.

Except there was just one more thing he wanted to know. A mere curiosity—but it pricked at his mind . . .

"Tell me something."

"Is that an order?" Bob glared flatly at him.

"No. Please." Sonny held up a hand. "I mean—I would like to know. If you would like to tell me. The story I heard about you and the leprechaun . . . "

"And the honey jar?"

"Yes. Did it happen? Really?"

"Well . . . the insides of my ears are sticky." He snorted. "And I occasionally attract the attention of amorous bees. You tell me."

"How did you get out?"

"May the gods bless progress." Bob raised his eyes to the

ceiling. "Eight or nine years ago some bullyboyo contractors came along and built a five-star resort and golf course on the very site. The day they broke ground, they broke my jar!"

Sonny laughed despite himself.

Bob shrugged. "It's a very nice course. I'm sure the patrons wonder, though, why they lose so very many balls. And the plumbing in the clubhouse tends to be . . . quirky."

"Never cross a leprechaun."

"Right."

"What did you do to raise his wrath?"

Bob's expression went stern. "That I will not tell you."

"But why—"

"What I *will* tell you is this. Are you listening?"

Sonny nodded silently. The Faerie's stare was so intense that Sonny almost felt it as a physical sensation.

"Once upon a time," the boucca continued, "I was Auberon's henchman, much like you. But I was *never* Auberon's fool. And I am not entirely without compassion." And then Bob, who was called Puck, who was called Robin Goodfellow, laughed gently and leaped gracefully from his perch, disappearing up into the shadows of the high stage rigging. His last words echoed down through the darkness.

"Take care of her, Sonny Flannery," he said. "I did. . . . "

XI

Kelley showered in the tiny bathroom attached to her dressing room and blow-dried her hair. Of course, when she glanced up at the high, tiny window, she noticed sourly that it was suddenly raining buckets. Good thing her jacket had a hood, she thought, because her umbrella had gone missing days earlier. She suspected Bob.

With a sigh, she packed up her stuff and got ready to head home for a nice, quiet evening spent figuring out how to get a full-grown horse out of the bathtub—and the apartment—without alerting the neighborhood.

Standing in the doorway, watching a curtain of water sheeting off the sloped roof, Kelley briefly contemplated sleeping in the theater that night. What with the stormy weather and the no doubt stormier roommate . . .

Coward.

Squaring her shoulders, she yanked up her hood and stepped out into the sleeting rain. Instantly it felt as if she was running underwater. She could barely see through the downpour; ducking her head, she darted into the side walkway, where the eaves of the Avalon offered a scant bit of protection. As she glanced up from the puddles, Kelley halted, startled by the sight of a figure perched on an old wooden crate and peering through the grimy leaded-glass window that looked into one of the theater's rooms. Her dressing room.

Where I just spent the last fifteen minutes standing wrapped in a towel!

Kelley stifled a gasp with one fist while her other hand went to the overstuffed bag hanging from her shoulder, with her can of mace buried somewhere deep inside. She tried to back away as silently as she could, but the figure stiffened, as if he had heard her sneakered feet over the rattling sound of the rain on the trash cans. Kelley turned to make a run for it back toward the stage door. Somehow the man made it off the crate and was blocking her way before she had taken a step.

How could anyone move that fast? she thought.

Then she looked into his eyes, and every other thought melted away.

Handsome Stranger.

His face was exactly as she remembered—from both the park and her midrehearsal dream. This time his gaze flashed not with compassion or sympathy, but with danger. His beautiful mouth was drawn into a thin, tense line.

His expression put Kelley on guard.

"Well if it isn't the FTD florist," she said, tilting her chin up defiantly. "What are you doing here?"

"Looking for you."

Three words that made her heart hammer painfully in her chest. Kelley had to stop herself from backing up a step. This was not exactly how she had wanted to run into Handsome Stranger again. This felt dangerous.

"What were *you* doing in the park after dark last night?" he asked, his tone sharp.

Anger took hold of Kelley. "What makes you think I was in the park after dark?"

"I know you were. I know you stayed there after I left you in the garden, and I know you found . . . something." He was watching her very closely. "I need to know where it is. Tell me. Now."

"Get lost."

"Excuse me?" He blinked, startled. The blankness of his expression made him seem suddenly boyish, and Kelley realized that he couldn't be that much older than she was, maybe eighteen or nineteen—not that his age necessarily made him less threatening.

But Kelley had been raised by a fiery Irish aunt. She enunciated each word as she repeated, "Get. Lost."

Handsome Stranger looked confused, as if he'd never had someone tell him to take a hike before. "You don't understand. I need to know what you found. It's for your own good—you need to trust me."

"Trust you? You're *lurking* in an alley, for God's sake. You obviously followed me here from somewhere, and you were looking in my dressing-room window when I was getting changed! I don't think 'trust' is the issue here!"

"I wasn't watching you get changed."

"Sure you weren't."

At least he had the good grace to blush, Kelley thought.

"All I saw was you leaving the room. I wanted to see if you were alone so I could talk to you."

"Right!" Kelley scoffed. "So you could 'talk' to me?"

In truth, he'd looked startled enough by her accusation that Kelley was inclined to believe him—she just wasn't much inclined to care.

"Is that why you were skulking around backstage earlier?"

The question didn't prompt any kind of reaction Kelley could have expected. His eyes flew wide and he pulled back sharply from her—almost as if Kelley had physically struck him.

What the hell?

"Are you stalking me?" She glanced over her shoulder to see if any of the cast or crew were still around. But the rain had driven everyone away or indoors.

"Of course not!" he said, sounding shocked.

He took a step toward her, and Kelley skittered backward. "You even *try* to touch me, and I scream like a banshee."

That stopped him. Again, there was that confused, boyish expression on his face.

Kelley hazarded a glance back up into his eyes, and the breath caught in her throat. The blazing intensity of his gaze was like being caught in a searchlight. He was threatening her. And yet all she wanted was to reach out and touch his face.

What thou seest when thou dost wake . . .

Kelley shook herself from the unwelcome reverie. She backed away as she watched him visibly clamp down on the urge to shout at her.

"It's getting late and I don't have time for this," he muttered impatiently, shooting a brief glance skyward.

Kelley found herself following his glance. *How on earth can he tell what time it is?* The sky had been the same dingy shade of pewter-gray all day.

He took another step toward her, and all of Kelley's nerve endings jangled like car alarms, urging her to flight. She felt a strange tingling along her spine, down to her fingertips, as though she were actually trying to grow wings. But her feet remained rooted to the ground and, locked in his gaze, she held her breath.

He reached out a hand toward her, his fingers brushing her arm. All of a sudden an electrical shock jolted him backward, his whole right side jerking away. He flinched, and as he broke eye contact, suddenly Kelley could move again. But with preternatural speed he recovered and swiped a hand in her direction, catching her hood and a handful of her hair. He yanked her backward, and Kelley felt a snap as the catch of her silver necklace came undone and the four-leaf-clover charm fell off, landing in a puddle.

Anger flared in Kelley's chest, overriding fear, and she rounded on her attacker.

She swung a wild fist in a wide circle, and the young man flew backward through the air, slamming up hard into the brick wall of the theater.

"How *dare* you?" she shouted, the air around her suddenly as shockingly cold as her adrenaline-fueled rage.

His storm-gray eyes went wide with alarm at the sight of her . . .

XII

Light blazed like fireworks exploding in the alleyway.

"How *dare* you?" she shouted again, and her thunderous voice knocked him back against the wall a second time. Sonny threw an arm over his face to shield his eyes. The ground beneath him spun dizzyingly, and for a moment he thought he was going to be sick. Squinting against the glare, he glanced up at where, only a moment before, a girl had stood drenched and defiant. His jaw dropped open.

A nimbus of light flared all around her like diamond-bright wings.

He wanted to beg forgiveness. Offer up his life for

his grievous offense. Grovel. The creature that stood before him, glorious as the stars, was to be worshipped and feared. His chest ached as though he'd been kicked with stone boots, and tears of remorse welled in his eyes. It was as though he were a small boy again, running through the halls of Auberon's palace, knowing that he would never be one of the Fair Folk—a toy, a pet, but never truly loved by them. By creatures like the goddess who stood before him. Her light poured down on him, and he knew that he was massively unworthy. . . .

And then, just as suddenly as the starburst had shone, everything went dim again.

"Jackass."

Sonny shook his head, confused and disoriented, his field of vision still light dazzled and spotted with afterimages. He blinked at the girl, who glared angrily at him as she did the clasp back up on her necklace.

"You almost broke it!"

For an instant, Sonny thought he still saw a sparkling aura surrounding her. But it was faint, ghostly. Then nothing. She could not possibly have been hiding behind a glamour. Sonny's Janus sensibilities could rip through a Faerie disguise as though it were gauze, even this far from the Gate.

"Are you deficient?" The girl stuffed the silver pendant back down the front of her shirt. "What the hell are you staring at?"

Sonny climbed unsteadily to his feet. The girl had her mace

out now and was aiming the sprayer squarely at the bridge of his nose.

"What is it—drugs or something? What's wrong with you?"

"Who *are* you?" he asked, rubbing his arm where it still tingled.

"Shouldn't you already know that?" she scoffed. "I mean, seeing as how you're stalking me."

"I'm not stalking you." He shook his head. It did, he had to admit, probably seem that way. "Not exactly. I just thought you might be able to help me."

"Gosh, you know?" She tilted her head, eyes still bright with anger. "I'm really not feeling particularly helpful at the moment. Maybe some other time. Oh, wait. Maybe not."

Sonny moved off, frustrated and utterly out of his depth. "All right. I understand. I'm sorry if I frightened you."

"Yeah, well. Try not lurking. And not attacking. I'm outta here," she said, backing away. The mace never wavered. "And don't you dare follow me."

"I won't. I won't bother you again." Sonny held up his hands, palms out in a placating gesture. "I promise."

"You'd better not," Kelley said.

She turned and ran.

She ran away from him. She was afraid of him.

Sonny didn't like the feeling at all.

"I see that went well," Maddox said dryly as he dispersed

the veil that had kept him hidden from sight and stepped out from behind a Dumpster. Sonny turned to glare at him. "No, really. I think she likes you."

"Maddox . . ."

"I'm already shutting up."

"You were supposed to be keeping watch," Sonny muttered.

"I was. She's quick." He shrugged. "And anyway, *you* should've stayed veiled."

Sonny stared in the direction the girl had gone. "I'm not sure it would have made any difference."

"Why not?"

"She saw me. Standing onstage—she *saw* me. Through the veil. Did you . . . see *her*?" Sonny turned and grabbed his friend's shoulder, hard. "I mean—just now—did you *see* what happened to her?"

Maddox's expression was closed, inscrutable. The rain was lessening, but water still ran down both their faces. Neither of them noticed.

"I saw . . . something," Maddox said. His voice was flat, carefully stripped of audible emotion. But his next words made his feelings perfectly clear. "I'm pretty sure it scared the hell out of me."

"We should follow her."

Maddox was already vigorously shaking his head. "Oh, no. No no no. You just promised you *wouldn't* follow her. I'd think twice before breaking a promise to a sweet, pretty, incredibly *scary* kid like that. Especially when she can effortlessly toss you around in an alley."

"Look, I got nothing but vague, somewhat dire warnings about the kelpie from the boucca. But that 'sweet, pretty kid' knows more about what happened at the Lake than she's telling, and I think we should find out what that is." Sonny didn't bother to mention that Bob had also told him to "take care of her."

"Let it go, Sonn," Maddox said, and turned to walk in the opposite direction from where the girl had run. "I know trouble when I see it, and so do you. Put her out of your mind."

Sonny did know trouble. As much as he didn't want to admit it, Maddox was right. He followed reluctantly in the other Janus's wake, looking back over his shoulder as he went. In that moment, putting her out of his mind seemed like the hardest thing he'd ever had to do.

XIII

Standing before her apartment door, Kelley took a deep breath and turned her key in the lock.

"Tyff?" she called out tentatively. "Um . . . I'm home-and-really-sorry. . . . "

Silence.

"Tyff?"

"He ate my soap." Tyff walked slowly out of the bathroom, arms folded across her chest, the tone of her voice pleasantly conversational. "My eighty-dollar bar of hand-milled Japanese herbal complexion soap. From Japan. He ate it."

"Oh . . . "

"He also ate your two-dollar bar of Irish Spring. I *let* him eat that one."

"Tyff, I'm really, *really* sorry—"

"Actually, I gave it to him to eat." Tyff smiled sweetly. After a moment of staring honeyed daggers at Kelley, she frowned and said, "Did you know you're soaking wet?"

"I kinda got caught out in the rain. . . . "

"Go put on a robe or something before you warp the floor, will you?"

Kelley looked down at her feet and saw that there was a puddle forming around her. She scooted past Tyff, who stood in the bathroom doorway, shaking her head. Kelley heard a whinnied greeting from over Tyff's shoulder.

Stripping off her jacket and jeans, she slipped into her big fluffy bathrobe, thinking how much she was *not* enjoying coming home soaking wet twice in a row. A cup of tea would be nice—and give her an excuse to avoid the bathroom while she put the kettle on.

"Did . . . um . . . did he eat the oats?" she asked, smiling tentatively at Tyff as she edged past. "You know . . . after the soap?"

"He did not." Tyff followed her into the tiny kitchen. "However, in an effort to avoid the further consumption of toiletries, I tried giving him some of your ridiculous kiddie cereal." She waved at a box of Lucky Charms that was sitting open on the counter. "That seemed to go over well. So did scratching him behind his left ear."

Kelley glanced at her roommate, extremely surprised by how well Tyff was taking all of this.

"*Not* that I'm becoming attached or anything!" Tyff said. "Because I'm not."

"Okay . . . "

"I mean—even though he's been a very well-behaved horsie so far and hasn't even made a horsie mess—" Tyff stopped suddenly, realizing that Kelley was staring at her. "Never mind."

"Okay . . . ," Kelley said again. She turned to make the tea.

Tyff was silent for a moment. "Winslow . . . what *happened* to you today?"

"What do you mean?"

"You look kind of . . . spooked. Wiggy. And it's not because there's a soap-devouring pony in the apartment. What's wrong with you?"

Kelley bit her lower lip to keep it from trembling. Now that she was home safe in her own apartment, the thought of what had happened in the alley came rushing back. She suddenly realized what a very scary situation she had been in.

"Kelley?"

"There was this guy in the park yesterday. I've never seen him before, but he gave me a rose and . . . well . . . then he just sort of disappeared."

"So? What about him?"

"I think he might be . . . following me."

"Okay," Tyff said slowly. "I know you're new to the big city and all but, see, that's not a *good* thing, Kelley."

"He was in the alley outside the theater this afternoon."

"An alley? Oh, even better! Did you call the police?"

"No, but I told him to stop following me."

"Oh, *good*—you talked to him," Tyff said sarcastically. "*That's* nice and safe!"

"I know, I know. . . . " Kelley stirred distractedly at her tea. "But he had a lot of opportunity to hurt me if he'd wanted to. And he didn't. He said I should trust him."

"What? Trust him? He's not some guy your wacko aunt hired to follow you around or something, is he?"

"Like a detective?" Kelley blinked away the sting of unshed tears. It hurt her somehow to know that the random act of kindness he'd presented her with in the form of that beautiful flower might, in fact, have been just a calculated move to get close to her. It had seemed such a lovely gesture at the time.

"Yeah, or some kind of bodyguard," Tyff said. "We all know how deeply unenthusiastic dear old Auntie Em was about you moving here."

Kelley thought about that for a moment. "Maybe . . . ," she said. Emma *could* be freakishly overprotective.

Tyff sighed, checking the time on her watch. "I have to go. I have a date and, thanks to your heroic horse-rescue efforts, I'm going to have to shower at the gym. Are you going to be okay by yourself?"

"I'll be fine," Kelley said. She was feeling a bit better now that she was home and had told someone about her encounter.

It didn't seem quite like such a big deal anymore. Just Big City Weirdness, and she could handle that.

"Look—just do me a favor and don't do anything stupid?" Tyff said, swinging a pashmina over her shoulders and heading for the door. "Our little buddy in there might be well-behaved, but so far, he hasn't contributed to the rent, so I still need you around."

Kelley grinned and nodded. She couldn't believe how understanding Tyff had been so far, but she was grateful.

"Maybe you could spend the evening trying to figure out a way to get Mr. Ed out of the tub," Tyff suggested as she opened the door and stepped into the hall. "But if you do go out, watch your back, okay?"

"I will. I promise. Have fun tonight."

The door closed behind Tyff, and Kelley went into the kitchen. She picked up the box of Lucky Charms and shook it. It was half empty. At the sound of the cereal rattling, she heard an answering whinny. She headed toward the bathroom, poking her head around the door. The horse flicked his ears in her direction. He snorted, and a large, iridescent bubble appeared, inflating from his left nostril to the size of a small balloon before popping loudly. Kelley laughed out loud at the surprised expression on the animal's face, and he answered her back with a whinny that sounded distinctly like a bashful chuckle.

"Come on, horse."

Kelley felt stupid.

For one thing, the horse seemed as if he might be smarter than she was. He refused to fall for her trick of moving the handful of cereal farther and farther away in an attempt to get him out of the tub. He just stretched out his neck until she was out of reach and then tilted his head, looking at her with big sad eyes, until she relented and sat on the edge of the tub, feeding him marshmallow moons, horseshoes, and clovers.

For another thing, she couldn't just keep calling the horse "horse." It felt . . . well, rude somehow.

Kelley poured out another handful of Lucky Charms, holding them up to the velvety-soft muzzle. The animal's eyes seemed to brighten with enthusiasm, and he nuzzled around in her palm. It tickled and Kelley laughed. A name occurred to her.

"Lucky," she murmured.

The horse lifted his head as though responding and gazed at her, munching placidly on the sugary treat. Well, it kind of fit. He was lucky that she'd been in the park that night, and he was lucky that Mrs. Madsen in the apartment next door hadn't heard all the commotion and called the cops. He was lucky that the landlord hadn't paid a visit. And he was extremely lucky in that Tyff, for some unfathomable reason, hadn't killed either of them yet. Lucky.

Kelley scratched behind his left ear, and Lucky whickered softly with pleasure. Kelley got the impression that if he were a cat instead of a horse, he would've started to purr.

I just hope for both our sakes that you're a "Good" Lucky, Kelley thought, *and not a "Bad" Lucky.* She was perfectly well aware that luck could go either way.

XIV

Sonny dropped painfully to one knee to avoid having his head bitten off.

The boggart he was fighting had burst forth from a rift in Strawberry Fields. It was covered in venomous thorns and had a prominent set of gnashy teeth. Hissing at him, the boggart hurtled off into the dark. Sonny swore and broke into a sprint to chase it, trying hard to concentrate—and forget about that strange, infuriating girl.

The boggart snarled, bounding through a thicket, and Sonny cursed and followed. The clearing beyond was empty, but Sonny could smell it—like the stench of milkweed. The thing was hiding, but it was still close.

There was a rustling in the trees above his head. Sonny glanced up, only to realize too late that the boggart had led him straight into a trap.

A cloud of ravens swirled in the air overhead, and Sonny went cold with apprehension. These were no ordinary ravens. They were creatures of Mabh, the Autumn Queen of the shadowy Faerie Borderlands. Huge birds with oily black feathers, they had red eyes and claws like scythes, and a terrible hunger for human flesh.

The boggart must have been one of Mabh's minions as well, Sonny thought as he frantically pulled out the bundled branches from his satchel. At his incantation, they transformed once again into the silver-bladed sword.

On the other side of the clearing, the boggart emerged, lifting its gnarled hands into the air as though signaling troops. The ravens attacked.

Sonny's sword flashed through the air as he whacked two of the murderous birds out of the sky. He cut through several, but others followed, and he thrust sharply, impaling them on the end of the blade. He ducked away from another attack, narrowly missing losing an eye.

Kelley's face appeared before him in his mind. This time Sonny didn't try to fight it. Thinking of her smile, he redoubled his efforts. The ravens came at him again, and his sword whirled, a shining arc in the darkness.

* * *

The light from the rising sun was pouring through his windows when Sonny stepped through the door into his apartment. Out on the balcony, the elegant figure of the Unseelie king sat on a lounge chair. Sonny wearily threw his jacket and satchel on the settee and went onto the terrace.

"Mabh is mightily annoyed with you, young man," Auberon said, his words colored with a chilly merriment. "She is very fond of her pets."

"Next time tell her to keep them home. Or, if she really wants to test me, to send bigger birds." Sonny stretched his tired back. In truth, the murderous ravens had taken a great deal of skill to handle, but Sonny was pleased with the outcome. Not a single one had gotten past him.

When she had roamed the mortal world freely, Queen Mabh had been the stuff of nightmares. Her transgressions against mortals had grown so terrible that Auberon and Titania had been forced to join together and imprison Mabh within the confines of the Borderlands, her own darkling realm. But Mabh had still relished the pleasure of sending her minions through the Gates to wreak chaos—which she would track with her scrying glass, as though watching horror films.

The thought of Mabh's creatures being loosed upon the world again made Sonny take his duties as a Janus very seriously. He might not want to live in this world, but he did not wish it harm. Especially not when it had such creatures in it as his Firecracker. . . .

Sonny felt Auberon staring at him. He had a disjointed

sensation that the king had asked him a question and he hadn't even heard it.

"My lord?" Distracted, Sonny looked up. Into the eyes of his king.

"Tell me of the girl," Auberon said.

Sonny had not meant to think of her. He had certainly not planned to mention her to Auberon. But his mind, it seemed, was a problem in that respect. And he had made the dangerous mistake of exchanging glances with the Unseelie lord.

"I can see her. In your eyes." Auberon's dark gaze held Sonny like a fly trapped in amber. He could not look away, even as he felt Auberon's mind stabbing into his own. "Who is she?"

"I don't know."

"Do not lie to me, lad." The king's voice remained easy, but Sonny knew that, Janus or no, he was in a great deal of peril in that moment.

"It is no lie. She is . . . an actress. Just a girl from the park, really." Sonny expected that at any moment Auberon would shred through his formidable mental defenses as if they were paper and learn everything he knew about her. Even though that wasn't much, Sonny unaccountably did not want the Faerie king to take any sudden great interest in finding out about his Firecracker.

"Hmm," Auberon murmured.

Sonny felt the pressure inside his skull lessen. He raised himself up off his knees—he hadn't been aware that he had fallen to them—and shook the tension from his shoulders.

"I cannot gather her from your mind," the Faerie king mused, sounding intrigued. "And yet, you hold her image there."

"She is pretty." Sonny shrugged with what he hoped was an appropriately casual air. "For a mortal."

After a long, weighty moment, the king's lips twitched in the ghost of a smile. "Not so pretty, I hope, as to make you forget yourself, Sonny Flannery. Or your duties."

Sonny bowed his head slightly in deference. "Of course not, my lord."

"Good. Because I have an unsettling sense that Mabh's harbingers are simply that—heralds of things to come. There is a great deal of unrest in the Faerie realms, Sonny. And the closing of the Gates, while I deemed it necessary, has become a thing of contention and a rallying point around which my enemies gather. If my Janus Guard falters, it will go hard."

"We will not, my lord."

"That would be best," Auberon said. "And what news, else?"

Sonny hesitated for an instant, but only for an instant. Auberon was his king. His very purpose as a Janus was to serve him. Why was he even *thinking* about dissembling? Bob the boucca's words were a tiny echo in the back of his mind, and Sonny pushed them away.

He told Auberon about his encounters at the Gate. The king already knew about the boggart and the birds from

Mabh, so Sonny told him, instead, of the swarm of piskies, mildly chagrined by his amusement at the tale—much like Maddox's. Then, swallowing nervousness at the thought of his failure, Sonny told Auberon of the Lake and of the creature that he—and, indeed, all the Janus—had somehow missed entirely: the kelpie that had escaped through the Gate and disappeared into the night.

"Kelpie are dangerous, surely." Auberon shrugged, unconcerned. "But not smart enough to evade my entire Janus Guard for long, I wouldn't think."

"I'm not sure that it was just *any* kelpie, my lord," Sonny said. He stood and went back into the apartment to retrieve his messenger bag. He drew the three onyx gems from the inner pocket of the bag and, returning, placed them in Auberon's upturned palm. A few coppery strands of horsehair were still tangled in the beads. "I found these talismans in the mud by the Lake. I don't think I've ever seen their like before."

"I have," the king murmured.

Sonny wouldn't have thought it possible for Auberon's face to turn a paler shade than it already was, but it did. The tall brow remained smooth, the regal face impassive. But the air on Sonny's balcony plummeted to glacial temperatures.

"The Hunt . . ."

Sonny had to strain to catch the words. "My lord?" he asked.

"These are charms of making." The king's eyes were midnight pools. "They can call the Roan Horse into being."

Sonny's blood froze in his veins. He knew, suddenly, what the glittering black jewels meant. "But . . . the Roan Horse leads the Wild Hunt." His voice came out in a rasping whisper.

"Yes. It does." Auberon's hand clenched into a fist around the beads, then he dropped them to bounce along the flagstones at his feet.

He stood and stepped to the edge of the terrace, looking down on the park, and it seemed to Sonny that the Faerie king had forgotten that he was even there.

"Oh, Mabh." Auberon's voice was harsh, his expression stricken. "Is this what your folly has brought us to now?"

There was a blur of motion, and Sonny threw a hand up in front of his face to shield it from the sudden ice-sharp wind. When he lowered it, the king was gone, his cry melting into the keening of a falcon.

XV

The Avalon was on fire, and there was nothing Kelley could do about it.

All of Manhattan was on fire.

Brighter than day, the night sky was orange with the light of the flames, leaping to singe the clouds. Terrible music thundered; pipes and drums and skirling voices clawed the air with triumphant, horrific noise. There was the sound of hooves. She looked down at the ground, far, far below, and saw that the streets of the city ran red with blood.

She could not stop it.

She didn't want to.

A savage glee filled the space where her heart should have been, and Kelley opened her mouth wide to add her voice to the sounds of the war cries ringing through the air all around her.

"Hey, Winslow—get some sleep last night?"

Kelley looked up, jolted from the remembrance of her disturbing dreams. "Hey, Alec," she sighed. Scenes of carnage had paraded through her head all night. "Yeah, I slept. A ton. Wish I hadn't."

Alec regarded her with a grin. "You are an odd, odd girl."

Kelley smiled back. "That's what I was thinking of writing for my bio in the show program. You know, that and only playing this part 'cause the real actress went *snap* . . ."

"Hey! Don't kid yourself—I think you're a smokin' Titania. And just between you and me? Before she went *snap*? I shuddered at the thought of having to do the bower scene with Crazy Babs every night. With you it'll be fun!" Alec leaned beside her against the wall. "Wanna go practice? It'll only take a second to grab my ass . . . uh . . . head. My ass head."

Kelley threw back her head and laughed, her mood brightened. It was becoming pretty obvious that, bad jokes notwithstanding, Alec would have cheerfully run off to a darkened corner of the theater to "rehearse" with her. She chose to ignore that and punched him lightly on the shoulder. "You know I'm still the *only* hired help around here, right?" She waved one hand in an airy gesture, intoning imperiously, "I,

Titania, Queen of the Fairy Realm . . . had better go mop the stage before Mindi sets my wings on fire."

With that, she made her escape, surprised to find that her heart was pounding a little too fast in her chest. He was cute . . . but it wasn't the thought of rehearsing in dark corners with Alec Oakland that set her heart racing.

She ducked Alec after the end of rehearsal, too. Another day of having Lucky stuck in her tub had led Kelley to the conclusion that the only way she was going to get rid of him was if she could find out to whom he actually belonged. She had spent the morning on her computer, printing up fliers on hot-pink paper with a picture of Lucky (taken with her camera phone) and just enough information to hopefully get someone to call her without calling the police or a mental institution. After rehearsal, armed with the fliers, a stapler, and a roll of tape, she hit the park and headed toward the few scattered public bulletin boards so that she could post her notice. She started at the south end of the park and sneaked a look at her watch, wondering despite herself whether . . .

Cue actor—enter stage left.

Sure enough, she'd been in the park only about five minutes when an increasingly familiar reflection appeared over her shoulder in the glass-cased bulletin board.

Kelley didn't even turn around.

"Don't you have a home?" she asked, awash in studied nonchalance. She opened the glass and stapled a pink flier over a free-concert notice from last summer on the corkboard.

He answered her question with a question: "What are you doing here?"

"I'm posting information fliers," she replied, waving the little sheaf of paper she held. "Not that it's any of your business."

"You shouldn't be here."

Kelley glanced back to where he stood behind her, brooding.

"Nice to see you again, too," she said as she walked away.

He'd caught up to her before she'd taken five full steps. "That wasn't what I meant," he said, a note of frustration in his voice.

She couldn't tell whether he was frustrated with her or with himself. She realized she felt almost exactly the same way. The crisp fallen leaves crunched under their feet as they walked side by side in what, under any other circumstances and with any other guy, would have felt like companionable silence.

"I'm sorry about yesterday," he said at last.

"What, exactly, are you sorry about?" Kelley didn't slow down, and didn't look at him.

"Uh . . . I'm sorry that I frightened you." His voice was gruff, awkward, as though he was unused to having to apologize.

Kelley was determined not to make this easy. After all,

he had frightened her—badly. Why was she even talking to him? "Apology not accepted."

Beside her his steps faltered, and he fell a bit behind as he said, "Oh. All right. I . . . understand."

"No, you don't!" she called over her shoulder, and kept up her pace.

A moment later and he was back at her side, his long stride having made up the difference without effort. He walked silently beside her for another moment. "You're right," he said finally. "I really don't."

Kelley sighed. "I don't see any reason to accept an apology of that kind from a total stranger, under these particular circumstances. I can accept 'sorry about that' from the guy who bumps into me on the subway car. *That* is entirely appropriate." She shot him another brief glance. "However," she continued, "'sorry about that' from some mysterious guy who gives me a gift, then disappears, then shows up at my place of work, then disappears, then shows up lurking in the alley beside my place of work, then disappears—"

"*You* ran away that time!"

"Don't interrupt."

"Sorr— Er, go on. Please."

"And *then* shows up again, as if by magic, when I am running errands in the park—" Kelley stopped abruptly and held a finger up to his chest. "Well, I do *not* accept a bland, measly, unembellished, unexplained 'sorry about scaring the hell out of you' apology from *that* guy." She turned away again and continued her swift progress down the path. "As a matter of fact, I'm not even going to accept the shiny, impressive, embellished, explained apology from that guy. Not without knowing who, exactly, that guy is. Your choice."

After she had gone several more yards, he put a hand on her arm and pulled her to a stop. "Sonny."

Kelley looked up.

He shook his head, smiling a little, and tapped his chest. "My *name* is Sonny." He paused, his expression turning just a bit cautious. "Sonny Flannery."

"Kelley," she said slowly. "Kelley Winslow."

"And you're an actress." The tone of his voice made it almost a question, as though she was really something else entirely and he just wasn't sure what.

"Yes . . . ," she answered hesitantly. "You saw me at the theater, right?"

"Right."

"About that, . . . Sonny." It felt funny suddenly knowing his name. "Seeing as how you know way more about me than I know about you, how about returning the favor?"

His brow clouded. "There is nothing the least bit interesting about me."

Kelley laughed. "I'm pretty sure that's not true!"

Sonny remained silent.

"Okay. So . . . do you go to school? College? Work? What do you do?"

"I'm a . . . a guard." He shrugged, feet scuffing through fallen leaves. "Of sorts."

"Like, security?" Kelley asked.

Sonny hesitated for a moment and then nodded. "Like security . . . I suppose."

"Fine. So you're a night watchman."

His mouth quirked. "Yes."

"Nothing wrong with that." Kelley turned to continue their stroll again, and Sonny fell into step beside her. She remembered Tyff's theory that Sonny was some sort of junior PI or something, hired by her crazy aunt to keep an eye on her. It made a certain kind of sense—especially if he worked for a security firm. She tried to picture him wearing an ill-fitting rent-a-cop uniform with scratchy gray polyester pants and decided, just for the sake of her own imagination, that he worked plainclothes.

They took the path that led east around Bethesda Fountain and down through a leafy stone archway, skirting the north side of Conservatory Water. Usually there was a smattering of toy-boat hobbyists, sailing remote-controlled yachts on the shallow pond, but it was deserted so late in the day. Kelley hugged her elbows.

"It's going to be chilly again tonight," she said.

Sonny froze in his tracks as if she'd uttered some kind of

curse or spell. He turned his face from her, shoulders stiffening. Kelley was startled by his sudden change.

"Damn it," he muttered under his breath.

She looked around but couldn't, for the life of her, figure out what was wrong. Everything seemed utterly still and silent in the park.

In the distance, a dog howled.

"You shouldn't be here," Sonny said, his voice harsh, as he looked off in the direction from which the sound had come. He seemed a thousand miles distant. Closed off. Hard.

The abruptness of Sonny's mood shift caught Kelley off guard and swung her sharply back into defensive mode. Had she offended him somehow? *How?*

Still, she tried to keep her tone light. "You know, the last time I checked, this was a *public* park. I"—she pointed to herself—"am public."

The dog howled again, closer this time. Kelley *knew* it was a dog because she was standing in the middle of one of the largest cities in North America. If she'd been back at home in the Catskills, she would have said it was a coyote.

Sonny turned to her, his gray eyes dark. He pointed very deliberately to the west. "The sun is going down."

Kelley crossed her arms. "It does that, I've noticed."

He suddenly seemed years older. He frightened her. "I'm glad. Now you should go before you get yourself into any more trouble. Like you did the other night."

"What? That was *not* my fault!" Kelley was flabbergasted enough not to bother questioning how he knew about her near drowning. "How was *that* somehow my fault?"

"Whose fault was it then?"

She glared at him pointedly.

"What?" he yelped, jarred for an instant from his menacing attitude. "You can't possibly think to blame me for . . . I'm not even sure what you're blaming me for."

Kelley was irate. "Okay. You see, if *you* hadn't been all Mr. Chivalry in the first place—with the romantic gesture and the rose and the lilty voice and the eyes and everything—then *I* never would have hung around here long enough to have found Lucky and he wouldn't be standing in my bathtub and I"—Kelley dug through her bag and pulled out the slightly rumpled pink sheets she was supposed to be posting—"wouldn't have had to come back here with these stupid fliers. Which means we wouldn't have run into each other again, and I'm starting to think that would be a really good thing!"

" 'Lucky'?" Sonny looked lost.

"He's a horse." Kelley shook the handful of fliers at him angrily.

"Of course."

"*Don't* start that."

"I'm not starting anything. Wait . . . " Sonny's eyes went wide. "Do you mean to say you have a *horse* in your *bathtub*?"

"Don't look at me like that. Animal Control didn't believe me either."

"Is there water in the tub?"

"Yes!" Kelley blurted, surprised. "How did you know? Every time I try to pull the plug and drain the bath, he nips at me and manages to turn on the taps with his nose. I think he's a circus horse or something. But I worry he'll get hoof rot!"

"He'll be fine. I mean, as far as his hooves are concerned, anyway. . . . You don't know what you've gotten yourself into!"

Kelley snorted and shook her head, refusing to indulge any more of this kind of crap. She turned sharply on her heel, heading north up the path.

Sonny shot out a hand and grabbed her, stopping them both in the shadow of the park's famous *Alice in Wonderland* statue. "You can't go that way."

"I can go any way I damned well please!" Kelley erupted, shaking loose. What was *with* this guy?

Sonny huffed. "Why? *Why?*"

"Why what?"

"Do you see anyone else here?" He flung out an arm.

"What does that have to do with anything?" Kelley was mystified and angry, although she had to admit that they did seem to be the only living souls around.

"Most of your kind avoid this place like it's plague ridden at times like this!" Sonny snarled. "Why did *I* have to get the one nutcase mortal who thinks it's somehow fun to fling herself repeatedly into the midst of dire peril?"

Kelley stared at him, openmouthed in her astonishment. "I'm not even going to pretend I know what you're talking about." She stabbed a finger at her chest. "And *I* am clearly not the 'nutcase mortal'— Wait a minute! What the hell does that even mean?"

"What—*nutcase?*"

"No! *Mortal!*"

"Aren't you?"

"Of course I am!"

Sonny shrugged and muttered, "It's getting harder and harder to tell."

Kelley took a deep breath and said, "Okay. Okay, I'm going home now." She took a few steps and then turned back. "Do I even need to tell you not to follow me again?"

"No." Sonny wiped his forehead with the back of his sleeve. He looked upset and relieved at the same time. "I promised the first time I wouldn't, and I haven't."

"So what *is* this then?" Kelley cried. It made no sense to her—she barely knew him—but this *hurt* her. "What is this *constantly* running into you? Coincidence? It's a big park, Mr. Flannery. It's a big city! And yet, somehow, *you* just happen to find me here. Just like you managed to track me down at the Avalon—"

"That was planned. I told you; I went looking for you. And *this* was not coincidence because there is no such *thing* as coincidence," he said bitterly. "*This* is *your* stubbornness and *my* sheer, bloody-minded bad luck. The Fates have it in for me. What did I ever do to them?"

"Why do you hate me?" Kelley's voice was very quiet in the still air. "I don't even know you!"

And there it was. That look. The look from her dreams, the one that broke her heart. Sonny's face became open, wounded, his expression wide with longing and a strange anguish.

"Oh, Kelley," he said. "I am so very far from hating you that I think it would be a great deal safer if I did. For both of us— *Get down!*"

Suddenly he launched himself in a running dive through the air, knocking Kelley off the path toward the Wonderland statue. Her head bounced off the cap of the Caterpillar's mushroom, and all the breath was driven from her lungs. Kelley fell to the ground, gasping, head swimming from hitting solid bronze.

The howling creature charging out of the night's thin air had barely missed her—thanks to Sonny's shove. The enormous thing spun with an agility that belied its size and sprang at Sonny, slamming him to the earth about ten feet away from her with such force that Kelley was sure his spine must be broken.

Sonny lay on the gravel path, unmoving, as the rabid thing swung its buffalo-sized head in her direction, fastening red eyes upon her. Its slavering jaws opened impossibly wide.

Kelley stared in utter disbelief at its huge, hairy paws. They didn't seem to be touching the ground. . . .

Through a fog of paralyzing terror, Kelley heard Sonny shout something that sounded like, *"Turn, hell-hound!"*

She thought to herself, *That's the wrong play. . . .*

That's from Macbeth, *not* Midsummer. . . .

I'm in the wrong play. . . .

As the beast lunged at her, the dull ache in her head suddenly flared into blinding agony.

XVI

From outside his immediate sphere of concentration, Sonny saw that Kelley had blacked out, and was grateful for that. He didn't want her to see what happened next—whatever the outcome.

As the creature lunged for Kelley, Sonny leaped and locked his arms around its massive torso. He threw his weight sideways, rolling with the wolflike animal, taking it as far away as possible from the unconscious girl. The roll ended with Sonny on his back. He threw his forearms up in front of his face as the thing snapped at his trachea.

Its fetid breath poured over him like swamp fog, its sharp-toothed jaws straining to close on his flesh. With his arms crossed in a defensive shield, Sonny reached for both of the creature's ragged ears. He grabbed, pulling hard in opposing directions. The thing yelped in a disturbingly dog-like fashion and flung itself onto its back. Sonny leaped to his feet and aimed a kick at the thing's ribs. It grunted in pain and lurched to its feet, where it hovered several inches above the ground and gathered itself, swinging its head to and fro. Backing up on its raised hindquarters, it hunched in preparation for another attack, growling hideously deep in its throat.

Before Sonny had a chance to draw a weapon, it leaped again. Arching its heavy body in midair, it twisted past Sonny and went again for Kelley. Sonny flung himself in another tackle, one-armed, grabbing frantically with his free hand at the small of his back, where he carried a sharp dagger in a sheath on his belt. The move left the right side of his chest unprotected for an instant, and Sonny felt the bloom of searing pain.

Losing his bearing, he collapsed. Face pressed to the ground, he heard the sound of running feet and more snarling. Dimly he heard fighting and then silence.

After a moment, Sonny was able to raise his head.

Maddox stood above him, holding out a hand to help him stand. A heavy mace dangled from a thong at his other wrist.

"Bellamy and Camina must have sensed you needed help at just about the same time I did, I guess," he said, gesturing down the deserted path. "They've gone after—"

Sonny cut him short. "You didn't *kill* it? Did you?"

Maddox wiped his brow. "Nah—wounded maybe, not sure . . ."

"Where did it go?"

"Yonder. I'll go help them. You can stay with—"

"No! It has to be me."

Maddox's head snapped up at the tone of Sonny's voice. "That was a Black Shuck! It didn't tag you, did it?"

Sonny pulled aside his coat and watched as his friend's eyes went wide with alarm. He looked down and saw the dark red lines of blood through the slashes in his T-shirt. He could feel the poison of the shuck's claws seeping, a terrible numbing cold growing slowly, spreading up toward his shoulder.

"Go," Maddox urged him, near panicked. "Go! I'll take care of the girl."

"Get her home. Find out where that is."

"Don't worry about that right now—"

"She has a *horse* in her bathtub, Madd," Sonny said urgently.

"Ah." Maddox blinked, understanding. "Well then."

"Be careful, Maddox. That shuck? It had a purpose and it didn't come after me. It went straight for *her*. Ignored me like

I was a stone. It was tracking her."

"Seven hells. Tracking her for *whom*?"

"Dunno . . . "

Sonny staggered a bit and almost fell to one knee. Maddox put out a hand to steady him. In the distance, they heard baying.

"Go now, Sonny," Maddox said. "I'll try to signal Bell and Camina—tell them to hold off on killing the damned thing. But even still, you've only got till midnight if they don't take it out first."

Sonny nodded and took one last glance at where Kelley lay on the ground. Then he pushed all thoughts of pain from his mind and took off at a run down the path, hoping desperately that he would not be too late.

The Black Shuck had given the Janus twins one hell of a merry chase up and down the park. When Sonny finally found them, Camina and Bellamy had the thing cornered on the terrace of Belvedere Castle. By that time Sonny was a lurching apparition, heaving himself up the worn stone steps with the very last of his strength. Camina was about to send a slender spear hurtling down the thing's gaping maw.

"Camina!" Sonny managed to rasp. "I need it. I need the kill. . . . "

"Oh, Sonny!" She took in his appearance with one swift

glance. "Bell, hold up!" She turned and called to Sonny over her shoulder, "You'd better hurry. You won't be able to kill in another moment, from the look of you."

His sword was out in his hand already and he brushed past the other two Janus, not even bothering to feint or dodge. The mental image of Kelley, unconscious and at the mercy of the beast that now stood snarling in front of him, was all he needed. He took two steps, slashed upward with the silver sword, and then down again. The demon dog's head slumped to one side, its body to the other.

In the few seconds before the gruesome thing began to fade from existence, Sonny went around to its long, shaggy tail and, with the edge of his bloodied blade, sheared off a length of the coarse black hair. He held out the handful of wiry strands to Camina and sank to his knees on the hard stone, his head drooping.

"Could you . . . ?" he mumbled, the fire of the shuck's poison burning in his veins.

Camina knelt in front of him, and Sonny watched through a fog as she went to work with swift, capable fingers. Soon she was tying a ribbon of braided dog hair around his wrist with an intricate knot.

"'Hair o' the dog that bit ye,'" she said, lifting his face gently. "You'll be all right now."

Slowly, Sonny's vision began to clear. He stood dizzily and thanked the twins for their help, wishing he could go home to bed. But the night wasn't over yet, and there was still the rest of the Gate to be guarded until sunrise. As Camina and Bellamy prepared to return to their patrol, Sonny raised a weak hand, forestalling them.

"Be careful," he said. "Very careful. Auberon thinks that someone may be trying to wake the Hunt."

XVII

Kelley heard the whispered murmurings of a hushed and hurried conversation. Sonny. And someone else. Then someone was shaking her gently, calling her name.

She blinked and struggled to sit up. A huge pair of hands grasping her shoulders helped, and she found herself staring up into the open, guileless face of a man maybe twenty years old with ginger-sandy hair and a nice smile.

"Hullo," he said. "I'm Maddox. Friend of Sonny's."

"What are you doing here?" Kelley asked, deeply confused.

What had happened? She must have hit her head when that *thing* . . .

"I was on my way to meet your man Sonny," he said, squatting beside her. "I saw that stray dog attack you both and came running."

"That was a . . . dog?"

"Bull mastiff by the look of it—big one—and rabid as a bat, most like. Nothing to worry about now, though. The proper authorities are on it, lass." He stood and held out both hands to help her up. "Now c'mon, let's get you out to the street and hail a cab. I'll take you home."

"Where's Sonny?" Kelley thought she must have hit her head harder than she'd realized. Everything seemed fuzzy and confused.

Maddox laughed—a low, pleasant rumbling sound deep in his broad chest. "Off chasing the dog. He'll keep an eye on it until the dogcatcher shows. Make sure it doesn't hurt anyone."

"What if it hurts *him*?" She glanced around a little wildly, a fluttering panic crowding up her throat.

"Now, now," Maddox soothed. "Ol' Sonn—he knows how to take care of himself. Don't fret. Come on, lass. Here, let me help."

Maddox tilted her face up so that he could stare directly into her eyes, and Kelley suddenly felt all of her questions and fears slip into the background.

Let me help you, Lady, she thought she heard him say, although she was fairly convinced his lips hadn't moved.

"What did you call me?"

"Uh . . . you mean 'lass'?" Maddox frowned in confusion.

"Never mind," Kelley murmured. "He *told* me I shouldn't be here now. . . . "

"And so you shouldn't, lass. The park is no place for a lady after nightfall. Come along now."

Kelley felt herself slump against his side as Maddox put a muscled arm around her shoulders, and she let him lead her east along a well-lit path toward the edge of the park, where he hailed a taxi. Somehow she wasn't surprised or worried when he climbed in as she was giving her address.

Just as she got out of the cab in front of her building, she remembered something and, leaning down to the half-open window, said, "He's not my man."

"Sorry?"

"Before—you said 'your man Sonny' to me."

"Ah, right. An idiom, that. Figure of speech, lassie." But as the cab pulled away, she thought she heard him say, "I hope."

Inside the apartment, Kelley heard a whickered greeting from the bathroom.

"Hi, Lucky, I'm home," she murmured. She still wasn't sure if she had actually heard an exchange between Sonny and his friend in the park or if she'd dreamed it all up. Kelley ran a shaky hand over her face, trying to remember exactly what it was the big guy—Maddox?—had called the creature in the whispered conversation she'd overheard between him and Sonny. Not *mastiff* or *dog* like he'd told her. To Sonny he'd called it by another name. *Black* something.

Black . . . Shuck.

What the hell is a Black Shuck?

She went into her bedroom and flipped open her laptop. While she waited for it to boot up, Kelley opened the bathroom door to check on Lucky. The horse swiveled his ears in her direction, bobbing his head in greeting.

"Hi, pal." Kelley couldn't help but smile. She was really becoming quite fond of the wayward beast. She went to give him a scratch, but as she approached, Lucky suddenly arched his neck, and his eyes rolled until she could see white all the way around. He shuffled his feet in the soapy water, trying to back up in the bathtub even though there was no more room. Kelley jumped as the horse began making distressed, high-pitched noises and tossing his head violently. He flared his nostrils so wide she could see the network of veins stretching in the delicate skin, as if he scented danger.

Kelley sniffed hesitantly at her clothing. She couldn't smell anything, but that didn't mean Lucky couldn't. Kelley supposed that the scent of the . . . whatever—she was content, for the moment, to keep referring to it as a dog—might have clung to her clothing.

She backed out of the bathroom, away from the agitated horse, and went back to her bedroom, stripping off her jacket, sweater, and jeans and exchanging them for a robe. She would have had a shower but, well, not really an option. Instead she went into the kitchen and scrubbed at her skin with the liquid soap there. It seemed to work—Lucky was a great deal calmer when she returned to the bathroom, shaking a fresh box of cereal.

Lucky sniffed at her, snorted a few times, and sneezed. Then he nuzzled around in her palm and ate the cereal, seemingly mollified by the scent of Spring Rain liquid soap on her hands. She couldn't figure out exactly why the horse would eat nothing but frosted cereal. Nor why, when it did, what little went in . . . didn't come out. The messy logistical difficulties of keeping a horse in the bathroom never seemed to materialize. Which was suitably mystifying and yet, Kelley supposed, good news—considering that their landlord would have them out on the street in a flash if Lucky's presence was discovered.

Kelley might not have admitted it openly to herself, but she was starting to appreciate having Lucky around. There was something strangely soothing about the big animal's presence. Something . . . familiar, almost. Her rational mind may have shied away from the notion, but especially in the wake of the frightening episode in the park, it was comforting to come home to the horse in her bathtub. Almost *normal*, even.

Having fed the horse, Kelley went back into her room and pulled up Google, entering the phrase "Black Shuck." As she read, a cold dread filled her stomach. Beyond a sparse

Wikipedia entry, one of the first websites that came up actually looked fairly scholarly—even though it was devoted to supernatural sightings and the paranormal.

Black Shuck: a spectral being, doglike in nature, big as a Shetland pony, with fiery red eyes and sharp, venomous talons. Shuck and their ilk, so-called demon dogs, have been known to roam the hills and moors of Continental Europe and, in particular, the British Isles for centuries. They travel swiftly, often without touching the ground, and are frequently considered harbingers of doom. In Faerie mythology, they are often seen accompanying or preceding an appearance of the fearsome Faerie war band known as The Wild Hunt. Shuck were used by the Hunt to track and flush quarry, much like mortal hunting hounds; they would corner their prey, keeping it at bay until the Faerie hunters could make their kill. *See also Hellhounds, Gwyllgi (Welsh), Dog of Darkness, Herne the Hunter's Hounds, the Barghest (Yorkshire), etc. . . .*

Kelley switched on a lamp to dispel the shadows in the room. *This is ridiculous,* she thought, suddenly angry with herself. A horse in the bathtub was one thing, but "demon dogs"? That was just the same kind of silly "ghost story" superstition she'd fought to outgrow as a kid. Kelley closed her laptop and went to sit on the side of the bathtub for a while, breathing the comforting scent of her horsey companion, soothed by his steady breathing. Exhausted by the events of the afternoon and evening, by the strangeness of her encounter with Sonny—at least she could finally stop referring to him as Handsome Stranger—and the unfathomable animal attack, Kelley finally stood and tiredly bid Lucky good night.

XVIII

"The Wild Hunt?" Camina whispered. "Who would *do* such a thing?"

Sonny looked at her bleakly. "Who do you think?"

"Mabh wouldn't dare."

"Auberon seems to think she would." He shrugged. "And why not? She's the one who created the Wild Hunt in the first place."

"But, Sonny—this city is so crowded, " Bellamy protested. "To loose that insatiable, death-mad Faerie war band on an unsuspecting mortal populace here—the carnage would be unspeakable, the death toll catastrophic!"

"And bloodthirsty old Mabh, the Queen of Air and Darkness, would *never* do a naughty thing like that, now would she?" Heavy sarcasm infused Sonny's weary tones.

Behind the twins, Sonny saw Maddox standing with his arms crossed. The look on his face told Sonny that he had heard their conversation.

Maddox and the twins exchanged worried glances, then Camina and Bellamy left to continue with their patrol, talking in low voices as they departed.

Maddox was silent for a moment. Then, "Can I give you a piece of advice?"

"No."

"You stay away from that girl."

"I *said* no—"

"Because if you don't"—Maddox shook his sandy head—"you're going to make a mistake. And any mistakes you make are liable to have dire consequences."

"I'm not afraid," Sonny said firmly.

Maddox stared at him, unblinking. "I didn't mean for you. I meant for her."

"Did you see her safe home?"

"I did."

"Then you know where she lives—"

"Did you *hear* what I just said? Let one of the other Guards fetch the damned kelpie!"

"I don't care about the damned kelpie. If it hasn't tried to hurt anyone yet, then I'm betting it's safe for the time being. *She* isn't."

"And who's going to make her safe—you? Look at you!"

Sonny weakly batted away Maddox's hand and, with considerable effort, thrust his arms through his jacket sleeves, trying not to wince. "Do you honestly think she's going to be safer without my protection than with it?"

Maddox ignored the question. "You know you're going to need suturing, right?"

"I hope you're handy with cross-stitch." Sonny glared at the other Janus.

Maddox rolled his eyes and shrugged, giving up the fight.

"I've a kit at the penthouse. D'you think the others can cover for us for an hour or so while you knit me back together?"

At first glance, there was probably nothing too out of the ordinary about Sonny's first aid kit. It contained bottles of iodine and rubbing alcohol, bandages, scissors, and the like. Beneath all that, however, was a small bottle of two-hundred-year-old Irish whiskey; long wooden matches in a waterproof box; three pure, rolled beeswax candles; a spool of red-and-silver thread; a small sheaf of dried rosemary, verbena, marigold stems, and mistletoe; a braided ring of marsh grass; a blown-glass phial of coarse sea salt; and a tuning fork, all of which lay on top of several large squares of gossamer—real gossamer. Plus six aspirin wrapped in a tissue.

Sonny downed four of the aspirin, swallowed a mouthful of the whiskey, and lay back on the couch as Maddox went to work on patching up the damage done by the shuck. It was substantial.

"You said you thought the demon dog was sent for her," Maddox murmured, his mouth a tight line as he concentrated on the job at hand. All of the Janus were trained in basic medicine, and Maddox's big fingers were surprisingly dexterous.

"It went right for her at the first. And then again after I'd knocked it on its big ugly arse. Why? I was the biggest threat to it. It should have gone straight after me."

"Unless you're right about someone having specifically sent it to track her. There's something about that girl, I tell you. She's bad business," Maddox said as he took the red-and-silver thread and pulled a long length from the spool, threading it expertly through the eye of one of the longer suturing needles.

"You don't know that." Sonny looked away as he felt the first sharp bite, and the tugging sensation that followed as Maddox began to sew.

"You said Auberon asked about her. That he saw her in your gaze."

"I don't know if he was able to get much of a read on her," Sonny said. "I don't think he found much that piqued his curiosity."

"So you don't think that he might be the one after her, then?" Maddox asked. Tying off the last knot, he crushed a few sprigs of rosemary and verbena between his fingers and sprinkled them over the wounds, both for their antiseptic and their magical properties. Then he covered everything with several of the diaphanous sheets of gossamer.

"For what earthly purpose?" Sonny scoffed. "I cannot see any possible reason for taking an interest in some quirky little teenage actress. No matter how pretty she is."

"Are you talking about Auberon, now? Or yourself?"

Sonny glared balefully. "Madd . . . she's just a girl."

"Right. A girl with a Black Shuck hunting her."

"If it was truly her it was tracking."

"You said it was. Which seems to indicate that someone is planning to awaken the Wild Hunt and set this girl up as their quarry," Maddox countered as he unwrapped a roll of sterile bandage. "My money's on Queen Mabh. This kind of thing seems right up her alley."

"I don't know, Maddox. I've been wrong before."

"No, you haven't. And if you are *now*, well then, that in itself is a worrying thought." Maddox placed an edge of the bandage over Sonny's ribs. "Hold that." He circled Sonny's chest with the strips of fabric. "You can't afford to be wrong, Sonny. And you can't afford to make mistakes. None of us can." He finished wrapping the bandage and neatly tucked the end in, securing the dressing. "Not during the Nine-Night."

"I know. Come on." Sonny struggled stiffly to his feet and went to put on a fresh long-sleeved T-shirt. "We'd best get back out there. It's getting late, and the others could probably use our help."

"For all that *you* can barely stand," Maddox muttered, and helped Sonny put his arm through his coat sleeve. He handed Sonny his messenger bag, but stopped him at the elevator. "Mark me, now: I've no burning desire to stitch you closed again tonight. So you keep your head down and in the game. And get that girl out of your mind!"

They made their way down Central Park West toward the Columbus Circle entrance to the park, past a trio of street musicians and a singer performing mellow jazz standards. They were good, Sonny noticed idly, despite the fact that the drummer was using an old hard-sided suitcase as his bass drum.

"Oh, sweet goddess," Maddox murmured under his breath as they passed.

Sonny followed his gaze. Bathed in the light of a street-lamp, the willow-thin singer swayed gently to the music. She was dressed in a long, clingy sweater and ground-sweeping skirt; her hair swung like a pale curtain in front of her face, partly obscuring her features as she sang with closed eyes.

Still, Sonny knew her. All the Janus did.

She was a Siren named Chloe. One of the first of the Faerie to escape from the Otherworld after Auberon closed the

Gates, she had crossed over to be with a mortal man, forsaking her deadly ways because of love. Unable to return after her lover's eventual death, she lived on in the mortal realm. Her home, it was rumored, was in one of the underground water caves deep beneath the park, connected through tunnels to the Hudson and East Rivers and so, eventually, to the sea.

She still made a living off her voice, but at least she no longer used it to lure unsuspecting sailors to their doom.

That's her *story*, Sonny thought. He didn't trust her.

Sonny turned back to find Maddox gazing at her, a dreamy expression on his face.

"Maddox?"

The other Janus sighed, his head nodding in time to the song.

"Maddox!" Sonny's voice turned sharp. "Snap out of it!"

"Hmm? Oh. I'm good. . . . "

The music drifted over to where they stood, coiling through the late October night like a slow, lazy serpent. Beautiful, a little disturbing. Sonny closed his eyes for a brief second and shivered, opening them again before the sinewy melody had a chance to take a firm hold. When he looked over at Maddox, he saw that the other Janus's eyes were completely closed. The planes of his face had relaxed, and a smile curled about his lips.

Sonny elbowed him sharply in the ribs. "Stop that!"

"What?" Maddox stood up straight. "I'm not doing anything."

"You're *listening*. That way madness lies."

"It was only a second."

"*Mad*ness."

"Right. So *you're* the only one allowed to go all moony over a girl, then?"

"Shut up," Sonny muttered, glancing back at the temptress. From behind the silky veil of her hair, he thought he saw her wink at him. "And Chloe is not a 'girl.' *Chloe* is a Siren. She used to lure men to their deaths, you idiot."

Maddox looked mulish. "I hear she's changed."

The song ended and there was a smattering of applause from the small, mostly male, audience that had gathered to listen to the band and its enchanting chanteuse. They dug into trouser pockets for bills and handfuls of change, grinning sloppily as Chloe sashayed coquettishly before them with a tip basket.

The band launched into another song. This one started off melancholy, hardly any percussion and only a few drifting strains from the double bass. Then with the slow, mournful fall of notes from the sax, Chloe began to sing. The melody was dark, compelling . . . familiar.

Sonny gasped.

He'd heard that song before.

It had the exact same tune as the "Philomel" lullaby from Kelley's play.

* * *

146

"Where did you get the music for that song?" Sonny said, dragging Chloe off the moment the band finished. Maddox followed close behind.

Chloe smiled. "Same place as all the others. Plucked it from the memories of a drowning soul."

Famous as Sirens were for the beautiful voices they possessed, they didn't actually have any music of their own. Their music was stolen—pilfered sounds taken from the minds of drowning mortals.

"I thought you were out of that business," Maddox said, a strong note of disappointment in his voice.

"Don't look at me like that." Chloe pouted. "I had nothing to do with it. Not as if *I* lured her into the water. Took the plunge all on her own."

"Who? When?" Sonny leaned forward, despite his aversion to Sirens and their ilk.

"Pretty thing." Chloe regarded him through sloe eyes. "On the first night of the Nine. I almost had to let her die."

"Why?" Maddox frowned.

"She was helping a kelpie." The Fae shrugged. "Kelpie bite. Naughty things—*especially* that one. I was wisely trying to keep my distance."

"But you didn't." Sonny stared at her. "You saved the girl?"

Chloe nodded.

"Why did you change your mind?"

"Mmm . . . " The tip of the Siren's pink tongue ran across the edges of her kitten-sharp teeth. "I heard her music. Pretty

pretty music," she mused, remembering. She hummed a bit of the tune.

Sonny felt a stab of longing and could almost see Kelley's face in his mind.

"Wonderful. Strange and wondrous . . . " The temptress opened her eyes and glanced sideways at him. "Too pretty to let die."

"What happened that night? With the girl." Sonny grabbed her by the shoulders. "What did you do to her?"

"I saved her life!" she said indignantly. "Don't I get points for that? Against my nature and at great risk of injury from kelpie teeth and hooves!"

"And then you took her song."

"Only a tiny bit," she said, unwilling to meet his stare. "Fair bargain, I thought, and it didn't hurt her."

"*Didn't* it?" Sonny sneered. A Siren could steal all or part of the music from a person's memories. Stealing only fragments wouldn't necessarily cause death, but it would still hurt like hell.

"It didn't hurt her because of what she is. She doesn't *know* what she is." Then Chloe did raise her gaze to meet his, her eyes glinting. "I do."

"You do?" Sonny felt his heartbeat quicken.

Chloe must have heard it. She leaned toward him. "Oh, *yes* . . . I tasted it."

Sonny released her. "What is she?" he asked.

Chloe's eyes were golden, he noticed. She sidled toward

him, suddenly dangerous. "I'll bet you've got a few sweet tunes stored up in that pretty head of yours, Sonny Flannery. I'll tell you what I know if you give me just a little taste. . . . "

"Now just a minute, there!" Maddox spluttered.

"You're not my type." Sonny held his ground.

"Yeah, you're not," Maddox agreed feverishly. "You're really, really not."

She shrugged a thin shoulder and spun on her heel. "Then the girl's story stays with me." She moved swiftly up toward West Sixty-second Street.

"Damn," Sonny swore softly.

He ran down the sidewalk after her.

Chloe slowed when she heard his footsteps, and turned.

From a distance, Sonny thought that he saw her eyes go red, hunger glowing in their depths. But by the time he reached her, they were just the flashing golden color they had been before.

"Just a taste," she said in a low throaty voice.

Her arms wound around his neck like a strangling vine. Chloe fastened her lips on Sonny's, and he felt the inside of his mouth go numb. A hollowing, paralyzing sensation crept down his throat, flooding through his chest. The terrible cold spread upward into his brain, a wave of ice behind his eyes. Helpless in the Siren's iron grip, he felt her sifting through his memories. There was a tearing sensation deep in his mind and then a small, aching emptiness.

She'd taken a lullaby. The only memory he possessed of

his mortal mother from when he was a baby. From far away, he heard himself sob once. Then he was falling backward; Maddox caught him and lowered him gently to sit with his back against the stone wall surrounding the park.

Through watering eyes, Sonny looked up to see Chloe standing statue still, eyes closed, her long fingers pressed to her lips. Maddox glared at her before turning back to Sonny, concerned.

"I'm all right," Sonny said, trying to make himself believe it. "I'm all right."

Chloe opened her eyes. "I'll tell you now about the girl, Sonny Flannery."

"Do you think she was telling the truth?"

"I didn't hear a lie in her voice. And I don't think you did either, Sonn."

Sonny was silent.

"Sensitive information," Maddox said carefully. "And it's probably safe to assume, based on the Black Shuck attack, that we're not the only ones to possess it."

They leaped—Maddox nimbly, Sonny less so—over the stone wall and dropped into the undergrowth.

"Someone *is* after that girl, Sonny," Maddox continued. "And now we know why."

Sonny feared that Maddox was right, and that fear sent a wave of sick misery washing over him. "Do you think Chloe has told anyone else?"

"Dunno. She's still alive, so . . . probably not." Maddox put a hand on Sonny's shoulder. "Doesn't really matter. One way or another, somebody besides us knows. And word like that gets out. Won't be long before the whole of the Otherworld knows."

Sonny nodded, lost in the enormity of their discovery.

"Sonny . . . you've found the Faerie king's daughter."

XIX

"Ill met by moonlight, proud Titania!"

Gadzooks! Kelley smiled to herself. *Jack really does have a great set of pipes!*

She composed her expression into one of ethereal displeasure. "What, jealous Oberon," she intoned with silky anger as she stepped from the upper platform down to where Gentleman Jack awaited, elegantly arrayed in a velvet cloak. His thick hair was swept back from his regal brow, and he looked every inch a king.

Kelley hoped she could pull off "regal" even half as well.

She stood as tall and straight as she could and, as she reached the platform where Oberon stood, threw herself into the scene.

"Nice work, Kelley—you looked *born* to fairy royalty out there today." Jack saluted her with his coffee cup. They were on a break and had retired to the greenroom after Quentin had finished running the scene through a few times.

Kelley leaned back in her chair and returned Jack's salute with the cup that he'd poured for her out of his treasured thermos. It was awesome coffee. And, Kelley thought, what the heck: she actually deserved it. Despite another night of bad dreams—including the live-action ones—Kelley had to admit she'd done a wicked job in that scene.

Even Quentin had been uncharacteristically generous in his praise of her.

"Hnng," he'd muttered. "You missed the hot spot for your light cue. Half a step downstage next time, please."

For the Mighty Q, *that* was positively effusive.

And it had been so easy. The entire scene was about Oberon and Titania and the fact that the Natural Order of Things was being turned inside out by the squabbles and quarreling of these two powerful beings—all over the matter of a changeling child. The scene was fraught with stubborn pride and miscommunication. Kelley had drawn on personal experience and channeled all of her frustration and annoyance with Sonny Flannery into the scene and her relationship with Oberon. Talk about motivation.

After the break, Quentin wanted to go over the whole scene once more with the addition of the fairy attendants and Puck, so Kelley had remained in costume. But the brocade corset made her warm, so she went out into the courtyard for some air before they called her back to the stage.

Sitting on one of the old stone benches was a slightly bedraggled-looking Sonny Flannery. Kelley bit back a smile. But as she approached, she could also see that his expression was drawn. She stopped in front of him, sipping the last of her coffee.

"You're a real glutton for punishment, aren't you?" she asked.

"You have *no* idea," Sonny muttered through clenched teeth, not meeting her gaze.

"If you're here to apologize for last night, forget about it." She couldn't help the tone of her voice—she felt immediately defensive, remembering how he'd spoken to her the night before. "Your friend saw me safely home and, since I didn't hear about anyone getting bitten by a rabid dog on the news this morning, I assume that Animal Control took *your* call seriously, at least."

Kelley leaned on the back of the bench and regarded him. Sonny sat with his elbows resting on his knees and his fingers laced. He seemed as though he was struggling to find something to say. Or, perhaps, to find a way to say it. Kelley wished he would just talk. The silence stretched out between them.

"Kelley . . . ," he said finally, "you're in great danger."

She straightened up and turned to go back inside.

"Kelley, wait!" Sonny was in front of her, blocking her path. Fast—but maybe not as fast as she was used to with him. "Didn't you hear me?"

"I heard you. I'm just trying to be polite." She stared up at him. "My parents taught me that it's not nice to laugh at people."

Sonny grimaced in frustration. His eyes, she noticed, were red-rimmed and gleamed with an almost feverish intensity. "Your parents didn't teach you that."

"Pardon?"

"They—whoever raised you—they were not your real parents."

Kelley blinked at him.

"Did you hear me?" Sonny demanded. The vein at his temple pulsed, and Kelley thought he might actually have some kind of a meltdown right there in front of her. His breathing was ragged. "Did you?"

"Stop asking me that!" She took a step back. "What on earth are you talking about?"

Sonny pitched his voice low, as if he was afraid to be

overheard. "Kelley . . . look, I know that this will come as a complete surprise to you. But . . . you are the daughter of a king."

She tried not to laugh. "I'm the daughter of a doctor."

Sonny shook his head. "I know that's what they told you, and I know that's what you want to believe, but—for your own safety—you must trust me."

"Because I'm the daughter of a king," Kelley answered back, matter-of-fact, and crossed her arms over her chest, ignoring the pull of the elastics holding on her fairy wings. She suddenly wished she'd taken them off before coming outside. "A real king?"

"Yes." He nodded.

"I understand." Kelley smiled sweetly.

"You do?" He breathed deeply, a glimmer of relief shining in his eyes.

"I really do. You are a mental case."

Sonny's expression hardened again. "They *lied* to you. They did it to protect you, but it was a lie."

"Sonny—"

"Your father is a very, very old power and he is not from this realm."

"You are *actually* trying to tell me that my father—wait, sorry, my 'real' father—is from another country?"

He nodded. "Another world entirely. Actually."

Kelley was speechless, her patience reaching its absolute end.

Sonny took another deep breath and barreled through his next words. "Your father—yes, your *real* father—is a king, and his name is Auberon—"

Kelley laughed out loud.

"Yes, I know—but Shakespeare *didn't* make it all up, Faerie tales *are* sometimes true, and *you* are the heir to the Unseelie throne of the Faerie realms—"

"Stop it."

"Kelley—"

"Stop. I said stop!" She held a hand up in front of his face as he opened his mouth again. She got it now. The gauze wings on her back suddenly felt like lead weights. "I don't want to hear any more. I don't want you to say my name. As a matter of fact, I don't want to hear you say *anything*. Look . . . I don't know if you're a weirdo or a liar or just crazy, but you have to stop talking to me. You have to stop coming around here. I have a job to do and I can't do it with you near!"

"Funny, I feel exactly the same way about you every time I see you in the park," he muttered, turning away. But then he turned back to her, and his storm-gray stare fastened on her like a vise. "Kelley. *Listen* to me."

"No. This is insane. I mean, okay, I get it. You're very amusing, Sonny. A real practical joker." She struggled a bit frantically at the knotted laces that held her wings on. "What kind of an idiot do you think I am? Do you really think I'm naïve enough to fall for this particular line of BS? Did you and your buddy Maddox come up with this over beers or something?"

"What? No!"

"Ha-ha, very funny—let's mess with the girl who thinks she's a fairy queen! I'm an actor. This is a role." She shrugged out of the costume piece with violent, jerking motions, and threw the wings at Sonny. They hit him in the chest and fell to the ground at his feet. "And you can go to hell!"

"You think I'm delusional? You think I'm crazy or something? That this is all a joke?" His hands shot out and he grabbed her roughly by the shoulders, shaking her. Then he released her and his long fingers moved down the front of his shirt, unbuttoning it with a lightning swiftness. He yanked the fabric aside, and Kelley gasped despite herself. His chest was heavily bandaged. There were dark stains seeping through in parallel gashes over the right side of his ribs. He flung his arms wide so that Kelley couldn't help but see the blood. "Was that creature in the park a delusion? A joke? Funny. Those claws felt awfully real to me."

"It was a *dog*," Kelley protested weakly, her stomach heaving at the sight of Sonny's blood. The Black Shuck web entry she had dismissed as fantasy suddenly flashed unbidden into her mind.

"Sure it was. A dog the size of a hay wagon with talons and glowing red eyes and—oh! I almost forgot—it ran without touching the ground."

"It was dark. . . . "

"*I* saw it just fine. Of course, I got a nice, close-up view as it was trying to rip my throat out. It won't be trying that again." The tone of his voice made it pretty clear what he meant by that.

"You killed it?"

Sonny held up his arm: His wrist was encircled by a band of coarse black hair, intricately braided and knotted. "I got lucky. But, by all means, if you really don't believe me, and don't believe that I was trying to protect you—that I'm trying to protect you now—just say so. And then, maybe next time someone from the Otherworld—that's the place your father *the Faerie king* rules—tries to have you killed, I won't even bother coming to your rescue. I could probably save myself some pain and suffering that way!"

Kelley was silent. Whatever Sonny saw in her eyes in that moment, her expression made him shrink from her— as though he had just slapped her across the face and regretted it profoundly. Shame coloring his cheeks, Sonny dropped his gaze and buttoned his shirt back up. He reached out a hand to Kelley in a gesture that might have been a silent apology, but she turned and walked back toward the theater.

Jack was standing on the steps when she got there. Wordlessly, he held the stage door open for her.

159

Once inside, Kelley stood with her head pressed against the wall, feeling a bit faint. From the other side of the door, she heard Jack's voice, not so mellow at that moment.

"I don't know what you said to upset her so, young man," he said. "I don't need to. All I need to know is that you aren't going to be coming around here again. Because if you do, there's a fairly good chance I will forget that most people call me *Gentleman* Jack. Do you understand?"

Kelley peered through a crack between the theater's old oak doors and watched Sonny wordlessly hand her wings to Jack. Then he turned and walked out of the Avalon's courtyard without once looking back.

Kelley shut the door to her dressing room and picked up her cell phone.

Her aunt answered on the first ring.

"Kelley?" she asked immediately. "Is everything all right?"

Kelley didn't answer the question. "Emma . . . Was I . . . adopted?"

There was a pause. *"What?"* Emma's voice, when it came, was pitched too high. "Oh, my dear! Why would you ask such a—"

"Don't lie to me, Emma." Kelley cut her aunt short. "I know about . . . about *them*. I know."

"Oh, Kelley . . ." The long, sad sigh on the other end of the line told Kelley everything. Sonny had spoken the truth. As insane as that seemed, as much as Kelley had wanted it to be some elaborate practical joke, she knew suddenly that Sonny hadn't lied.

"Em?" Kelley asked again, her voice quiet. Calm. "Please. Tell me."

"You weren't adopted, Kelley. Not exactly." Emma's voice, on the other hand, shook with emotion. "More like . . . "

"Abducted."

"I . . . " The tremor stopped just short of becoming a sob. "Yes. You were stolen. I took you from them—from *him*—because he took my child from me."

"How . . . Oh, Em—how *could* you?" Kelley didn't even know what else to say.

"Madness. Grief." The pain in her aunt's voice reflected an old wound that had never fully healed. "I only wanted someone to love. It's not an excuse, and I won't blame you if you hate me forever."

The crackling hiss of the phone connection stretched out in the silence that followed.

"I don't hate you, Em," Kelley said finally.

"I've denied you your birthright." Emma was weeping. "Your destiny. I thought that I was doing a good thing, but it was all kinds of evil and I see that now. I only hope you can forgive me one day."

It broke Kelley's heart to hear her aunt's grief. "Tell me about this 'birthright,' Emma," she said gently.

She had to wait for a minute while Emma struggled to get hold of herself, but eventually her aunt was able to speak.

"Do you remember the stories, Kelley—the ones I used to tell you about the Fair Folk?"

Of course she remembered. The fables. Folklore . . . cautionary tales of the fairies and their wicked deeds. She'd grown up steeped in it. Given even half an ear, Emma would rabbit on and on about the subject until her listener's head exploded. Eventually Kelley had become immune to it.

And to all the rest. She'd learned to ignore . . . things, things that lurked in the half-forgotten memories of her childhood. Things once kept at bay by the constant presence of rowan switches and iron charms near her bed, warded off by pots of wild marigold and primrose kept growing on the sills, and by Emma's whispered invocations every night at the door of her room.

Later on, when she'd give fleeting thought to those days, Kelley remembered Emma's "superstitions" as quaint. Once she'd grown older and stopped believing in things she'd once seen in the woods around home with her own eyes, Kelley had written Emma's stories off as just that: stories. And her own encounters, the product of an overactive, childish mind. She had made herself forget. But *now* . . .

"I remember voices. Outside my bedroom window."

"You used to tell me that." Emma's voice was choked with memory. "When you were young, you told me that. And it scared me half to death. I knew that you could see . . . *them*. Hear them. I could too—after I'd been to their world."

"Faeries."

"Yes, dear. The ones that came around the house were harmless, really. Only curious because they knew you were different. They just didn't know why, exactly. We tried so hard to keep you hidden. Safe."

"We?"

"Me. And your mum and dad . . . "

"You mean the Winslows."

"Don't be angry with them, Kelley," Emma pleaded. "They loved you. And they tried their best to do right by you. By both of us. When they died in the car accident, I was heartbroken."

"How . . . how did . . . " She didn't even know how to phrase such a question.

But Emma knew what she asked. "They found me wandering, half out of my mind, in the middle of that great bloody park with you tucked in my coat, and they offered to take me in—back to their place in the country."

"Why? Why didn't they call you an ambulance? Or the cops?"

"I wouldn't let them. I was confused. Frightened. Thousands of miles and a hundred years away from my own home . . . "

"I don't understand."

"That place. The *Otherworld* . . . " Emma's voice went soft with remembered wonder. "It isn't like it is here, Kelley. It's beautiful there . . . *too* beautiful, somehow. Such a strange,

163

dreaming place, and—just like in a dream—time is meaningless there. You see, once I had crossed over to steal you and then crossed back again, well . . . the world—*this* world—had changed. Decades had passed. I wasn't even in my own country anymore. Dr. and Mrs. Winslow, I'm sure they thought I was just some poor unfortunate soul gone clear out of my head. But they told me they'd help me." Emma's laugh was a weary, battered sound in Kelley's ear. "They'd been wanting a child themselves, you see. Desperately. But it was not to be. Until they found me. And you. We . . . made an arrangement."

"I see."

"They would take care of us, keep you as their own. With me close by to help raise you. I didn't know what else to do, so of course I said yes. And it worked out all right. We were happy. You were happy." She sighed. "But I see now that we were just selfish. We were all so selfish. You, poor thing, were the only one that no one seemed to give much of a thought to. I see that now." There was another long, crackling pause. "Kelley . . . I'm so sorry."

"It's all right, Em," Kelley said. "I'm all right. Really."

"I hoped you'd never have to know. Never have to remember."

But it seemed as though she was going to have to start remembering, even though it was the last thing she wanted to do. Although she loved her dearly, Kelley had never wanted to grow up to be like her sweet, crazy Aunt Emma who believed in fairies.

And who, it turned out, maybe wasn't so crazy after all.

Kelley needed time to process the enormity of what she now knew and told her aunt so. But before she hung up, Em stopped her to ask, "Who told you these things, Kelley?"

"A friend. I think." Kelley hated the thought that Sonny could be something unfriendly.

"Oh, be careful, my girl," Emma said. "Promise me."

"I will, Em. I promise."

"Your necklace, dear, the amber clover—you do still wear it, don't you?"

"Yes. Why?"

"Don't take it off, Kelley. Please. For . . . luck."

"I gotta go, Em."

"We'll talk later?"

"I think we'll probably have to. Yeah," she said, and snapped her cell phone shut. She heaved a shuddering sigh and looked at her reflection in her dressing-room mirror, letting numbness take over. It was strange that she looked exactly the same as she had the day before. How could that be? Surely, if she wasn't who she thought she was—and never had been—shouldn't she look different? . . . Wait. Hands shaking, Kelley lifted her hair back from her face and examined her reflection.

The tips of her ears were ever-so-slightly pointed.

"Oh God," she whispered. "It's really true."

The makeup lights glinted off her four-leaf-clover necklace. The green amber glowed warmly. Emma had told her when she was a little girl that amber was really "the blood of very old trees," and Kelley had thought that a lovely idea.

She frowned at herself in the mirror and reached up under her hair. Before she could unfasten the clasp, Bob appeared— still dressed all in green—in the reflection, standing close behind her. She didn't move as he reached for her hands and gently plucked her fingers away from the catch on the chain.

"Best listen to your auntie, luv," he whispered in her ear, "and keep that on."

"Why?" Kelley stared at Bob in the mirror, somehow unsurprised to see him there.

"Because . . . " He stared back at her, intense, and answered her question with a line from Shakespeare. "'Light thickens, and the crow makes wing to th' rooky wood. Good things of day begin to droop and drowse, whiles night's black agents to their preys do rouse.'"

She blinked. "You are the second person I've heard quote *Macbeth* in two days. Why do I keep getting the feeling I'm in the wrong play?"

"Oh . . . you're not. Quite the contrary—you're in exactly the right play," he murmured. "It's just that there aren't really any turns of phrase in *Midsummer* quite so poetic that I could think of, off the top of my head, to warn you with."

"Warn me?"

"Watch your back in the days to come, girl. And the *nights*."

Kelley swallowed a sudden lump of fear in her throat.

"You could have just said *that*," she whispered.

"'Thou marvell'st at my words; but hold thee still.'" Bob smiled mirthlessly, finishing the ominous quote. "'Things bad begun make strong themselves by ill.'"

And then he was gone.

As long as she lived, Kelley would never know how she made it through to the end of rehearsal without crying or screaming. Emma's words, and Sonny's, ricocheted around her skull as the company went through Oberon and Titania's argument scene again.

Titania's lines tumbled from her with a ferocity that her previous rehearsals had only hinted at. As she ripped into Oberon, Kelley felt as though, somewhere deep inside her, there was thunder stirring.

"The seasons alter," she cried, an impassioned plea. Her arms spread wide in a gesture that encompassed the wrongness of it all, her Titania despairing that their conflict had sent nature itself into a perilous spin. "The spring, the summer, the childing autumn, angry winter change . . ."

She leveled a devastating sadness at Oberon, whom Titania loved, but whom she could no longer bear to keep company with. "And this same progeny of evils comes from our debate, from our dissension; we are their parents and original."

Her voice cracked only a little on the word *parents*.

XX

Sonny walked back to his apartment from the Avalon, head down, shoulders hunched. Along the way, he spotted several Lost Fae: a dryad in an empty lot offering encouragement to a sickly-looking juniper bush; a winged boy crouched atop a fire hydrant who watched him pass with big, glistening eyes; the fruit seller at a corner market who hid his taloned, feathered feet beneath an impressive glamour and a long white apron. . . .

Where Sonny went, reputation preceded him. As he passed the Fae on the streets, they gave him a wide berth, even though Sonny had no quarrel with them. Most had already had to fight against the Janus to cross over, and it wasn't an experience any of them wanted to repeat. There were also those of the Otherworld who had been trapped in the mortal realm more than a century ago through no fault of their own. Some would even have gone back, were it not for Auberon's harsh decree of banishment that had accompanied his closure of the Gates: If a Faerie had gotten caught—consorting with humans in the human world—then they could stay there.

Still, not wanting to appear to his remaining loyal subjects in the Otherworld as overly vengeful, Auberon had left it to his Janus to decide whether or not a Lost Fae would go on to pose an actual threat to the mortal realm. Most of them didn't, and so the Janus left them in peace.

Even so, the Lost Fae remained almost universal in their passionate hatred for Sonny's kind. He felt a familiar twinge of regret about that as he stood in the swiftly ascending elevator to his floor.

At the entrance to the penthouse, he sensed a presence even before he'd turned the handle on the door. It was warm inside, almost oppressively so. Sonny could feel the hair raise up on his arms as he stepped cautiously through the doorway.

A Storm Hag hovered a foot and a half off the floor in the middle of his living room.

"Hag," he hailed her blandly.

"Watch thy mouth, fleshling," she hissed. Tiny spears of lightning sparked from her fingertips, and her dusky robes billowed around her like gathering thunderheads. Servants of Mabh, the Storm Hags had long ago been chained to the mortal realm by their harsh mistress to carry out her commands. The hags communicated with Mabh, herself confined to her own grim realm, through enchanted mirrors. They were malicious creatures but—because they were Queen Mabh's direct emissaries, answerable only to her and not to Auberon or any of the other Courts—they were untouchable; the Janus were forced to leave them in peace.

Which made it particularly frustrating when one showed up uninvited in the middle of your living room, Sonny thought.

"Queen Mabh sends a greeting."

"Queen Mabh sent her ravens first." Sonny crossed his arms and leaned against the bar, not in the mood for this. "A greeting might have been welcome *before* an attack."

The Storm Hag's gray lips stretched in a ghastly parody of a smile. "Be thou lucky Mabh turns any attention on such a crawly worm as you. She is mighty as she is merciless. She is the Darkling Queen, the Queen of Air and Darkness, bringer of storm and war—"

"I don't need to hear her résumé. Just tell me what she wants and get out."

"An alliance," the creature snarled. "This realm hides something that belongs to Mabh. You know this?"

The kelpie. Sonny went cold despite the room's temperature. *Auberon was right! It was Mabh.* He nodded slowly.

"She wants it back. It should never have been sent here. It was a mistake. Find it. Return it. And the queen will grant you a boon."

Sonny wasn't entirely sure he wanted Mabh's favor. But still, a boon granted by a queen of Faerie . . . that was a valuable thing. And Sonny had a feeling that such a gift might come in handy. He had to consider Mabh's offer carefully.

"What say you, fleshling?" the Hag hissed wetly.

"I say call me that again and Mabh will have another minion to put back together with her magicks."

Sonny walked a few steps away, thinking hard. Bargaining with the Faerie was always bad business. If a deal was ever broken, the consequences could be dire. An unfulfilled agreement was considered an unforgivable transgression by Faerie laws. If you wanted to break a bargain with the Fae—and couldn't find a loophole by which to do it—then you risked granting the wronged party unlimited power to seek redress. It was always best never to enter into a deal with the Faerie in the first place, but here was an opportunity to not only eliminate the threat of the Wild Hunt waking—by getting the kelpie back to the Otherworld—but also earn a favor of a Faerie queen.

"All right," he said. "I'll get Mabh what she wants—but

only because it's for the greater good. She can send me word of time and place."

He turned away.

"Now get out of here and stop drooling on my rug."

XXI

She had to talk to Sonny.

Kelley waited on a bench by the carousel, wondering how long it would take for him to appear. She'd fled the Avalon the moment rehearsal ended, heading for the park. It wasn't even ten minutes before Sonny stepped out from beneath the trees and walked toward her.

Kelley stood. "That was fast."

"I was . . . hoping." He shrugged.

Kelley walked a few steps away and said, "Okay. So. It wasn't a dog that attacked me."

"You can call it a dog if you want to," Sonny said encouragingly. "Some people call them demon dogs, or the hounds of Herne. I call them Black—"

"Black Shuck. I know," Kelley interrupted him. "So what exactly is this Herne, then? Is it a person? Did he send that thing? Is he a . . . Faerie?"

"Herne? No. Herne is . . . " Sonny paused. "Are you *sure* you want to hear all this stuff right now?"

"No time like the present."

"All right." Sonny sat down on the bench and waited until Kelley relented and joined him. "Herne was once a man. He became . . . something else. You would probably call him a god."

"A . . . god."

"But he wouldn't have sent the shuck," Sonny assured her. "They are only called *his* hounds because they run with the Wild Hunt. And a very long time ago, Herne used to lead the Hunt."

"I see." Kelley crossed her arms and chewed on her bottom lip, trying very hard to follow what Sonny was saying. She vaguely remembered something about a Wild Hunt from the web entry on the shuck. "The Wild Hunt. Sounds like some kind of party."

"A war band, really," Sonny said. "They are an old power. Very dangerous."

"I see," she said again.

"You do?"

"I really don't." She sighed, giving up.

"We could start with the basics," Sonny suggested.

"Okay," Kelley agreed. That might be a good idea. "Let's just say—for the moment—that I buy into this whole I'm-a-Faerie-princess thing."

"You are."

"So what are you, then? Like a Faerie prince or something?" She frowned. "That sounds *so* wrong. . . . "

"I'm not Faerie." Sonny didn't look at her, but his mouth quirked up at the corner. "I'm certainly not a prince."

"Then what are you?"

"I'm what's called a changeling." He kept his eyes focused on the ground as he spoke. "I was . . . I was taken by the Faerie from the human world as a baby and raised in the Other-world."

"Taken?" Kelley looked at him sharply. "You mean *stolen*?"

"I . . . Yes. I suppose so."

So I'm not the only one, Kelley thought. It made her feel a bit queasy. "So they just come and go as they please?" she asked finally. "These Faerie?"

"They used to," Sonny said. "You see, the Celts, the Elizabethans, the Victorians . . . they all believed in the existence of the Faerie. More than believed—they shared their world with them."

"But not by choice." Kelley tried, but she couldn't keep

the disdain from her voice.

"No. Since the earliest days, the Faerie had always been there. And they had always *taken*."

"Creeping across thresholds to steal children away from their families."

Sonny looked uncomfortable with the way the conversation was going. "Taking them away to live forever, yes!" he said. "In a place of beauty and majesty where time has no meaning and dreams come true . . . "

"Even the bad ones?" Kelley watched him for a moment. "Yeah. That's kind of what I thought. Go on."

Sonny avoided Kelley's gaze. "By the beginning of the twentieth century, as the Victorian age was coming to a close, the human world began to stop taking an interest in the Faerie world."

"But not the other way around?"

"No. The Faeries still came. They still . . . took. And then, one day, a mortal woman took something back."

"Me."

"Yes."

Sonny told her that after she'd been spirited away from the Unseelie Court, her father, Auberon, in grief and fury, had tried to cast an enchantment that would seal the passageways between the worlds. "But Auberon's enchantment was flawed. And so, for one night every year, the Samhain Gate—for that is what this park is—swings open."

"When?" Kelley asked.

"From sundown on October thirty-first to sunrise November first."

"Halloween, huh? Cute."

"It used to be called Samhain," Sonny said quietly. "Back in my day."

Kelley looked at her watch. "Timing's off. It's only October twenty-sixth."

"That's the thing about magic, Kelley. It's tricky stuff, even for a Faerie king. Part of the flaw in Auberon's spell casting means that once every nine years, the Gate stands open for the nine nights leading up to Samhain. We call it the Nine-Night."

"That's original. So, nine whole nights, huh? That sounds like it was a pretty *big* flaw on dear old Dad's part, wouldn't you say?" Kelley snapped.

Sonny grimaced but remained silent.

Kelley closed her eyes, shaking off the brief flare of anger. "Okay. Moving along. What's your part in all of this?"

"I work for your father."

Stiffening, Kelley pulled away from him.

"I told you the other night that I am a guard, and that was the truth. Auberon decreed that there would always be thirteen changelings—Janus, we are called—whose duty it is to guard the passage and keep the Faerie from crossing through the Gate."

"How do you do that?"

"By any means necessary."

"So you're like, what, enforcers? Auberon's gang of hired thugs?"

"That is unkind," Sonny said, looking at her finally. "I didn't ask for this, Kelley. I don't belong in this world, your world. Only now, because of what I have become, I am no longer welcome in the place I called home."

For a brief moment, a naked look of homesickness crossed Sonny's face. It made Kelley wonder just what the Otherworld was *really* like. It certainly seemed to hold a powerful attraction for Sonny, even if he couldn't return there.

"Because I am a Janus, I am hated and feared among the Fair Folk," he continued. "But I would have thought *you'd* be a bit more understanding."

Kelley dropped her gaze, shame burning in her cheeks.

"Especially considering last night's little adventure." Sonny stood and looked as though he would leave. "Do you really want that kind of creature roaming free in New York City?"

"I'm sorry. You're right." She put a hand on his arm. "I am sorry. This is all just . . . "

"I know."

Kelley looked up at him, wishing he would sit back down. "That thing," she said. "The Black Shuck—did *it* come through the Gate?"

"It would have had to, yes." Reluctantly, Sonny sat beside her on the bench.

"And Lucky?" Kelley asked.

"I wouldn't exactly call a Black Shuck 'lucky.' . . . "

"No, no." She waved a hand in the vague direction of the Upper East Side. "I mean the horse. In my tub."

"The kelpie? It's not exactly a horse. Actually . . . it really is a very dangerous creature—"

"Oh, he is not!" Kelley laughed, amused for the first time.

"Listen to me, Kelley—your new pet may look like just any other pretty little pony, but he's not. He's dangerous. He's dangerous all by himself and he's even more dangerous because of an enchantment cast upon him. You can be as cavalier about the situation as you want, but by doing so, you put not only yourself but every living soul in this city at terrible risk."

Kelley fell silent, shocked. "What do you mean?"

Sonny reached into his messenger bag and pulled out three glittering black beads. "You asked me about Herne and the Wild Hunt," he said. "Let me ask you this: Do you recognize these?"

She leaned over and nodded. "Lucky's got dozens of them braided all through his mane and tail."

He returned the onyx charms to his bag, his expression grim. "They are talismans, charms used by one of the queens of Faerie to cast a spell. Once upon a time."

Kelley watched as Sonny's gaze drifted over to the carousel. He looked as though he had never noticed it until that moment. It was open for business, although only a lone ticket-taker was to be seen. Most children were still in school. Kelley looked back and forth from the carousel to Sonny's face.

"'Once upon a time'?" she asked warily.

Suddenly Sonny stood and, without waiting to see if she would follow, started in the direction of the cheerful calliope music. "Come with me," he called over his shoulder.

Flustered, Kelley caught up to him as he paid for two tickets. He held out a hand, helping her up onto the wooden platform where the brightly painted steeds awaited. Kelley felt a little foolish, undecided about which of the horses she should choose, although it wasn't for lack of selection; they were the only two people on the ride. Eventually Sonny just grabbed her around the waist and lifted her effortlessly up onto the back of a prancing pony. Then he leaped up onto the steed beside hers.

The carousel groaned and the platform began to slowly spin. Kelley stared at Sonny, who sat easily on his mount, like a knight in shining armor on the back of his charger.

"Let me show you something, Kelley," he said, reaching up to touch the iron medallion at his throat. "Let me show you the story of the Wild Hunt."

"*Show* me?" Kelley asked, bewildered.

Sonny fixed her with his piercing gaze, the expression in his gray eyes wild and a little frightening. He said, "Don't be afraid."

The merry-go-round whirled and spun, and Kelley's heart galloped in her chest. The music spiraled around her, dizzying; the carousel horse shivered beneath her, rising up in a slow leap.

Sonny's eyes went from that extraordinary silver-gray to

almost black. Kelley felt, for a brief, disorienting moment, as if they rode through a mist-filled tunnel . . . and then everything cleared. She glanced around.

The carousel was gone. New York was gone.

The horse beneath her, no longer a painted wooden thing, tossed its head, and she could feel its muscles bunch beneath the saddle. Kelley gasped and scrambled to grab on to the horse's reins as, all around her, visions of a lush green forest rushed past at breakneck speed. The sounds of bird and beast filled her ears. She could smell the freshly rain-washed leaves of the trees as they whipped past and she felt the wind on her cheeks. In the distance the sound of a horn rang through the air like the chiming of church bells. She heard the frantic baying of hunting hounds.

Sonny's mount thundered along beside hers through the trees and, over the sound of the wind in her ears, she heard him speak—telling her the story of Herne and the Wild Hunt even as she herself rode right into it.

XXII

"Herne was a mortal. A prince in the world of a very long time ago. . . ."

Sonny's voice echoing all around, Kelley bent low over her mount's neck as the horse pounded through the trees and out into a wide-open clearing in the forest. As their horses cantered to a stop, she saw that they had become part of a hunting party, magnificently dressed and richly outfitted.

Kelley felt the rustle of silk and, looking down, saw that she was clothed in a russet gown that draped behind her, trailing over her horse's back. The hems of her sleeves and skirt were heavy with gold-hued seed pearls and amber. She looked over her shoulder—her hair was dressed with gossamer veils. At her side, Sonny was clothed in a flowing, laced shirt and supple leather breeches and boots. Silver flashed at his throat and wrists as he leaned from his saddle, reaching for the reins of her horse. He pulled them both to a stop at the fringes of the hunting party.

The rest of the hunters dismounted amid much laughter and merriment. Kelley stared in open amazement at them, realizing with a start that they were not human. Like clouds of brilliant butterflies, they shimmered and shone in the dappled sunlight. Some even bore the delicate traces of jewel-bright wings unfurling behind them.

Sonny chuckled at her expression as he swung a leg over his mount's flank and dropped lightly to the ground. He reached up to help Kelley do the same, steadying her as her feet touched down on the mossy sward. She looked up into Sonny's eyes and saw the wonder in her own reflected back at her.

"How . . . ," she began, but turned at the sound of deep, booming laughter. It came from a tall, handsome man clothed in deep green and bearing the horns of a king stag on his bright helmet.

"That is Herne the Hunter," Sonny murmured in a low voice shaded with reverence. "The Faerie Folk call him the Horned One."

"I thought you said Herne was mortal," Kelley whispered back.

"He is . . . at least, he *was*. At this point in his life."

Kelley understood then that somehow Sonny had conjured up a vision from Herne's life, when the Hunter had been a prince. "And the Faerie don't—didn't—have a problem hanging out with him?"

Sonny smiled at her choice of words. "Faerie and mortal used to . . . 'hang out' together quite a lot. In the days before mortals grew fearful."

Isn't that because the Faerie grew frightening? Kelley thought as Sonny took her by the hand, leading her toward the center of the meadow, where fine tables laden with a fantastic banquet stood.

"Can they see us?" Kelley asked as they passed among the Faerie.

"No." Sonny shook his head. "They do not see us as we are—because we're not really here. They probably see us as companions of that long-ago day."

"How are you—"

"Magick. Auberon taught me small things—party tricks, really, compared with what the Faerie can do—when I was a boy." He shrugged. "Things like conjuring visions. I had a certain aptitude for it, although, I confess, I've never really tried anything *this* complicated before. Now come . . . let's at least enjoy our time here while we can. This is not a story with a happy ending."

About to ask him what he meant, Kelley's breath caught in her throat at what she saw next.

How, she thought, *could anything possibly go awry when*

the world has such creatures in it?

"Mabh!" Herne shouted in a joyous greeting, his voice filled with the unmistakable warmth of his feelings for the woman, flame haired and fantastically beautiful, who stepped out from beneath the shadows of the trees. "My Queen! My love . . ."

Kelley had never seen anyone with such fierce grace and majesty as the Faerie queen of the Autumn Court. Mabh was like all the poignant glory of the fall season distilled into a single being. She lifted her arms in welcome to the Horned One, and her smile filled the grove like sunshine.

Kelley forgot Sonny's foreboding words. In fact, she forgot almost everything—she even almost forgot that she'd ever had another life—as day upon day passed blissfully in feasting and hunting and song. At night, Herne and his companions, Sonny and Kelley among them, would lie on richly woven blankets under the stars, listening to the crackle of the bonfires and the strange, beautiful music of the Fae. By day, they would ride through the forests at great, reckless speed, whooping and laughing in sheer delight.

It seemed to Kelley that time passed and, yet, time stood absolutely still.

Then came the day when Mabh, clothed in a midnight-hued gown and smiling a secret smile, bent to kiss the Hunter Prince's brow as he lay on the mossy bank of a spring pool, his head in her lap, smiling up at her. All about them, the glittering coterie of Faerie royalty—Herne's hunting companions—lounged indolently, watching with idle amusement as the Faerie queen laughed and rose to her feet. With movements so graceful she seemed almost to dance, Mabh circled the pool. Lifting her voice in a chant of power, she pulled forth handfuls of glistening jet-black beads from hidden pockets in the folds of her skirts.

Propped up on one elbow beside Kelley, Sonny went stiff with tension, and she suddenly remembered what he had told her about this tale not ending well.

Her green eyes glittering, Mabh held both hands over the surface of the pool and, opening her fists, let fall the jewels into the spring. The surface of the water rippled and then boiled, foaming white and hissing steam. Rising to her feet and straining to see, Kelley glimpsed something moving in the inky depths.

A kelpie emerged from the spring, called forth by the chant of the Darkling Queen. Kelley glanced down at Sonny, speechless with apprehension, as Mabh cast her spell, enchanting the water spirit with her talismans, changing it with her magicks into a spirit of fire.

Sonny rose and watched with Kelley as the creature writhed and whinnied and blurred like smoke, transforming from something that closely resembled the sweet-tempered animal back home in her apartment into a ferociously beautiful creature—a stallion with a coat as red as a sunset, and fiery, flashing hooves.

"My Queen," protested one of the Faerie hunters uneasily. "This is an *impossibility*! It should not be—"

Mabh silenced him with a look.

Approaching her, Herne's eyes lit with joy at the sight of his lover's extravagant gift. The Hunter vaulted onto the back of the magnificent roan stallion. Mabh threw her arms into the air and laughed with an almost girlish delight as, together, the Hunter and his horse leaped into the sky, galloping swiftly over the treetops. In the forest glade there was a flashing blur of motion—like the beating of ink black wings—and Mabh disappeared. In her stead, a raven flashed through the spaces between the trees, following in the wake of the Horned One and his steed.

"This is unheard of," murmured the Fae who had uttered the protest. "To bestow a gift of such extravagant and danger-ous magick upon a mortal . . ."

"Mabh is besotted," said the Faerie beside him, shaking her head.

"Oh, come! The Horned One is no mere mortal," said another, laughing as he mounted his own horse, hurrying to follow in Herne's wake.

Most of the other Faerie seemed to agree and, in a flurry of activity, swept forward to join in the merry chase of their mor-tal companion and his new prize. Caught up in the excitement and not wanting to miss a moment of the story, Kelley picked up her skirts and ran for her own horse, Sonny at her heels.

The party galloped in pursuit of the Hunter. As the woods opened up into a wide expanse of rolling downs, all of the Faerie mounts leaped into the sky, their hooves pounding the air above the treetops as they took flight.

Her heart in her mouth, Kelley gripped the reins, white-knuckled, and hazarded a glance left and right. On either side of her, Herne's hunters rode, starry-eyed and ethereal in their beauty, with excitement-flushed cheeks, streaming hair, and expressions uniform in their fierce elation. Kelley had never seen anything so glorious, never done anything so exciting as ride through the skies with that shining host.

The days and nights continued to pass in an intoxicating blur. Not only did Mabh give Herne the roan horse, she provided him and his companions with the most extraordinary quarry to hunt. The Darkling Queen commanded her minions capture Faerie beasts from her own lands in the Otherworld and set them loose to roam the forests of Herne's mortal realm, all for the sake of her lover's sport. Magnificent animals: stag and boar and bear.

And what had once been folly and fun soon became a pursuit in deadly earnest. The hunters became consumed, riding in the chase with the mortal prince and his fantastic steed—huntsmen and -women, hounds and horses, riding with wild abandon above the forests of that ancient world.

The branches of the trees caught at Kelley's silk sleeves as the hunting party thundered to a stop. They were at the edges of a forest glade where a pure white monarch stag stood defiantly, held at bay in the clearing by a ring of enormous hunting hounds. For three days, Herne had led the hunt in a mad, exhilarating chase of this regal quarry.

Kelley had been as caught up in the excitement as anyone, but now all she felt was a painful tightness in her chest. She watched helplessly as, urged on by his companions, the Horned One drew an arrow from the quiver on his back. Herne's missile flew with deadly accuracy, striking unerringly, deep into the King Stag's throat. The snow-white creature bellowed and fell to its knees, its blood flowing in a silver river down its hide to pool like molten metal on the grass.

The Faerie hunters cheered their prince's triumph and two beautiful Fae rushed up to Herne, throwing their arms around him, even as the image of the dying stag almost broke Kelley's heart. Beside her, Sonny made a soft sound of protest. Kelley looked over at him and saw his silver-gray eyes flash with anger and sorrow at the sight of the downed beast.

Kelley felt other eyes upon them and turned her head to see Herne staring at Sonny—and then, briefly, at her. The Hunter's brow creased in a furrow beneath the rim of his bright helmet. After a moment, he smiled and turned back to his companions, leaving Kelley to wonder what he'd seen.

Herne approached the body of the stag, stopping at a distance of a few feet. There was a long, stretched moment of silence in the forest, for even the birds had stopped singing. Kelley raised a shaking hand to her forehead and realized she had been clutching the reins so hard they'd left red marks on her palms.

Suddenly the animal twitched and shuddered where it lay upon the ground. The majestic white creature drew breath again and churned its legs, lurching back up onto its feet. The stag pawed the turf and shook its head. Kelley could scarcely believe her eyes. It was alive again!

The Hunter lifted his bow in salute, and Kelley looked over at Sonny, feeling the corners of her own mouth turn up in response to the wide smile that suddenly spread across his face as the stag bounded off into the forest once more, leaving nothing behind but a trace of silver blood on the grass.

The Faerie hunters cheered, and all was well. Herne turned back to his companions, flinging an arm over one of the beautiful huntress's shoulders as the group burst into song. But from the corner of her eye, Kelley saw a blurring of darkness flash through the trees—a raven, flying off into the depths of the forest, its cry echoing harshly.

Later, once the sun had set, a great, lavish banquet was spread out upon a high hill. Herne was particularly merry that night, calling for games and music; he was never alone, constantly surrounded by the shining Fae who doted on him. One lovely Faerie girl had removed Herne's horned helmet and was weaving a crown of leaves through his hair as he laughed at a story another hunter was telling.

Over on the other side of the hilltop, on a wide stretch of flat earth, a furious game of hurling—something resembling field hockey but played with a silver ball and wide-bladed sticks made from polished oak—was being played at full tilt. Kelley's untutored eye could discern few if any rules as the battle for possession of the shining ball raged between two groups of Fae. It seemed like gleeful, dangerous chaos to her, and she kept her distance. But she couldn't help noticing how Sonny drifted over to the margin of the pitch to watch them play. His expression turned wistful, and Kelley guessed that he was thinking of his own childhood in the Otherworld where, no doubt, he had played this game or one like it.

Not wanting to intrude on his reminiscence, Kelley walked a little away from the revelers and stood at the edge of the hilltop. Looking down, she saw the lights of a small village nestled in the valley, bordered by the thick forest where they had hunted that day. The full moon illuminated the houses, and Kelley could just make out the figures of two villagers emerging from their cottage to peer up at the hill. *They can hear us*, Kelley realized, unsurprised, for the Fae's laughter and carousing had reached raucous levels.

Kelley's skin prickled, and she looked up, toward the horizon, and saw Mabh standing alone on a barren hilltop in the distance. The Faerie queen's dark cloak spread out behind her on a cold wind as she watched Herne's festivities from afar.

Anger, palpable as a thundercloud, gathered around her. In her fist, she gripped a slender, silver-tipped spear. But Kelley also thought she saw the Faerie queen's shoulders hunch beneath her cloak—as though Mabh wept.

Kelley's heart went out to her.

But as the dawn approached, her sympathies for the Autumn Queen vanished. As Herne and his hunters slept, full of meat and mead and sparkling Faerie wine, Kelley awoke from an uneasy dream to see Mabh stalking silently among her lover's companions. Her lips moved, the breath hissing between her teeth, as she knelt down before each sleeping Faerie hunter, tying charms around their throats. Black, glittering charms.

Kelley froze, realizing the queen was casting a terrible curse as she wove a path through the sleeping Fae. Once she had passed, Kelley dared to sit up, and looked at the Faerie asleep on the ground. Horrified, she watched the exquisite beings amid whom she had been living change before her eyes—becoming terrible in their beauty. Dark. Dangerous. The queen's magicks had transformed them; no longer care-free, they were cruel looking even in sleep.

Creeping silently to the edge of the hunters' camp, Kelley

watched Mabh stride down the sloping hill to the forest below. Reaching the edge of the trees, the queen waved a hand and conjured an ugly, gaping rift in the wall between the mortal world where the hunters slept, showing glimpses of a dark, forbidding Otherworld realm beyond. Mabh put two fingers to her lips and whistled—soundlessly, to Kelley's ears. She was answered by a pack of vicious hounds—Black Shuck—who bounded from out of the rift between worlds and into the forest.

Crouched at the edge of the hill's precipice, Kelley saw Mabh's hounds drive the hunters' noble quarry out from beneath the sheltering trees, herding them like cattle. As the Black Shuck snapped at the silvery heels and exquisite hides of the magical animals, Mabh waved her arm again and the shuck drove them through the rift. The sky began to lighten in the east just as the last of the quarry—the white King Stag—leaped through.

"She will hide them in her own lands, the Borderlands, in places where the sight of neither men nor Fae can find them." Sonny's voice was grim. He appeared out of the predawn mist at Kelley's side, watching with her.

"And then what?" she asked, not sure if she really wanted to know. "What will happen now?"

"Mortal beasts are . . . no longer challenging to the hunters," Sonny said softly as he unclasped his cloak and draped it over Kelley's shoulders.

He must have seen her shiver. She didn't tell him it wasn't from cold.

"They will seek other prey," he said.

But as he spoke, the sun was already rising. The hunters were awakening.

Herne and the transformed Faerie greeted the day with bloodlust shining in their eyes. Mounting their horses, they set off at breakneck speed for the forest with a newfound grimness underscoring their elation. Sonny and Kelley mounted their steeds, too, but kept well behind their now-frightening companions.

Searching everywhere for their enchanted quarry but finding none, the spell-ensnared Fae howled with madness and rage at their spoiled pursuits. Thundering to a halt at the ragged edge of the woods, they looked up and saw, atop the hill where they had camped, the Dark Queen standing, still as any statue.

Mabh smiled coldly and put a tall bronze war horn to her lips. Kelley had to drop the reins of her horse and cover her ears as the queen blew three earth-shattering notes, calling the Wild Hunt to war.

Herne and his hunters seemed to go mad at the horn's terrible sound, tearing up into the sky and brandishing swords suddenly livid with flame. Some of the treetops caught fire as they passed, casting an orange glow on the bellies of low clouds and painting the Faerie with lurid, angry light. The Hunter and his once-beautiful companions, features now twisted with hate, turned malevolent eyes toward the human village that lay just to their west—the village Kelley had observed during the night.

Horrified, she turned desperately toward Sonny, who grabbed the bridle on Kelley's mount as her horse reared in distress. Kicking his heels into his own mount's flanks, he wheeled the horses and led Kelley away from the Hunt as fast as their steeds would carry them.

"This can't be happening," she gasped, breathless, as they reached the cover of the forest and she hauled her charging horse to a stop, forcing Sonny to circle his mount and return to her side. "They're not going to kill those villagers? Sonny?"

Sonny could not answer.

"Oh, my God . . . ," Kelley whispered, twisting in her saddle to look back through the trees as she heard the first shrieks of hunted humans echoing down the wind.

"Mabh turned them from a hunting party into a deathless, death-mad war band," Sonny spat, his bitterness palpable. "Waking nightly with the rising of the moon to ride out with a singular purpose: to kill."

"But after that?" Kelley whispered, pleading for a glimmer of hope. "What happens *after* that? It can't just end there . . ."

"No." Sonny had grown very pale, and his voice sounded faint and far-off. He stared, his gaze unfocused, at the scudding clouds. "The High Courts of Faerie will finally be forced to action. They will gather together in council and—in an utterly rare moment of accord between the Seelie and Unseelie kingdoms—Auberon the Winter King and

Titania the Queen of Summer will combine their efforts and cast Herne down from the sky, from the back of his fearsome horse."

A sheen of sweat on his brow, Sonny pointed up into a sky suddenly full of shifting, thunderstorm hues—where the last, ghostly remnants of the vision he had conjured wavered before Kelley's eyes. She saw another gaping rift open between the worlds and a great whirlwind of light and sound poured forth. She saw Herne thrown from his charger and watched as he plummeted to the earth far below, a falling comet.

Without his rider, the Roan Horse suddenly became nothing more than a lowly kelpie again. It vanished at a command from Auberon, leaving behind nothing but glittering black jewels that twinkled briefly like stars in the night sky before disappearing themselves.

"And Mabh?" Kelley asked, her throat dry.

"Confined by Auberon and Titania to her own realm, where she remains," Sonny murmured, "a prisoner in her shadow kingdom to this day."

Kelley did not find that as comforting a thought as she was perhaps meant to, but there was no time for more questions. Sonny was bent low over the neck of his mount, and he looked dangerously close to slipping from his saddle.

"We have to go," he said as he reached out, hooking his fingers around her horse's bridle. He turned his mount and led them toward a bank of fog that was rising over the moors.

The swirling mists closed around them, and Kelley felt the horse beneath her gradually stiffen and change—reverting back to the wooden carousel horse it had once been, what seemed like so very long ago.

XXIII

The fog dispersed and Herne's ancient world faded into nothingness. The pictures in Kelley's mind disappeared and, with them, the silken princess gown. She found herself sitting once more astride a painted carousel pony, bobbing gently up and down as the ride wound to an end. She looked over and saw that Sonny's eyes were closed, and there was a grayish pallor to his skin.

"Did it work?" she demanded.

His eyes snapped open, and he struggled to focus his gaze on her.

"Sonny?"

"It did. Leaderless, the power of the Hunt itself was diminished, thrown into chaos and confusion. Auberon and Titania were then able to weave an enchantment that would lock them away, forever sleeping in a place that is not in this world, not in the Other."

"And Herne?"

"Free. Ultimately . . . ," Sonny said sadly. "But even though he was released from the horrific enchantment, Herne was broken in spirit and body. Despairing of the crimes he had committed as leader of the Wild Hunt, he retreated deep into his forests. After so much time spent in the company of the immortal Faerie, Herne found that he himself was unable to die. But he faded, century after century, until he was no more than a shadow of his former grandeur. And the Hunt has remained locked in enchanted slumber."

"So . . . where's the problem then?" Kelley asked, although she had the uneasy feeling that she already knew the answer.

"As per Mabh's vile enchantment, they will only stay that way as long as they remain leaderless."

"Okay . . . " The uneasy feeling deepened in the pit of her stomach.

"And they will only stay leaderless as long as the Roan Horse remains riderless."

"But I saw the Roan Horse go *poof*!" Kelley protested.

"It did." Sonny nodded, the color slowly returning to his

cheeks as he swung himself out of his saddle. "The Roan Horse was destroyed. But the magick that Mabh used to *create* the Roan Horse remains."

"And . . . it's all tangled up in Lucky's mane. Isn't it?"

"I'm sorry."

Bad Lucky, Kelley thought.

Sonny helped her down off the back of her painted mount, and she found that her knees were shaky. He put a hand on her shoulder to steady her.

"It's not all bad, Kelley," he said. "Not yet. The creature is safe as long as he stays in your bathtub. Water is a gateway— if he stays standing in it, he's not in this world and not in the Other. As long as he stays that way, even if someone *were* to blow Mabh's war horn, the call of the Wild Hunt can't touch him."

"So I have a Faerie water horse stuck in my tub for the rest of eternity?"

"No. Just for the rest of the Nine-Night, until the door to the Otherworld shuts again. Then there would be no way for the Wild Hunt to cross over, and we could try to remove the enchantment."

"And if the unthinkable happens? If he gets out somehow and he's still enchanted?"

"Then if someone were to sound Mabh's war horn, Lucky would transform and become *the* Roan Horse," Sonny said in a quiet voice. "The Roan Horse seeks out a Rider. Once it has a Rider, the Wild Hunt wakes. Once the Wild Hunt wakes, they come thundering through the Gate on the backs of their shadowy steeds, and they kill. They are insatiable and they are unstoppable. The whole of this city—the whole of the mortal realm—could conceivably be destroyed."

Images from one of her recent nightmares flooded back into Kelley's mind: Manhattan awash in blood and fire; herself staring down at her own hands grasping, white-knuckled, the tangled strands of a fiery mane. . . .

She shuddered and looked up at Sonny. "And is it, then, some kind of lunatic coincidence that the Roan Horse is in *my* tub? And *I* just also happen to be the daughter of a Faerie king?"

"I don't know. But I don't believe in coincidence." Sonny smiled at her wryly. "No—I do think the two things are connected. Because I'm reasonably sure that, insofar as you *are* a daughter of the Faerie king, someone wants you dead. I believe that is why a Black Shuck was set to track you. To lead the Wild Hunt to find you specifically"—his expression darkened—"among whatever other quarry they might find to give them sport."

Kelley stared at him, her eyes wide. "Isn't that a little like hunting quail with a cannon? Haven't these people ever heard the phrase *collateral damage*?"

"I suppose. But for someone like Mabh, for instance,

collateral damage is the fun part. And she *does* hold something of a grudge toward your father. The whole imprisonment after the Wild Hunt thing."

"Oh, right." Kelley hugged her elbows, possessed of a sudden deep chill, and muttered, "She sounds delightful. But she's still locked up?"

"She is confined. Within her own realm, a grim place called the Borderlands. But she has outside agents through whom she can still work her will." Sonny scowled. "Auberon suspects her of trying to wake the Hunt. If he's right, she will most likely try to do it on Samhain—when the Gate is open widest."

Kelley shivered. "You know, New Yorkers take Halloween pretty seriously. There are going to be a lot of hapless partygoers and trick-or-treaters on the streets come the thirty-first. Sounds like a recipe for a whole lot of collateral damage."

"The Janus Guard will also be out that night," he said, one hand reaching out to squeeze her shoulder. "Just as we have been and will be for every night of the Nine."

"Good."

"Speaking of which—Kelley . . . " Sonny seemed suddenly exhausted. He turned his face to the west, and she could see the fatigue etched into the lines and planes of his face. "It's getting late. You need to leave the park. Please. Don't argue with me this time. Just go. The sun will set soon, and I have to go to work."

He squared his shoulders as though he expected her to put up a fight.

She did—a little—but only out of actual concern for him. "Shouldn't you be taking it easy? I mean, you try to hide it with the whole tough-guy-swagger thing and all, but I saw the bandages. You're really hurt. Aren't you?"

"It's not so bad."

"Wow. You are a terrible liar."

He frowned fiercely at her.

"You also look like you haven't slept in a week." She took a tentative step toward him and put a hand on his chest, looking up into his silver-gray eyes.

He put his hand over the top of hers, and she could feel the rhythm of his heart beating under her palm, through his shirt and the bandages.

"I'm fine."

"Are you sure?"

With his other hand, Sonny reached up and brushed a stray auburn curl out of her eyes. "I'm sure."

He smiled down at her, and she felt her insides melt a little. His whole face changed when he smiled. It was like the sun coming out.

"But," he continued, "I'll be even better if you are safe at home and I don't have to worry about you for tonight."

"I can take care of myself, Sonny Flannery," she bristled, halfheartedly.

"Please?" He turned up the wattage on his smile.

"I . . . okay." She felt her own lips turn up in a shy, answering smile. "I'll be good. This *once*."

"That's my girl."

Kelley was silent. Those three words of Sonny's had managed to render her utterly speechless.

XXIV

That night proved easy by Janus standards.

By the time Sonny saw Kelley out of the park at East Seventy-second, the shadows had grown long again, and he'd gone to work. He'd only had to draw his sword once and he'd even been able to actually *talk* a bevy of wood sprites into returning back through the rift whence they'd come without any of them so much as lobbing a pinecone at his head.

Maybe they'd felt sorry for him, he thought as he walked up Fifth Avenue after sunrise and passed his reflection in a shop window. He really did look terrible: bone-deep weary, his eyes circled with shadows like bruises.

He knew that sleep would be the best thing for him, but as the sky brightened over New York and the day began anew, Sonny headed instead in the direction of the address that he'd finally been able to pry out of a reluctant Maddox.

The fire-escape landing outside the fourth-floor apartment could be accessed by two windows. One, the bathroom window, showed Sonny a glimpse of reddish horsehair: a tail swishing back and forth through the gap between the wall and the shower curtain. He heard a gentle, regular rumbling—the kelpie was snoring in his sleep. Sonny briefly thought of doing . . . something . . . but the thing was safe for the moment. And he had begun to shy away from any thought of violence toward the creature, for Kelley's sake.

Kelley . . . The other window was hers. The gap in the curtains showed her curled up in her bed, sleeping peacefully. When she shifted in her slumber, the silver-and-green amber pendant she wore slid along the chain around her neck, coming to rest in the graceful, hollowed contour above her collarbone. In the dim light of the room, the little charm seemed almost to glow.

Sonny closed his eyes and reached toward her with his inner senses. With Kelley asleep, it was easier for him to get a read on her. . . .

There she was, like brilliant little sparks in the darkness, her explosive brightness kept in check, Sonny was sure, by the sputtering fuse of the charm around her throat. She was almost completely hidden.

Swinging himself off the iron stairs and down to the ground, Sonny decided that he wouldn't be going back to his apartment to rest that morning.

The Avalon Grande proved easy to break and enter, but the fact that it left him even slightly out of breath gave Sonny pause. His Janus training should have made it effortless. His injuries had made it hard.

You're only human, he thought. It left a bitter taste in his mouth. Especially now that he knew that Kelley wasn't. *Which one is really Kelley?* he wondered. The apprentice actress at a tumbledown theater, or that incandescent creature in the alleyway—the one he'd glimpsed when the veil that kept her hidden had slipped?

Sonny was pretty sure that Kelley didn't have the vaguest idea what she truly was—what she could be. What would happen, he wondered, when she discovered it for herself? Would she change? Become like those same Faerie he had worshipped as a child? He was not so sure that he would want Kelley to become like them.

It had been difficult for Sonny, living in the mortal realm for the past year. Everything seemed just slightly shabby to his Otherworld-accustomed eyes. Still, he found himself, more and more, entertaining the thought that perhaps the Faerie realm—in all its wild, magical splendor—

208

was not exactly the glorious place his childhood memories made it.

He thought of Kelley drifting through the halls of her father's shining palace. He pictured her as she might become: a perfect being, but distant. Cold. Aloof. Wanting for nothing but, by the same token, dreaming of nothing . . .

He pushed the thought away and hid himself in the darkened upper balcony, resting his arms on the worn wood of the pew in front of him and relaxing as the morning stage crew began to trickle in. Kelley hadn't yet arrived—it was still too early—but Sonny was filled with a warmth of anticipation. Not that he was going to let her know that he was there; he was finally getting the sense that Kelley might not take entirely kindly to his watching out for her. Also, the man playing Oberon had been fairly explicit in his warning to stay away. Not that he posed any kind of threat to a Janus, but Sonny respected the man's desire to defend Kelley. The shadowy balcony provided an ideal vantage point.

It was also dark and warm. When Sonny woke up hours later, it was only because Bob the boucca was poking him in the shoulder with a wooden prop sword. Sonny sat up with a start, but the ancient Fae put a shushing finger to his lips.

"Heigh-ho, Faerie killer," Bob whispered, a mocking grin stretched across his face. "Thought you might be up here."

"Seven hells . . . " Sonny glanced around blearily and

scrubbed a hand over his face. Some bodyguard he was! "Does she know I'm here?"

"No. But if you'd kept on snoring like that, she was bound to find out. Didn't think you'd want that. She fancies herself all kinds of self-sufficient. You may have noticed."

"She doesn't know what she's up against."

"Do you?"

"I have theories, but . . . I could use your help."

"I'm not known for giving it."

Sonny chose his words carefully. "I think you're the victim of—what do they call it?—bad press. I think you're a great deal more helpful that you let on. I know why the leprechaun shut you in a jar, for one thing." He nodded toward the backstage area, where he could sense that Kelley was in her dressing room. "The charm on Kelley's necklace. The shamrock. It's been hiding her, protecting her."

Bob gave Sonny a long, appraising look. "Technically it's a four-leaf clover. Shamrocks have only three leaves. But the four-leaf—"

"I know, I know," Sonny murmured impatiently. "Powerful magic. Strong protection. The leaves represent the Four Gates, the Four Feasts, the Four Courts of Faerie—"

"Also hope, faith, love . . . and luck. It is powerful in any case, but *that* particular charm is exceptionally potent. The little green finks do good work, I'll give them that."

"You *stole* it from a leprechaun?"

"Yes. And, contrary to popular opinion, I make a lousy

thief. He figured out it was me pretty quickly and was waiting for me when I got back."

"That was a heavy price to pay."

"You have *no* idea." Bob's face scrunched up in misery. His eyes glowed with a sullen green fire. "I hate honey. Can't stand the stuff."

"Why did you do it then?"

The most notorious boucca to ever make mischief in the mortal realm stared up at the vaulted ceiling. His voice when he spoke was barely audible.

"I let myself become fond. Of a mortal."

"Who?" Sonny asked. Something deep within him whispered that he already knew the answer.

"Your mother, Sonny."

"My . . . "

Sonny felt as though all of the air in the theater had been sucked out. His chest hurt.

"The sweet and lovely Emmaline Flannery . . . " Bob sighed. "I made the mistake of passing by her village a second time, not long after Auberon had sent me to fetch you in the first place—"

"You mean *steal* me."

"Steal you. Yes."

Sonny's earlier conversation with Kelley came rushing back to him.

"I didn't think much of it at the time," Bob said. "You were just another piddling human bairn to be cradle-took. Not like

I hadn't done it a dozen times before. More . . . " The ancient Fae's timeless features grew contemplative. His pale eyes filled with memory. "But this time . . . well. After I made the mistake of going back, I couldn't get the sound of your mother's cries out of my ears. Hmph—much like the honey now, I suppose."

Neither of them laughed at the joke.

Bob sighed. "It tore at me. I couldn't close my own eyes for fear of seeing hers . . . pretty blue eyes, red with weeping." The boucca shook his head, memory and regret chasing themselves across his face.

Sonny looked away. His hands, he suddenly noticed, were curled into tight fists.

"Well, time—or what passes for time, at least, in the Faerie realm—moves on," Bob continued. "You were already toddling about when Auberon went out into the forest one day and brought a wee tiny princess home to Court the next. An heir. But it was not the joyous occasion it might have been, if it had been, say, Titania's babe as well."

"Kelley. Whose is she? Who is her mother?"

"Never knew." Bob lifted a shoulder. "Never asked—not the kind of thing you *would* ask the good king Auberon. Not and still keep your noggin on top of your shoulders."

"He never said who her mother was?"

"Could have been a lowly wood nymph for all we knew. Auberon's dalliances were legendary back then, what with him and Titania always quarreling."

"Why didn't he keep the baby hidden, then, I wonder?" Sonny asked.

"Well, that's the thing about Faerie royalty, boyo," Bob replied. "They don't tend to stay inconspicuous for very long. And this tiny thing glowed like a new star. She wouldn't have stayed hidden—even if Auberon had tried."

Sonny knew that was the truth from experience. The sight of Kelley, revealed in her glory in the alley, was imprinted on his mind like the afterimage of a flash photograph. "So what happened? How did she wind up hidden in this realm?"

"Because the lord of the Unseelie, in his immeasurable wisdom"—Bob's voice was heavy with sarcasm—"set *me* to nursemaid the wee thing. Punishment for some sort of passing wickedness on my part, no doubt. Auberon was not noted for a long supply of affection—paternal or otherwise. And he seemed quite content to spend what little he *did* have on you."

"Why?" Sonny had always wondered. He'd just never asked the question out loud before. "Why me?"

The boucca shrugged. "Who knows? Whimsy? The novelty of raising a son who was not an heir? And you were an amusing pet: fearless, stubborn. He doted on you. All while his own daughter lay shut away in the nursery—wailing in the cradle, night after night, alone."

213

"You felt sorry for her."

"Bah! I tell you, I'd already gone pudding-soft by then!" Bob's face twisted into an expression of disgust. "It drove me near mad. Cries of the babe mewling in my ears, cries of your mother still howling in my mind . . . The two things just seemed to add up and make a sudden sense."

"And so you helped my mother steal the heir to the Unseelie kingdom right out from under the Faerie king's nose." Sonny knew that he was staring at the boucca with his jaw hanging open, but by that point he couldn't help it. "By all the gods, that was brave *madness*!"

"I would have tried for you, but as I say, Auberon barely let you out of his sight. So instead, I stole a charm from a leprechaun, grabbed your mum, and snuck her straight into the palace nursery. Big, cold room full of sharp, pretty things and not even a wee baby rattle in sight. Emmaline takes one look at yon sad little princess and her heart starts to mend right there. I put the clover charm around the baby's neck to veil her brightness, and that was that. Away we ran!"

Sonny could only gape; the sheer audacity of the thing overwhelmed him.

"Easier than I thought it would be." Bob grinned sourly. "At least, at first. In, out, off we went . . . until Auberon got wind of it. There he was shutting the Gates one by one— *clang! clang! clang!*—as we run. I tumbled out the Beltane

Gate, right back in Ireland where we'd started, and over my shoulder I saw Emmaline and the babe caught in between the worlds and just able to leap through the one crack left in the Samhain Gate."

"A hundred years later in time and an ocean away from her home," Sonny said quietly, understanding.

"Aye, and *that* was what mucked up Auberon's spell. Like sticking your foot in a closing door, it jarred the Gate off its hinges a bit, I suppose. There I was, unable to do a damned thing about it, stuck in the past and fending off a hopping-mad leprechaun." Bob waved a hand in the air. "Unsuccessfully. That about sums it up."

"And Auberon never tried to find her or his daughter."

"Oh, he threw all manner of tantrums, I hear. Issued decrees. Heads rolled. Blah-blah-blah. Put on quite a show of paternal grief, considering he'd never paid the poor wee thing an ounce of attention when she'd been under his own roof. It wasn't about the girl, you see—it was all about his own wounded pride. And, sadly, it also gave him a convenient excuse to tighten his grip on the rule of the Fair Folk."

Sonny could hardly argue that point.

Bob sighed. "Well. That's the last time I get sentimental."

"And yet, I noticed that you *are* still keeping an eye out for the well-being of a certain princess."

"Rule of the Faerie kingdoms is passed only through the

direct bloodline; you know that." Bob cast a shrewd glance at Sonny. "Who knows—our girly might just knock the Unseelie throne out from under her dad's chilly bum one day. And I'd cheerfully take the job of right-hand sprite to the new Unseelie queen if it's offered."

Sonny's mind was reeling with the implications of Bob's tale.

"I love this scene," the boucca murmured, leaning over the pew to watch the stage, his eyes glinting with amusement. "I remember the first time I ever saw them do this. . . . Old Willie himself played Bottom. The man's timing was flawless."

Below them, onstage, the Mechanicals were enacting the play within the play. It was a tragicomic story about two lovers, Pyramus and Thisbe, kept apart by their cruel, disapproving parents and forced to whisper their devotion to each other through a crack in the wall that separated their houses. The scene was supposed to be funny, and yet Sonny found himself oddly affected by the lovers' plight.

The "play" ended with a prolonged, purposefully hilarious death scene from Bottom, who flopped around on the stage like a landed fish, a wobbly rubber prop sword protruding out from under one arm. Then all of the actors froze in place.

For a brief moment, Sonny thought the tableau was just part of the performance, then he heard Bob whisper beside him.

"Oh . . . *shit*."

The temperature suddenly plummeted to freezing. The theater echoed with rolling *boom*s like a glacier breaking apart. The double loading doors at the back of the stage flung wide, and a cold, baleful light poured over the threshold. Puck made a sign in the air with the fingers of one hand and clutched the back of Sonny's neck with the other. Sonny knew that Bob had cast a powerful veil—powerful enough to shield them from the awareness of the Unseelie king.

"What are you doing?" he whispered. "I'm a Janus—there's no reason for me to hide from my king."

"Oh, really?" Bob whispered back. "Somehow I get the feeling that your king would not approve of the company you keep. I stole his daughter, remember? Nor, I think, would he appreciate the fact that you've yet to tell him of your discovery."

"I was going to!"

"When?"

"After Kelley's had a chance to get used to the idea," Sonny said, although he wasn't entirely sure he believed his own assertions. Why *hadn't* he told Auberon straightaway?

"Well, never mind that now," Bob said, peering through the balcony rails. "I think she's about to receive a little fatherly face time, whether she's used to the idea or not."

Down on the stage, all of the actors, the crew, and the director stood frozen like statues in a garden. Auberon stalked among them like a predator, searching their faces. He cast a glance up toward the balconies.

Bob's spell held. The king turned and kept walking, heading toward the dressing rooms and Kelley.

XXV

Kelley didn't mind that she still had to help out backstage, even though she was now playing a lead. She was good with her hands and she hummed as she plugged in the glue gun and went to work peeling back the faux fur on the left ear of Bottom's ass head. It kept drooping in front of her face in their scenes together.

The wave of arctic air hit her like a physical assault.

"Hello, Kelley." The voice was sonorous with a faint crackling hiss. "I am Auberon, King of the Unseelie Court of the Realm of Faerie. I am also your father."

Kelley felt a surge of fear tighten her stomach and willed her hands not to shake. She'd been half expecting this. She looked up from her work.

"My father was a doctor."

The Faerie king chuckled. "A healer of the sick. How noble. *You* do not get sick. You have no need of such creatures. And *I* am your father. None other."

"My *father* was a doctor," she said again. Her hand went white-knuckled on the glue gun as she squeezed out a bead of melted adhesive along the base of the ear. "When I was four years old, he taught me how to properly bandage my knee when I skinned it. My mother showed me later how to take the dressing off without it hurting. What have you ever done for me? *They* were my parents and they loved me. How dare you tell me that they weren't!"

Auberon took a step inside the room, over her threshold, and Kelley felt the clover charm at her throat spark and grow warm.

She glared balefully at the king. "Now that I'm, what, almost an adult? You suddenly appear in a puff of smoke and you want to assert some sort of parental claim on me? The Deadbeat Dad from Faerie Land? Whatever." She rolled her eyes. "I don't know you. I don't need to. You might have been responsible for my creation, but you certainly had nothing to do with what I've become. I plan on keeping it that way."

To her surprise, Auberon smiled. "I think that's an excellent idea," he said. "And I'd like to help you with that—if you don't mind."

Kelley put the glue gun down and stared at the Faerie king. "I beg your pardon?"

"Yes, you would," he said, a not quite subtle note of warning in his voice. "If you weren't my daughter."

Kelley blinked and dropped her gaze back down to the furry head in her lap. The hollow eyes seemed to stare back at her, full of caution.

"Kelley," the king said, softening his tone, "you know that you are in a great deal of danger because of the simple fact that you are my daughter, do you not?"

"In danger from whom, exactly?"

Auberon spread his hands before him. "There are those who would use you—hurt you—because of what you are. When you were stolen from me, I mourned. I . . . raged. But eventually, I came to see the theft as a blessing in disguise. I have always tried to govern my folk with a just hand, but the Courts of the realm are fractious and fraught with danger. As long as you remain hidden in the mortal world, you are safe."

"*You* found me."

"I found you quite by accident. And only because Sonny Flannery found you first. But you are right. There are others who might prove as clever. And that puts you in grave danger, my child. You must remain hidden. For your own sake, if not mine."

"And what if I decide to take my chances?" Kelley asked.

"Embrace my heritage—whatever that is?"

"Then you will most likely perish," the Faerie king said quietly. "I offer you a bargain. I can see to it that you keep your life—the life that you have made for yourself. I can make you as good as mortal. If you let me."

Kelley's tone was sharp. "You want to keep me from my birthright?" Almost everything she had learned about the Fair Folk over the last few days had served to scare the hell out of her—the Otherworld sounded like a place full of treachery and danger. But although she was loath to admit it, even among her fears there was a tiny part of her that remembered how truly awesome it had been to ride with the Faerie in Herne's hunting party. To be clothed in silk and jewels, galloping through the skies with godlike beings so beautiful they seemed made of starlight, laughing . . . Kelley closed her eyes and banished the seductive thoughts. No. She was pretty sure that she didn't ever want to become a princess of Faerie, but she wasn't about to let Auberon know that. "You want to make me 'normal'? How is that a good deal for me in any way? And in exchange for what? There is nothing you have that I want. Nothing."

"Not even a certain member of my Janus Guard?"

"You leave Sonny out of this! He's not yours to give."

"Perhaps not . . . " Auberon sank gracefully into a crouch in front of her chair and looked up at her. "But tell me this. How does he look at you now?"

"What are you talking about?"

"Now that he knows? Knows *what* you are."

Kelley swallowed to ease a sudden constricting of her throat.

"Oh, my dear girl," Auberon murmured, the chill in his voice suddenly thawing. She could imagine that she heard actual concern in his words. "I raised Sonny. I've watched him ever since he was a child. I know what he thinks of me and of my people. He respects us—and, indeed, there is a small, secret part of him that would sacrifice almost anything for the chance to *become* one of us. But he is not capable of loving us."

"Sonny's not afraid of you."

"No. He isn't," the king agreed. "In fact, he has spent most of his life learning to kill my kind. *Our* kind. He's very good at it."

"Well that's a marvelous legacy you've left him, isn't it?" Kelley refused to look away. She stared straight into his eyes, the fierceness of her emotions making her hands shake. "Way to raise up the kid you stole."

Auberon stood, rich garments falling in regal folds all around him. "I do not wish to quarrel with you, Kelley. I merely tell you this to save you further hurt. It is not within Sonny Flannery to love a Faerie queen. He cannot rise above his upbringing; and if you remain as you are, he will begin to resent that which you are. It is inevitable. If you retain your birthright, my dear girl, you will lose him. Maybe not at first and not all at once, but you will. But I can make it so that you need never see that coldness creep into his gaze."

"Get out."

"Consider my words." Auberon turned to go, but hesitated. "You have your mother's eyes, you know. . . . "

"Get *out*," Kelley said again through clenched teeth, closing her eyes as she turned away from him. When she opened them again, she was alone in her dressing room—shaking, a sticky mess of hot glue pooling on the counter in front of her.

"Kelley?" Sonny appeared at the door of her dressing room. "Are you all right? He didn't . . . hurt you, did he?"

Sonny . . .

She *had* seen how he'd reacted to her in the alleyway. In those brief moments when she'd felt . . . strange. She remembered the look in his eyes and she could not, in her imagination, convert that expression into one that could convey love. What if Auberon was right?

"Kelley?"

She thought suddenly about the rest of the cast and crew. If Auberon had been in the theater . . . "Is everyone okay?" She started for the door.

"They're fine. Bob is out there right now making sure."

"He's one of them, isn't he?" She felt for the charm around her neck, remembering Bob's words to her yesterday. "Bob . . . "

"He used to be called Robin. Among other things."

"Oh, God . . . ," Kelley whispered.

"He's sort of the reason you're in this world in the first place. Actually . . . we both are, it seems."

"I don't understand," she said.

"I didn't either, until he told me just now. Emma—your aunt—once went by another name. Emmaline Flannery."

"Flannery? But . . . " Kelley understood then. "It was you. Em took me because Auberon took you."

"Like I said"—Sonny smiled gently—"the Fates have an odd sense of humor."

"You look like her," she said. "Now that I know. I can see her in you. All that stubborn Irish crazy . . . "

There was a sheen to Sonny's gray eyes. "I'd like to meet her."

"You will."

Sonny cast a glance in the direction of the high window. "It's getting late."

"It keeps doing that. . . . " Kelley sighed. "You're going to leave soon."

Sonny nodded mutely and helped Kelley to her feet. He stood looking down at her and then took her face in his hands. Turning her head slightly, he ran his fingers through her hair, lifting back the loose auburn curls that fell around her cheeks. "You have his ears," he said, running a fingertip over one subtle point.

Kelley shivered. "And my mother's eyes, apparently."

"Did he say who—"

"No. And I didn't ask."

Sonny lowered his hands and they stood there, inches apart, for an awkward moment. Suddenly he gathered her into his arms and held her in a tentative embrace. Kelley felt her heart swell. "I have to go now," he murmured into her hair. "But . . . please be careful tonight. While I can't be there to protect you. Be *careful*."

XXVI

"I only need to know two things," the Fennrys Wolf growled, stalking back and forth in front of the other Janus. "Where do you want me, and how do I kill whatever needs killing?"

"Well, that's just it, Fenn," Sonny tried to explain. "The answers to your questions are: We don't know, and we don't know."

The Wolf rolled his eyes at that and retreated to perch on the back of a bench. The thirteen Janus had gathered after daybreak and a successful night's hunting at Sonny's request in a tucked-away bit of the park that offered enough seclusion for the Guard to assemble without the police thinking they were some sort of gang.

"By now, all of you have been made aware of the possibility that someone is trying to wake the Wild Hunt, right?" Sonny looked from face to face. "The likeliest suspect, of course, is Queen Mabh, although a visit I had from one of her Storm Hags seemed to indicate that it may have been a *mistake* on Mabh's part to release the kelpie into this realm. Or maybe she's had a change of heart."

"Mabh doesn't have a heart," Ghost said quietly.

"Good point," Aaneel agreed. "I can't help but think that she'd just laugh and kick her feet with glee if such a thing were to come to pass."

"Well . . . whatever game she's playing," Sonny said, "we've got more pieces on the board to worry about than just the Queen of Air and Darkness."

Maddox snorted. "I'll say. Tell 'em whom we stumbled across, Old Sonn."

Sonny took a deep breath and said, "The stolen child."

The circle of changelings stared blankly at him, as if he'd suddenly spoken in an incomprehensible language.

"Auberon's daughter?" Sonny prompted. "The lost princess. The reason the Gates were shut. The reason for *us*. I know where she is."

"Who is she?" Aaneel asked.

"She's . . . seventeen," Sonny said. "An actress. Sweet. Happy. And up until—well, up until I told her—she had absolutely no idea of what she is. Let alone who."

"How is that even possible?" Bellamy glanced back and forth between Sonny and Maddox. Beside him, his sister's brow was creased in a frown.

"She's been kept well hidden with the help of a powerful talisman," Sonny explained.

"Does Auberon know?" Beni asked.

"I didn't tell him—"

"Don't." The interjection came from Cait.

"Why the hell not?" the Fennrys Wolf snapped, his pale eyes fierce.

Cait ignored him. "The poor girl! If Auberon finds out about her, he'll want her back. The Unseelie Court is such a cold and joyless place."

"Cait's right, Sonny," Camina agreed, the frown still shadowing her brow. Her eyes were troubled. "Don't tell him."

"Have you two gone insane?" the Wolf asked, pulling out a thin-bladed dagger from his boot and testing the sharpness of the edge against his thumb. "It's the king's bloody kid. Unless you've all forgotten, we serve at the pleasure of the king."

"We've never had much choice in the matter," Cait said, her cheeks coloring with emotion.

The Wolf scoffed at that. "We might not like it much, but that's the way it is. Serve or die. I say let the bastard take her. Maybe it will end the nonsense of guarding this damnable Gate. And then *we* can all go home."

"Home, Fenn?" Maddox suddenly rounded on him. "What

is that exactly? Where is it? And when? We've none of us homes now but *this*. This here and this now. We had our homes taken from us." He turned to face the rest of the Guard. "I've seen this girl, and she belongs in this realm. Would you have the Faerie king take her away from everything she has ever known?" He turned back to the Fennrys Wolf. "Would you honestly wish *our* fate upon her?"

There was a murmur among the circle of Janus, and Fennrys spun the knife in his hand and returned it to his boot. "All right, all right," he said. "It wasn't a serious suggestion. Bunch of whining—"

"Shut up, Fenn," Godwyn said, fixing the muttering Janus with a warning stare.

"But what about the king?" Selene asked. "He'll *take* his daughter back to the Otherworld, whether she wills it or no."

"He hasn't yet," Maddox said. "Auberon knows about her—he already went to the theater where she works and spoke to her—but she's still here."

"Why?" Bellamy asked.

"Because he probably wants to make her think it's her own idea when she does finally go," Aaneel said.

"She's not going anywhere!" Sonny snarled, surprising himself by the vehemence of his reaction. The one place Sonny did not want Kelley, he realized, was the Otherworld. He did not want her living her life among the Fair Folk, constantly exposed to their casual cruelty, their capriciousness and selfish nature. Sonny did not want Kelley to learn what it was to be like them, to become one of them. Especially not if *he* was still stuck in the mortal realm. Because, no matter what Fennrys might think, Sonny was not so convinced that Auberon would reopen the Gates and allow free passage between the realms if Kelley were to return with him—he too much enjoyed the tight control he had wielded ever since their closure.

Sonny took a deep breath. "Look, Auberon's in for a surprise if he thinks this girl will meekly put her head down and fall into step."

Beside him, Maddox chuckled. "I'll say."

"Even if he thinks what he's doing is for her own good," Sonny murmured, almost to himself.

"And why would it be that?" asked Aaneel.

Sonny hesitated; it was just a theory he had been mulling, but—as he'd told Kelley—he didn't believe in coincidences. "I don't think it's just happenstance that the Wild Hunt is stirring at the same time as the king's daughter makes a sudden reappearance. Queen Mabh has her spies in this realm. And she holds a pretty serious grudge against Auberon. What if she caught wind somehow that Kelley was alive—that she's living in New York, but Mabh doesn't know exactly where. Well, what's the easiest way to eliminate one person in a crowd?"

"Eliminate the crowd," Beni said grimly. "That's harsh."

"Not to mention messy," Bryan agreed.

"Mabh likes a good bloodbath every now and then. She

hasn't had much opportunity to wreak havoc since Auberon locked her away. Now here is a perfect opportunity for a little fun and a lot of revenge."

"It's certainly not beyond the realm of possibility," Godwyn said.

"Seems your little actress is in a world of trouble, Irish boy," Fennrys laughed.

"Maybe we could stand a guard around her," Percival suggested.

"We're going to have our hands full as it is," the Wolf protested. "Especially if this threat of the Wild Hunt comes to pass."

"But we're supposed to be watching out for people," Percival said, bristling. "Keeping them safe. And none of this is her fault."

"Perry's right," Aaneel said, rubbing at his chin. Then he turned back to the rest of the changelings. His next words were as good as orders. "We are a poor excuse for guardians if we sacrifice the few for the sake of the many in the course of our duties. The girl is blameless. She should be kept safe, if at all possible." He turned to Sonny. "Hide her again, Sonny. And hide her well."

"Where?" Sonny asked. "How?"

Aaneel thought about it for a long moment. The rest of the Janus stood by patiently and waited until he spoke. "Take her to the Green. She'll be safe there. She can hide out until the threat of the Hunt has passed, and then it will be up to her to decide if she wants to go with Auberon. And if she doesn't, then we'll at least have the time to figure out a way to keep her hidden permanently."

Sonny frowned but nodded. Aaneel was right. "I'll need passage."

"I can set you up," Cait volunteered immediately. She flipped open the top flap on her leather messenger bag and began rummaging in its depths. "I have enough payment for two safe passages. I was going to go there myself for my next birthday but, really? The last time I went, I didn't have such a very good time."

"Why not?" Maddox asked. "I've never been, but I heard it's something else."

Beside Cait, Selene laughed. "One of the waiters there is an overfriendly garden gnome. Wouldn't leave her alone."

"The little fiend," Cait muttered, and blushed crimson.

"He kept trying to look up her skirt and lick her ankles!"

"So *anyway* . . ." Cait glared at Selene as she handed over a red suede pouch jingling with coins. "Here you go."

"Thank you, Cait," Sonny said.

"Don't mention it." She smiled. "But do me a favor: If you see a gnome in a floppy orange hat carrying a tray of drinks about while you're there? . . . Trip him."

"Just for you."

Back at his apartment, Sonny grabbed several hours of rest-less sleep, forcing himself to stay in bed long enough to recharge his weary muscles.

When he got up, he took a long, hot shower, only to find a surprise awaiting him. He saw, written in steam on his bathroom mirror, a time and place—instructions from Mabh on when and where he would have to deliver Lucky to her minions, the Storm Hags. Wiping the mirror clear, he shaved and changed his shirt three times, trying to decide on something that—if he was honest with himself—he thought Kelley would like. Then he set out to find his wayward Faerie princess.

XXVII

There was a knock on the door.

"Just a sec," Kelley called, and put aside the old hairbrush she'd been using to try to comb the tangles out of Lucky's mane, with little success. The Faerie horse butted at her, and she affectionately scratched his nose.

There was another knock, more insistent this time.

Kelley got up and headed for the door. "Tyff?"

The door swung inward as Kelley gave it a pull, and she saw that it wasn't Tyff.

The largest bouquet of roses she had ever seen obscured the features of the person standing there holding them. The bouquet lowered slightly, and Kelley saw Sonny's eyes over the tops of the peach-colored blooms.

She was thrilled and simultaneously horrified. She hadn't been expecting visitors and was wearing yoga pants and a faded hoodie. She was also covered in reddish strands of horsehair and Lucky Charms sugar dust. Yelping, she jumped behind the door.

"Sonny! What are you doing here?"

"I came to see you."

"You can't."

"You've learned the art of invisibility?"

"What? No!" She blinked, and stayed behind the door. "Wait. Can I do that?"

"Probably."

"Oh . . . "

"May I come in?"

"No! I'm a mess! I mean—the place is a mess." She glanced behind her shoulder to the obviously immaculate apartment beyond.

She could hear the smile in Sonny's voice as he said, "I happen to think 'the place' looks absolutely wonderful," and stuck the bunch of flowers around the door. "May I come in?" he asked again.

"Yes," she answered. Surrendering, she plucked the bouquet from his fist.

He followed a few steps as Kelley went into the kitchen but stopped as a high-pitched whinny sounded from the bathroom. "Is that . . . ?"

"The only horse currently residing in my apartment?" she said, filling a vase with water. "Yup. Go say hi. Just, you know, watch out for the fangs and flaming eye beams."

"The *what*?"

"I'm kidding." She laughed. "Go. He's *harmless*. You'll see."

Sonny shook his head. "You've obviously forgotten that, in my line of work, fangs and flaming eye beams aren't necessarily uncommon."

As he edged into the bathroom, Kelley clipped and arranged the roses; she counted more than two dozen of them. She took them out into the living room and sat on the couch, placing the vase on the coffee table. Then she pulled the elastic band from her hair and raked hasty fingers through it. She heard water running in the bathroom sink and then Sonny came out into the main room, drying his hands on a guest towel.

"He sneezed on you, didn't he?"

"Yes. Yes he did."

Kelley tried to pull a straight face. "But I also notice he did *not* try to strip the flesh from your bones."

"I'd almost rather he'd tried that," Sonny said ruefully.

Kelley laughed, fidgeting with her placement of the vase. "They're beautiful," she said, failing "casual" miserably.

He shrugged and said, "I just thought—after the past few days you've had—that you could use something . . ."

"Nice?" she finished, remembering their first encounter. "Are you going to disappear again before I have a chance to thank you?"

"No."

"Thank you."

"For the flowers? Or for not leaving?" He smiled and sat on the arm of the couch. "Kelley . . . I have to take Lucky back to the Otherworld. To the court of Queen Mabh."

Kelley stared at him, a cold sensation spreading through her chest. "Mabh. Isn't she the one who is probably causing all these problems with Lucky in the first place? No. I'm not giving him to her." Kelley crossed her arms, prepared to fight.

Sonny put out a placating hand. "She sent one of her minions, a Storm Hag, to see me. The Hag said that the whole thing was a mistake. That it—that Lucky—should never have been brought to this realm."

"Couldn't this Storm Hag have been lying?"

"Faerie don't lie. They may not always be the most forthcoming with the truth, but they do not lie outright. Kelley, I know how fond you are of Lucky." Sonny moved from the arm of the couch to sit beside her and took one of her hands in his. "But he can't stand in your bathtub forever, can he? If he stays, he poses a grave danger to the whole mortal realm. He will be destroyed. He'll have to be. Otherwise he will become the destroyer. I know you don't want that."

"I just hate the thought of sending him back to that place. . . . "

"Mabh granted me a boon if I return him, and what I will ask is that she will see to it that he is well cared for, and that she will not subject him to further enchantment."

Kelley raised her gaze to meet his. "You'd do that? When you could ask her for *anything*?"

He nodded, and she could see in his clear gray eyes that he meant it. "He's important to you. So that makes him important to me."

Kelley rose from the couch and went to the bathroom door, leaning on the door frame. Lucky flicked his tail at her and blew a soap bubble out of his nose in greeting. He'd figured out how to do it on command and seemed to take great delight in the ability now. Kelley bit her lip, trying not to cry. It was silly. Sonny was right. She couldn't keep him standing in the tub.

"He'll sure be missed, and not just by me." Kelley sighed. "Tyff actually went out and stocked up on all his favorite cereal."

"Who's Tyff?" Sonny asked.

Before Kelley could answer, the front door swung wide and her roommate appeared in the doorway as if summoned. Sonny took one look at her and threw himself off the arm of the couch, sinking into a defensive crouch.

"Seelie witch!" he cried, striking a menacing *en garde* pose.

Tyff's eyes blazed like comets. Her beautiful face twisted in an expression of pure hatred. "Faerie killer!" she spat.

"One toe over that threshold and you die," Sonny snarled, interposing his body between Kelley and the door. "I see through your glamor, nymph—"

"I'm no lowly nymph, you changeling dog!" Tyff sneered. "I am Tyffanwy of the Mere, lady-in-waiting to Titania the Summer Queen! And you do *not* want to mess with me!"

"Go back to the Otherworld and tell Titania this girl is under my protection. You seek her at your peril."

Tyff blinked. "What?"

"Or is it Mabh you're really working for, harlot?" Sonny's voice was a low growl in his throat. "Your kind have slippery allegiances, I know. Well, the Darkling Queen can no more have her than can Titania. Kelley is no pawn!"

"What exactly are you talking about, you deranged lunatic?" Tyff shrieked.

"On my honor as a Janus Guard, I tell you I will not let you harm one hair on her head!"

"Sonny, she's not—," Kelley tried desperately to interject.

"It's all right, Kelley—you're safe."

"'On your honor as a Janus Guard'?" Tyff said sarcastically. "Oh, that's rich! Janus have no honor. Otherwise you wouldn't be standing in the middle of my apartment uninvited!"

"You lie. This is not your place—"

"She doesn't!" Kelley interrupted loudly. "It *is* her place." She turned to her roommate. "And he's not uninvited. I invited him in. Tyff, come inside and close the door. Mrs. Madsen down the hall is going to call the cops if you two don't pipe down!"

Sonny's eyes narrowed. "Kelley, she's more dangerous than you know—"

"Oh, stow it, fleshling." Tyff stepped over the threshold and slammed the door behind her. "You know what I am and so you know perfectly well that I am incapable of lying. Why the hell *would* I hurt her? She pays me outrageous rent!"

"What?" Sonny straightened slightly, looking utterly confused.

"She's my *roommate*. Wait a minute . . . are *you* the creep who's been stalking her in the park?"

"Yes—no!" Sonny protested. "I'm not stalking her!"

"Why the hell is one of Auberon's lackeys so interested in a silly little mortal girl?"

"Hey!" Kelley protested.

"Mortal?" Sonny's tone turned mocking. "You mean to tell me that you don't know?"

"Know what?" Tyff snapped.

"All this time living under the same roof, and it never occurred to Tyffanwy of the Mere, lady-in-waiting to Titania the Summer Queen, that her 'silly little mortal' roommate also just happens to be Auberon's lost daughter?"

Tyff stood there dumbly, staring at Kelley.

"Holy crap," she murmured at last. "When word gets out about this . . . Titania's going to kill me."

XXVIII

"How could you not have suspected that there was something just a little bit different about her?" Sonny asked.

"Look at her!" Tyff said. "She's so normal it's almost weird. No offense, Kell."

"Er, none taken. I guess," Kelley muttered.

Sonny snorted. To his eyes, Kelley was unspeakably lovely. "She *is* powerfully veiled, I grant you. A leprechaun charm—"

"Well, no shit, Sherlock!" Tyff groused. "I can see it *now.*"

"I would have thought that a High Fae like you would

have been able to figure it out." Sonny was rather enjoying himself.

Tyff glared at the Janus. "My senses have obviously been blunted by this world. I *have* been out of the loop for"—she counted on her fingers—"almost fifteen hundred years, you know!"

"Ah." Sonny nodded, almost feeling sympathetic. "I forget the story. You were, what, banished, was it?"

"In a manner of speaking." Tyff sulked. "But it *wasn't* supposed to be permanent. I was supposed to be allowed back. After I had . . . 'served time.' And then what happens? *Your* stupid boss goes and shuts all the doors."

"You could have tried to get back," Sonny said. "Made a run for it one Samhain."

"And risk running into one of *you* bloodthirsty maniacs? Thank you, no."

"What did you do to get banished in the first place?" Kelley asked, fascinated.

"Ask that Sir Lancelot creep," Tyffanwy snapped. "Wait—no, don't. It was complicated." She waved the matter away with a manicured hand.

"Ookay there, *Tyffanwy* . . . " Kelley threw her hands in the air. "Is there anyone I know who is actually a normal, non-freaky, plain old vanilla-flavored human?"

"I'm sure that one or two of your actor friends are border-line normal," Tyff answered, her tone doubting the assertion.

"They're actors," Kelley said. "They're not even *close* to

243

normal. And anyway, one of them is actually Puck. Apparently."

"What?" Tyff's eyebrows shot toward her hairline. "The Goodfellow? Oh, super. Listen, you keep that miserable boucca away from the apartment, or I will not be held responsible for my actions."

Sonny smirked. "What, did he stand you up for a date once?"

"Shut up." Tyff scowled at him. "Just what *are* you doing here, anyway?"

"I've come to take Kelley somewhere safe," he said. "And after that, I'll be back to take the kelpie."

"Over my dead, shapely body," the Faerie sneered.

"I mean him no harm. But I have to return him to the Otherworld." He told Tyffanwy about the Wild Hunt and watched her complexion drain to porcelain.

"Well. I think it's safe to say that, in my absence, the power grabbing and backstabbing and political intrigue has officially reached an all-time Otherworld high," Tyff said, rigid with anger. "This goes beyond bickering."

"It does," Sonny agreed. "Far beyond."

"I *hate* the Courts!" she spat. "Why can't they just leave off with all the stupid homicidal meddling?"

"I wish I knew," Sonny sympathized. He understood only too well. No doubt Tyffanwy had experienced the fear and hatred of *his* lord's realm and its people in much the same way that he had been made to fear and hate hers. He considered that for a moment and thought that perhaps, just this once, they could put aside those differences and work as allies. Maybe she would help him.

Or, more likely, maybe she would help Kelley.

Sonny suggested a plan.

"You want me to do *what*?"

"Just get all the charms unknotted from Lucky's mane and tail," Sonny pleaded.

Tyff crossed her arms and pegged him with a pointed, icy stare. "They're tied in with elf-knots. Do you have any idea how long that will take?"

"Tyff—"

"*Days*, Janus. I have a social life to maintain, you know. I have a date with an *ambassador* and you want me to cancel it so I can sit alone in this apartment, performing an equine comb-out."

"Tyffanwy . . . please? Once I get Kelley to the safe house and secure protection for her, I don't know how much time I will have left until Samhain falls."

"That's three nights from now!"

"I'm taking her to the Green, and time is tricky there. *You* know that."

"How many of the damned things are there, anyway?"

Sonny thought he could hear a note of relenting in Tyff's voice and he pressed on. "I asked Cait—one of the other Janus—about the enchantment. She knows her magicks and she figures that there should be nine times nine talismans. Eighty-one all together. I have three of them. Which means that there should be seventy-eight stones left."

"Can't you just rip them out? Like the ones you found at the Lake?" Kelley asked.

"I tend to think Lucky would react poorly to that, don't you? Mild-mannered he might be, but one well-placed kick from those hooves could be deadly."

"What about cutting them out?" she asked.

"Can't." Tyff's voice was flat. "'Cause that would be cheating. Right, Janus?"

"Tyffawny's right, Kelley. Magick like this tends to react poorly—dangerously—if one tries to . . . well, cheat. There aren't really any shortcuts—our only hope is to untie all the knots. The spell has to be completely unraveled, or there is still the chance it will remain potent." He turned again to Tyff.

"I hate you." Tyff glared at him.

"And?" Kelley demanded anxiously from where she'd sat silently on the couch, listening to the negotiations. "If all of the talismans are removed?"

Sonny looked at her. "Then he should pose no threat of becoming the Roan Horse of the Hunt."

"He'll just revert to a normal, garden-variety kelpie." Kelley was skeptical.

"Like I told you, I don't think Lucky is very normal, as far as kelpie go." Sonny smiled at her. "In fact, your Lucky is the sweetest-tempered monster I've ever encountered. I think some of your nature must have imprinted on him when you rescued him, Kelley."

Kelley looked at him. "Did you just call me sweet?"

"Maybe . . . "

"Oh, get a room, you two," Tyff said, disgusted, and went to the cupboard in the bathroom. She pulled a large-toothed comb and several brushes out of a basket, eyeing Lucky's shiny, potentially deadly accoutrements.

"Thank you, Lady Tyffanwy," Sonny said with genuine gratitude and respect, relief flooding his chest. He would have time. Kelley would be safe, he could return Lucky to the Otherworld without fear, and the Wild Hunt would slumber on.

"I hate you, Sonny Flannery," Tyffanwy said.

"Just remember to keep his hooves wet. At least until all the charms are untied."

"*Hate* you."

"All of them—the ones in his tail, too. Seventy-eight in all. And I'll be back as soon as I can," he promised. "Kelley . . . " Sonny turned to her. "You should go get ready so we can leave."

"What? Where?" Kelley blinked, startled.

"Out," he answered. "If you're all right with that."

"But it's almost sunset. Aren't you . . . you know, on duty?"

"I was curious about that too, Janus," Tyff said over her shoulder as she sat on the side of the tub, worrying away at a

247

knot. "It is the middle of the Nine-Night, after all. Aren't you a little too busy to be going on a date?"

Beside him Kelley stiffened and made a little squawking noise.

"I told you, I'm taking her to the Green, so I'll be within the boundaries of the Gate," Sonny said. "I'll still be 'on duty.'"

"I can't believe you want to take her *to* Central Park," Tyff said, "tonight."

"She'll be safe with me."

"You hope." Tyff gave Sonny a long, appraising look and seemed to be coming to a decision about him.

"Kelley?" Sonny said to her, ignoring Tyff's critical eye. "Why don't you go get dressed?"

"Make it something nice," Tyff said, turning back to Lucky. "Wait—never mind—you don't have anything nice." She put the comb down. "I'll get you something of mine."

XXIX

"Tyff?" Kelley asked as her roommate deftly pinned her hair up into a loose, artful cascade of curls. "How come *your* ears aren't . . . you know?"

"For the same reason that I never let anyone photograph me from the neck up," Tyff muttered around a mouthful of bobby pins. "Because I've been trying to pass for mortal for the last millennium and a half. I used to just cast a glamour or wear my hair down, but then I finally found this great cosmetic surgeon on Ninth. Used to be a Druid healer way back in the day, and he's *very* discreet. Hey, do you want me to set up an appointment for you?"

"Uh . . . I'll think about it." Kelley ran a finger over the tip of one ear. "They're not *that* pointy, are they?"

"Oh, honey, no!" Tyff assured her. "Actually, on you, it's sort of cute."

"Thanks. I think. And for loaning me the dress." It hung in a contour-hugging wave from slender straps to brush her ankles. "Are you sure it's not a bit much?"

"What, you don't want to look nice for your date?"

"Do you really think this is a date?" Kelley could hear the panic in her own voice.

"I think he's trying to take you somewhere safe," Tyff said. "I do."

There, see? Not a date. Damn it.

Still. He was taking her to a safe house? Putting her under some kind of guard . . . Kelley really wasn't sure how she felt about that. "Do you like him?" she asked.

"I wouldn't go that far."

"Do *I* like him?"

Tyff's mouth bent up at one corner. "You're going to have to figure *that* one out all by yourself, kiddo."

Kelley sighed. "Okay, but—seriously—if this *isn't* a date, then why am I dressed like I'm hitting the red carpet?"

Tyff chuckled and secured the last pin in Kelley's artfully tousled updo. "The Green is a little more upscale than the burger joints you're used to, Kell. Trust me. Sparkly apparel is like a kind of uniform there."

Kelley turned this way and that in the mirror. Shimmering, champagne-hued crystals caught and reflected the light, but the effect was still somehow subtle. Tyff draped a silky wrap over Kelley's bare shoulders and gave her arm a quick squeeze.

"How do I look?"

"Fetching. But don't ask *me*. . . ." Tyff stepped aside so that Kelley could see past her—to where Sonny stood, waiting patiently in the living room. "Ask him."

Sonny turned and his eyes went wide. The look on his face spoke volumes.

If it hadn't been a date before that moment, it certainly was now.

"How was last night?" Kelley asked, as Sonny put out an arm for her to take as they crossed Fifth Avenue in the waning light of late afternoon. She had been making all kinds of small talk since they'd left the apartment—mostly to avoid having to notice the fact that Sonny had barely taken his eyes off her. "Guard duty, I mean."

"Quiet, all things considered." He shrugged. "For me at least. Maddox and the others did most of the heavy lifting. He still thinks I need mending."

"Don't you?" she asked, hazarding a quick look into his face. *He's still staring at me. Maybe the dress really is too much. . . .*

251

Sonny smiled. "I need less mending than a regular mortal. I'm fine."

"Really? Then why is Maddox worried?"

"He's just being an old woman."

"You're his friend." She gripped his arm tighter, feeling a bit precarious in Tyff's high heels.

"I know. He's still being an old woman."

She looked up at him again. "You know, you *do* look a little . . . rugged."

"I . . . oh." Sonny frowned and looked away.

"It's okay," she assured him. "Rugged works pretty well for you."

There were dozens of carriages lined up along the curb at the southeast corner of the park. Some were pulled by lean, neat-footed ponies, while others were powered by larger draft horses. Sonny cast his gaze up and down the line and made a choice. Grabbing Kelley by the hand, he approached a white buggy adorned with garlands of pink and purple silk flowers. The driver was a tall, broad-shouldered woman with a keen glint in her ice-blue eyes; the horse was a proud silver-white beast who managed to convey a sense of dignity despite the jaunty fuchsia ostrich plumes waving from his bridle and the sparkly purple paint on his hooves. Probably a tourist favorite for the pure kitsch value, Kelley thought.

The horse tossed his huge, noble head, butting her insistently with his nose once she got close enough.

"You certainly seem to have a way with horses," Sonny whispered.

"Belrix likes you," the driver said to Kelley. "He's very particular."

"He's beautiful," Kelley said, scratching his hairy cheek.

"We'd like to hire his services. And yours, if you are available," Sonny said to the driver.

"We haven't had many folk wanting a ride through the park the last few nights," she said, her face a carefully composed blank.

"Due to the uncertain weather, most like," Sonny suggested politely.

"Aye. Most like . . . Hard to tell one season from another these days."

"Just so. Can you take us to the Tavern?" Sonny asked the driver.

"The Tavern on the Green?"

"You know the one I speak of."

Kelley was confused. There was only *one* Tavern on the Green. It was one of New York's landmarks.

But the driver nodded slowly. "I do. It will cost you extra to take *that* road."

"I'll pay," Sonny said, pulling out a small red suede pouch. He tugged open the drawstring and chose several coins, which he dropped into the palm of her hand. "For both of us."

"Fair enough," she said, and gestured with the little buggy whip she held. "Up you get, then."

Sonny helped Kelley climb into the cab and then sprang in behind her as the carriage began to move. The steady *clip-clop* of Belrix's hooves echoed beneath the trees as they wound through the park, passing familiar landmarks and features. They were on a road that took them past the carousel at a distance.

Kelley remarked, "You know that particular carousel is the fourth one to stand on that spot? It's burned to the ground twice in its history."

The driver turned and glanced over her shoulder. "I'm usually the one who gives the guided tour, missy," she said, sounding amused. "Are you trying to take my job?"

Kelley smiled. "No, ma'am. I just remember reading about the carousel in a brochure."

"Aye, well." The driver nodded and took over the narrative. "The story goes that the original merry-go-round used to be powered by a horse and an old blind mule that walked a circular track in an underground cavern beneath the ride. Indeed, old Belrix here gets touchy when I talk about the horse and mule." The big animal's ears twitched back and forth. "Seems to think that it wasn't exactly fair work."

Kelley shivered at the idea of those animals traipsing in an endless circle, one blind, led by the other, in sunless toil for the sake of other creatures' amusement.

"The carousel that stands there now was found disassembled on Coney Island," the driver continued. "They brought it back here and refurbished it. Lucky, that. The park would be poorer without it, to my mind."

"Yeah," Kelley murmured, thinking about a horse of another kind. "Lucky."

On either side of them the park vista passed.

"You know," Kelley said to Sonny softly, "I was fascinated by the park when I first moved here. I felt kind of drawn to it. I guess that's not exactly a coincidence, now. Seeing what this place really is. And who I . . . really am and all . . . "

"Well," he said, as he thought about it. "I told you that I don't believe in any such thing as coincidence. However, I also think that you may have felt drawn to the park for the simple reason that you just felt drawn to the park. A lot of people are, you know. People who aren't . . . like you. Just because of what you are doesn't mean that anything is predestined for you, Kelley. I'll help make sure of that."

"Would you say that even if I decided to embrace the legacy of my blood?" she asked, quietly, so that the driver wouldn't hear her. "If I took up the mantle of a Faerie princess?" A tiny fist of panic lodged in her throat as she said the words, and she found it hard to swallow. The carousel had reminded her once again of just what it might mean if she allowed herself to become one of the Fair Folk. Although Kelley could not deny that there was a wily, seductive appeal in that notion, it terrified her almost as much as it thrilled her.

"Kelley." Sonny looked her square in the eyes. He took her

hand in his. "I will help you be whatever you want to be. I promise."

Her fear vanished, and Kelley found herself mesmerized. His hair that night fell in loose, dark waves on either side of his face, and Kelley couldn't restrain herself from reaching out and tucking a stray lock behind his ear. His gaze deepened. Kelley felt suddenly breathless.

"Almost there," the driver called, and they reluctantly broke eye contact. Kelley thought she heard a strange, almost inhuman quality to the woman's voice. Belrix increased his pace to a trot.

Kelley sat up and looked around. The park appeared familiar and foreign at the same time. "*Where* exactly is it that we're going, again?"

"I told you. I'm taking you someplace safe." Sonny smiled at her gently.

"And you don't have to, uh, work tonight?"

"Tonight, you are my work."

"Oh." She didn't exactly like the idea of being some kind of assignment.

"What's the matter?" Sonny glanced down at the tone of her voice.

"Nothing. I just thought . . . never mind. I guess being a princess means I get to have a bodyguard, huh?"

"Something like that," he said. "The Janus all agreed. You should be protected."

"I see. The Janus all agreed, did they?" Kelley pulled away

from Sonny, hugging her elbows tight to her body.

"Did I say something wrong?" Sonny frowned worriedly.

"No." She sighed. "No . . . I'm just having a little trouble adjusting to all the fuss over me, I guess. I should have known . . . never mind. So where *exactly* are we going again?" He hadn't answered her question the first time.

Sonny stared at the road ahead of them. "Somewhere where there are others who can protect you. In case I'm not there. I hope I am. . . . "

"Why on earth wouldn't you be there?" she said, laughing. "You're always there. Even when I've told you to go away!"

Sonny took both of her hands in one of his. She could feel his long, strong fingers laced with hers, and felt her heart racing. Sonny laid the fingers of his free hand alongside her cheek and tilted her face up.

"Please be there," Kelley whispered, suddenly afraid.

"Believe me, Kelley. If I'm not . . . it's because I'm already dead." He stroked her hair, and she could feel his breath warm on her forehead, like a kiss. "Because anyone that would seek to hurt you would have to kill me first."

That is not *exactly the comforting notion that he thinks it is.* She shivered, and Sonny put an arm around her.

She thought about Auberon's words to her in her dressing room. About how it wasn't in Sonny's nature to love what she might become. Whatever *that* was. In truth, Kelley knew so very little about the world she was heir to.

Just as she thought that, Belrix rounded a bend, pulling the buggy up in front of the Tavern on the Green, and Kelley realized that she was about to find out a whole lot more.

Kelley had been to Central Park's famed Tavern on the Green once before. In the first week after her move to New York, Aunt Emma had come to town—a rare thing, since she hated the city—and taken Kelley for dinner there. Inside it was a maze of mirrored halls, rococo stained glass, stag antlers mounted on chestnut-paneled walls, and fairy-tale murals. The main dining room was a glass gazebo festooned with a whimsical assortment of chandeliers of all colors and sizes, fracturing light into rainbows that danced across walls painted with cloud castles and winged horses.

Outside in the courtyard, every tree was wrapped with strings of tiny electric lights, and garlands of paper lanterns swung between the overarching branches. The bushes that surrounded the garden were trimmed into fantastic shapes—a prancing horse, a mermaid, even—with a New York sense of humor—a great, green, shrubby King Kong.

It had all seemed so fantastical.

At the time.

But on this night, Kelley knew she was in for something infinitely *more* fantastical. For one thing, there were no cars in the parking lot. There was, however, an old-fashioned coach-and-four that looked like a movie prop from Disney's *Cinderella*.

Sonny swung himself down from the carriage, holding out

a hand so that she could step to the ground without injuring either herself or Tyff's gown. Kelley wasn't used to wearing shoes with such high heels. He stuck out an elbow, beaming, and Kelley took his arm. She felt as though she might actually be blushing so she looked away, in time to notice that the doorman in the green top hat and long frock coat wasn't wearing pants. He didn't have to—beneath the hem of his coat, his legs were shaggy with brown fur and ended in delicate, cloven goat's hooves.

"Master Flannery," he greeted Sonny. Kelley noticed that he raised a saturnine eyebrow at the Janus, a silent question implicit in the expression. "Long has it been since you have honored Herne's house with your presence. And the lady . . . ?"

"The lady is my guest. I would have her exceptionally well looked after. She is . . . important to me. To all of us, I think."

"Then she is welcome here, of course," the faun said as he swept his hat off in greeting to her. Kelley tried very hard not to stare at the tiny horns curling back from beside his tufted ears. The strange little doorman gestured them up to the front doors, which swung wide at their approach.

"Did he say *Herne's* house?" Kelley whispered as they moved up the steps.

"He did," rumbled a deep voice from beneath the archway. "I am Herne. Welcome to my Tavern on the Green . . . "

"My lord." Sonny bowed deeply to the magnificent figure standing before them.

Kelley felt her jaw drop. She sank into a curtsy, silently grateful for the semester of ballet classes she'd taken back in theater school. Herne was exactly as she had seen him in the vision Sonny had shown her, like nothing so much as a god from an old storybook of Celtic tales.

Herne the Hunter—in the flesh.

XXX

Herne wore a deep-green sleeveless tunic that fell in folds to the floor and was held together over his bare, muscled chest with a heavy gold chain. His breeches were of dark leather, with ragged unfinished hems over bare feet. His wrists were circled with thick gold cuffs, and around his throat he wore a heavy gold torc. His dark hair was swept back, and on either side of his head a pair of stag antlers arched from an elaborate headdress that circled his brow. His eyes blazed like a fire in a hearth as he welcomed them.

Sonny couldn't keep from gazing at the shining girl at his

side as she dipped gracefully in a curtsy of respect. Together they walked into Herne's Tavern.

Sonny took the Hunter aside and spoke to him in low tones, informing him of his companion's true identity, as he watched Kelley out of the corner of his eye. Her eyes tracked through the room, following the people—the *normal*-looking people—that drifted about all around them. They were insubstantial, almost shadows—ladies with handbags and high heels and men in suits and ties, they ate and talked at tables that were simultaneously plainly occupied by leaf-winged Fae and silvery-skinned selkie girls with big dark eyes, among others of the Fair Folk in all their infinite variety.

"Are they really here?" she whispered, indicating a shadowy young couple—tourists from the look of them.

"Almost," Sonny said. "Or, rather, *we* are almost *there*. Herne's Tavern and the Tavern in Central Park exist side by side, occupying virtually the same place—just in slightly different worlds."

"Are we in the Otherworld?"

"No. This is a place apart from any other realm. A kind of safe haven created by Herne where the Lost Fae—the ones who have crossed over and the ones like Tyff who were trapped or chose to stay when the Gates were shut—can gather without fear. It is still in the park but it is, well, sort of sacred ground, I guess you could call it. Sanctuary."

"He means the Janus cannot touch us here," said an ethereal girl who appeared suddenly at his elbow. She had skin the color of new leaves, and in her fist she carried a slender bow. "They cannot kill us here."

"Now, Carys." Herne's voice was gently chiding. He came and stood behind them. "I would not have you show disrespect to our guests."

"None offered, my lord," she said, but Sonny could see that it was plain in what regard the huntress Fae held the Janus.

"And none taken," Kelley said firmly, stepping up beside him and placing a hand on Sonny's elbow. "I understand that Sonny's isn't exactly the most popular profession among your people. I also understand that he wouldn't be what he is if he hadn't been *stolen* from his world by your people in the first place. By doing his job, he saved my life, and probably the lives of others, from a creature I believe you call a Black Shuck."

Carys's eyes went a bit wide, and Herne's brow clouded with an impressive frown. "The shuck have come through the Gate?" he asked.

Sonny cleared his throat. "Just the one, lord, as far as I could tell."

"A harbinger," the Hunter muttered.

"I hope not. The Janus are trying to keep it that way. But Auberon does seem to think that someone—perhaps Queen Mabh herself—is trying to wake your former companions, my lord."

"For what purpose?"

Sonny's gaze drifted to where Kelley stood by his side.

"The shuck was tracking Kelley. I believe *she* is the one being hunted."

"Then she is in great danger," Herne said. "And she is not the only one. The Wild Hunt will not be sated with a single quarry. This lady's world—and the lady herself—are in terrible peril."

"Which is why I brought her here."

"I will see to her safety, then, personally."

"Thank you, my lord."

Herne gestured them farther into the Tavern. Music wound around them as Sonny and Kelley walked out to the courtyard, where high, thin clouds stretched across the sky like torn lace curtains. Kelley gasped as she realized that the fairy lights in the trees were actually *Faerie* lights in the trees: thousands of tiny winged beings flitting to and fro among the branches.

"It won't be long now until I have to go and return Lucky to Queen Mabh," Sonny said. "But I want to show you around a bit first. You needn't worry—you're under Herne's protection here. He knows who you are and he is the most powerful guardian I can think of to trust you to. And this place should keep you safe."

"Even from something like the Hunt?"

"Don't worry about that."

"That was not answering my question. That was avoiding my question."

"I know." Sonny grinned, ignoring the look she shot him. "Come on. Let me show you around the place."

Over in the corner where, in the mortal realm, the King Kong topiary stood, a massive leafy creature crouched. Vines and vegetation clung to the giant, twining in the green ivy of his beard, sprouting like bunches of marsh grass on his huge mossy head and shoulders.

"The Greenman," Sonny said reverently. "He is an ancient spirit, older than all of this. The Greenman has been in the worlds longer even than the Fair Folk. He is the soul of the natural world. He also likes a good whiskey now and then." Sonny whispered, "Herne has an excellent cellar, I hear."

The Greenman winked at Kelley and raised an enormous earthen mug, and Sonny watched, grinning, as Kelley smiled shyly and waved the fingers of one hand at the leafy old god in return. They continued past him, toward where the splashy music of a fountain entwined with the sounds of tinkling laughter. They saw the flash of a long rainbow-silver fish tail.

"Was that a mermaid?" Kelley asked, moving toward the stone rim of the pool.

Sonny put a hand on her arm. "The Water Folk are . . . tricky. Dangerously unpredictable."

"I think I saw one," Kelley murmured. "A mermaid, I mean. The night I rescued Lucky from the Lake."

"That was a Siren," Sonny said, trying hard to keep the bitterness from his voice. "Her name is Chloe. She saved your life."

"I should meet her then," Kelley said. "Thank her."

"You should stay as far away from her as you possibly can,"

he said, and pulled her away from the fountain.

They approached a band of Faerie musicians, and Sonny smiled as Kelley swayed gracefully to the unearthly music. His Firecracker. He was painfully aware that she would in all likelihood not remain "his" for very much longer. Not if she decided to accept her true identity. "Take up the mantle of a Faerie princess," as she'd said earlier, in the carriage. It was a choice that bore consequences that remained veiled to him. Sonny made up his mind. Whatever path Kelley ultimately chose to walk, and whether he would take that journey with her, he certainly wasn't about to waste the time they *could* share together.

He turned to her suddenly and held out his hand.

Surprised, she glanced down at his outstretched palm and then back up at his face. Sonny knew clearly that he would do anything, give anything, just to be able to make those green eyes sparkle. He swept her a low, courtly bow and gazed up at her. She smiled down on him.

"Will you dance with me, Kelley?" he asked.

His heart swelled as she put her hand in his.

XXXI

T he band played beautiful music.
Time spun out around them.
The stars whirled overhead in the heavens.
And they danced.

On and on, they danced.

Sonny's hand at her waist was strong and steady, and Kelley let her head rest on his chest—carefully, mindful of the bandages under his shirt. She closed her eyes as she felt Sonny draw her closer. She thought that she had never felt so much at home as she did right at that moment. But it wasn't the place. It was the person.

"I don't belong here, Sonny," she murmured, her senses dazzled by the sights and sounds of their surroundings. "I mean, look at these people. . . . "

A troop of Seelie Fae swayed to the music, unearthly in their beauty. Kelley felt like one of Cinderella's stepsisters at the ball. She knew her big clumsy foot would never fit into the glass slipper, and the only thing she couldn't figure out was why the handsome prince was still dancing with her. Sonny said nothing, but she felt his hands slide up her shoulders and under her hair. He undid the catch on her necklace and eased the silver chain from around her neck.

He whispered, "My Firecracker . . . "

Then her own eyes went momentarily blind from the wave of iridescent brilliance that filled the room, flowing out from where she stood. All around her the brightness of the beautiful, wondrous Fair Folk seemed to dim and flicker—and then answer her own shining luminescence like moons reflecting the light of the sun.

Sonny's gray eyes blazed with fierce pride—and something else. As Kelley gazed into them, she felt her heart swell with unnameable emotion.

She felt tall. Ten feet tall. Taller even than Sonny, she realized, as she looked down at him. She was flying. Well— floating, at least, about six inches off the floor. Kelley gasped and kicked her feet, but that only served to send her another several inches into the air. At her elbow, Sonny held out a hand to catch her before she floated away. She twisted her head and saw a pair of delicate, fiery wings that seemed to have sprouted from her shoulders. They were ethereal, ghostly almost, and glimmering with iridescence and light, like the lacy wings of a silvery dragonfly.

Herne dipped his antlered head to her in respect.

All around her, the people of the Faerie realms knelt and bowed and smiled at her.

She blushed and felt her wings shiver and their strength give way, and she fell back down toward the floor. Sonny caught her in his arms and she clung to him.

"You'll have to work on that," he whispered in her ear as he clasped the chain around her neck. Her brightness dimmed, but it did not fade altogether. The music swelled once again, and they held each other and danced.

Later, when they sat watching others glide across the dance floor, Sonny started—as though suddenly remembering something—and reached into his leather satchel, lying on the bench beside him. He pulled out a much-rumpled stack of pages, held together with brass fasteners.

"My script!" Kelley exclaimed. "I was sure Bob had stolen it!"

Sonny laughed. "He tells me he's actually a lousy thief. I'm sorry; I've been meaning to return it. In all the excitement, I sort of forgot."

She took it from him and hugged it against her chest like a

treasure. "Thanks. I guess I'm not going to need it, though."

"You know all your lines, then?"

She chuckled dryly. "In theory . . . But let's face it, Sonny. I'm an awfully long way from the Avalon. I get the feeling I won't be wearing my little gauze wings again anytime soon."

Sonny stood abruptly. "Come with me," he said, and held out a hand. "There's one more thing I want to show you before I go."

He led her down an oak-paneled corridor that slowly transformed until, eventually, they found themselves walking through a green, leafy archway, a living tunnel.

"Where are we?" Kelley asked.

"Think of this place as something like the wall in your play. The one with the hole in it, through which Pyramus and Thisbe can see and speak to each other. Herne's Tavern rests on the very cusp of the Otherworld—like a little bubble suspended, balancing between the Faerie lands and the mortal plane. It is the one place in all of the worlds where the two realms meet and meld."

When they emerged from under the leafy canopy, Kelley found herself standing on a forested shore lapped by gently rippling water. Sonny pointed in front of them: there, across the misted waters of a still, silent lake, was an island. At first it looked to Kelley as though the branches of its trees were heavy with snow. But even from across the glassy water she could smell the scent of apple blossoms.

"This is as far as we can go," Sonny said. "Any farther and we would be in danger of crossing over and perhaps getting lost in the Otherworld. But I wanted you to see this place."

"It's beautiful. What is it?"

"A place of legend. The storybooks call it Avalon. Just like your theater—you see? Not so very far as all that."

Kelley gazed at the distant island and sighed. "Oh, Sonny . . . This place is so full of wonders. Why does it make me so sad?"

He thought about the question for a moment, his head lowered. "Maybe it's because it feels a little like home to you. The home you never knew was yours."

She shook her head, staring through tear-rimmed eyes at the island in the mist. "That Avalon is yours. Not mine. Mine's a rundown old theater full of a bunch of misfit actors and a crazy director. And I'm about to let them all down horribly. I'll never get to stand under those lights and wear those wings and speak those words."

"What makes you think that?"

"Don't lie to me, Sonny. You and your buddies seem to think I'm going to have my hands full just lasting the night. Let alone the next three."

"Two of which have probably already passed while we danced here."

"Really?"

"Really. See? You're not doing so bad with surviving so far."

"Okay, then basically the real danger is actually waiting for me back in New York at the theater."

Sonny looked at her quizzically.

"Missing dress rehearsal? If I *do* somehow manage to get back, I'll be lucky if Quentin doesn't flay me alive."

Sonny laughed. "You *will* get back. I promise you. So you'd better practice your lines." He pulled her down to sit on a grassy patch beside him and reached for her script, flipping through it for a moment as if looking for something. He stopped on a particular page. "Here, for example." He pointed to the lines. "This scene. I'll read it with you. Now don't argue." He held up a hand. "I'll play the ass—just this once. Indulge me, Kelley. Please? I'm feeling theatrical."

She plucked the script from his hand and scanned the page to see what scene he'd chosen. She giggled when she read her first line and handed back the script so he could read opposite her. "Oh, boy! No ego there, Sonny . . . "

"Shh." He gestured dramatically. "I need to concentrate. Begin."

Kelley opened her mouth wide in an exaggerated yawn and stretched. "What angel wakes me from my flow'ry bed?" She waited for Sonny's response, curious to see how he'd handle Bottom's silly song about a cuckoo.

Sonny's face fell a bit and he muttered, "I didn't know I'd have to *sing*. . . . All right, we'll just skip my lines. Jump to your next speech."

Kelley stifled a laugh at the seriousness of his expression, and continued with her next line. "I pray thee, gentle mortal, sing again. Mine ear is much enamoured of thy note; so is mine eye enthrallèd to thy shape."

Okay, that part's true. It's a very nice shape.

"And thy fair virtue's force perforce doth move me on the first view to say, to swear, I love thee."

Sonny frowned and held up a hand. "I don't think you got that last line quite right. Say it again."

"I *totally* said it right!"

He ignored her protestation and said, "Go from 'thy fair virtue's force.'"

"Sonny—"

"Unh." Up went the hand again. It was like he was channeling the Mighty Q, for crying out loud! "'Thy fair . . .'"

"Okay, okay!" Kelley rolled her eyes and went back to the line. "And thy *fair* virtue's force perforce doth *move* me on the first view to say, to *swear*, I love thee. Better?"

"Better . . . Intonation's just a shade off on the last three words. Try those again."

"What—'I love thee'?"

"Hm." He gestured again with one hand for her to continue.

She drew herself up and took in a breath, concentrating on her inflection so that she could indulge him in his game. Then she leaned forward and, in her best, most sincerely love-struck voice, breathed, "I love thee."

Sonny's face was just inches from hers. His storm-gray eyes flashed, and the dark silk of his hair drifted across his cheek as he leaned in his head. "Perfect."

So was the kiss.

Perfect.

At the press of Sonny's lips against hers, Kelley felt the world around her—*all* the worlds around her—melt. The sweetness of his breath filled her, and she could feel his heart beating loud as thunder against her own, hammering in her chest.

"I love *thee*," Sonny murmured, all pretense gone.

With those words, tears spilled down her face.

"Oh, my heart," he said, and gathered her into his arms, and Kelley wondered why she was weeping. It could have been with fear, or sorrow—fear of losing him, sorrow at what he had already risked for her . . . or maybe she just wept from pure, incandescent joy. She felt all of those things in that moment.

He held her close for an eternity that seemed like an eye-blink when they heard the approach of footsteps in the leafy forest passageway behind them. Sonny loosened his embrace but did not let her go, gazing down at her.

Behind them, Herne quietly cleared his throat. "Janus? I do not wish to disturb, but my doorman watches the skies of the mortal realm and informs me that there are Cailleach hovering over the park. Storm Hags. The time approaches for your departure, if you are to keep your appointment with the Darkling Queen's representatives."

"Thank you, my lord." With a reluctance Kelley could

feel, he gently disentangled his limbs from hers and stood. He slung his bag over his shoulder and held Kelley's script out to her. She shook her head.

"Keep it," she said, and folded his hands back over the rumpled pages. "Keep it for me. For luck."

"Only if you promise not to forget that one line," he said as he stepped close again.

Kelley glowed up at him. "Not on your life."

"I'll be back as soon as I can. I promise." Sonny's eyes shone with a whole book of unsaid things—promises of more than just his return. "Wait for me."

XXXII

Tyffanwy had gone so far as to tie a little red bow in Lucky's forelock. He looked like a Pekingese dog fresh from the groomer.

"I figured I might as well give him the full salon treatment." She snuffled a bit, and Sonny noticed that her lovely eyes were red-rimmed.

"Thank you for this, Tyff," he said. "I know you know how important it is."

"Yeah, well. You tell Mabh she'd better take care of him"—the Faerie sniffed fiercely—"or there'll be hell to pay! I have a few favors of my own that I can call in, should I find myself so inclined."

"I will," he said—and made a mental note to stay on Tyffanwy's good side. "C'mon, Lucky. Let's get you home and end this."

When Sonny pulled a slim rope out of his satchel and tied a loose loop around Lucky's neck, he seemed to understand. The kelpie lifted his delicate hooves out of the tub, one by one, and stepped lightly out onto the bathroom floor. Sonny eyed the window skeptically. It seemed far too small for the kelpie to make his way through, but Lucky trooped obediently over to it and nudged the pane. Sonny edged past and lifted open the casement, and the faerie horse ducked his red-maned head and, impossibly, squeezed through, out onto the fire-escape landing.

Sonny followed, noting how the kelpie made his way with some haste down the iron stairs. From the street, Sonny waved to thank Tyff then, concentrating sharply for a moment, he drew upon his power and cast a concealing veil over Lucky, rendering the kelpie invisible so that he could lead him through the streets of Manhattan, toward Central Park. Where he would hand the creature off to Mabh's Storm Hags.

He glanced nervously at the skies as he walked. In another few moments the sun would be down and it would be officially Samhain night. Scattered groups of costumed children and the odd bunch of party-going adults passed him on the street; there were more than a few carved pumpkins grinning at him from windows and stoops.

Mabh was cutting this awfully close, Sonny thought. Probably just to make him twitchy and satisfy her own perverse sense of humor. But none of that mattered now. Kelley was safe, soon Lucky would be back in the Borderlands, and he would be done with the threat of the Wild Hunt.

As he passed through the park, Sonny noted with dismay that there were a lot of humans in costumes wandering the pathways. He could see Belvedere Castle in the distance, lit up in garish shades of orange and purple. Some foolish millionaire had obviously decided to throw a great big Halloween bash in the park that year.

He followed his Janus senses to find the place in the park where Mabh's minions would be waiting. In truth, as he walked shadowy trails leading the placid, invisible kelpie, he felt a wash of guilt. The poor creature probably didn't even know the fate that awaited it. And if it did, it went to it with far more nobility than Sonny would have thought possible from a beast. He reaffirmed to himself his vow to Kelley that he would demand protection for Lucky.

In his mind, Sonny could sense three Storm Hags hovering near. He came out into a little round clearing by Turtle Pond, dominated by an enormous statue of a historic Polish king mounted on a warhorse. High in the air he saw the Hags circling like wispy gray vultures. He lifted the veil from the kelpie, and Lucky shimmered into view by his side. Sonny opened his mouth to call down the Hags, but suddenly his Janus senses jangled an alarm. A rift was opening nearby.

Very nearby. Right in front of him . . .

He took a step back and dropped into a fighting stance.

Wham!

It was not a small rift. The tearing sent out a shock wave that hammered Sonny to his knees. Beside him, Lucky whinnied in panic and half reared, pawing at the air with his front hooves. Sonny sensed that the entire Janus Guard had been alerted to the breach, and he knew that those who were able would come running.

The sky rippled. Looking up, Sonny saw the Queen of Air and Darkness herself, lounging on the statue high above the ground as if it were a throne. Mabh was silhouetted against the sky, framed by the two massive swords held crossed in the air by the statue of the king. Just for fun, Mabh had conjured up a pair of glowing-eyed jack-o'-lanterns and jammed them onto the tips of the statue's swords. They flared like torches, illuminating Mabh's makeshift court with a lurid glow.

"I hope this meeting was convenient for you, Sir Guard," she said in a languorous voice. "I was concluding a bit of business with a lady of my court, and we went a little over time."

By the flaring light of the pumpkin torches, Sonny saw a ghastly sight. From the long, taloned fingers of Mabh's fist,

Chloe the Siren dangled like a limp rag doll, hanging by the knotted mass of her blond hair. Blood seeped from her mouth and the scores of small wounds that marred her sleek limbs. She moaned senselessly in pain.

"My lady Mabh." Sonny struggled to keep his voice steady. "I was . . . unaware that you traveled the ways to the mortal world."

"Ooh, diplomacy," Mabh cooed. "How lovely. If you refer to the chains that Auberon and that witch Titania bound about me to restrict me to my realm, they are still there." She swung one foot carelessly, and Sonny saw a snaking silver chain attached to a fiery manacle that circled her ankle. The chain disappeared back into the boiling rift in the sky behind the queen, and there were fresh, angry red welts scoring her pale skin where the shackle bit into her flesh. "I'm still tethered, little Janus. But mark my words, not for long."

"My time is short, lady. I expected to meet only with your . . . emissaries."

"My Hags." She cast a glance at the sky, but the Storm Hags were nowhere to be seen. "Oh, they're about. Victimizing a partygoer or two, I should imagine. Never mind. Have you completed the task appointed you?"

Sonny glanced back at Lucky and said, "Obviously. First, the terms of your boon."

Mabh rolled her eyes.

"You will take care of it." Sonny ignored her disdain, his

voice firm. "Once returned to you, it will not suffer at your hands."

Mabh's eyes narrowed. "You dare call my red-haired beauty 'it'?"

"Insofar as your 'red-haired beauty' has incredibly destructive latent capabilities, I'd rather not elevate its status with a proper pronoun." It was best not to let Mabh know that the kelpie had made himself actual friends—such knowledge could be used against them all. Sonny kept his inflections carefully neutral, although, under his breath, he murmured, "Sorry, Lucky—no offense."

"What say you, Mabh?"

"You are disrespectful," Mabh said. She tut-tutted, a grin playing about her lips.

Sonny shrugged. "Give it to get it, lady."

The Darkling Queen laughed—a cheery, tinkling sound. "I like you! You're an angry little thing. And here I thought Auberon would raise you up all soft. Well then. The boon is granted. Now fulfill your part of the bargain. Give me my precious girl."

Sonny slipped the rope from Lucky's neck and nudged him forward with a slap on the rump. "It's a boy, actually—if you'd bothered to check."

Mabh looked back and forth from the nervous kelpie to Sonny. Then she turned a furious glare on him. "Your jest lacks a necessary component, my little changeling friend.

Humor. Now where is my daughter?"

"Your . . . "

Sonny's guts went cold. He replayed the scene with the Storm Hag in his apartment over again in his mind: "*This realm hides something that belongs to Mabh. You know this?*" the hag had said. "*She wants it back. It should never have been sent here. It was a mistake. Find it. Return it. And the queen will grant you a boon.*"

He had made the most basic error in judgment that one could make when dealing with Faerie. He had jumped to conclusions. Sonny had assumed that the Hag had referred to the wayward kelpie and had not bothered to clarify that point.

With sudden, crystalline clarity, Sonny realized that he had been wrong from the very beginning. It had *not* been Mabh who had sought to unleash the Wild Hunt after all.

Auberon.

For the sake of securing his own position on the Unseelie throne, Sonny thought, the Faerie king would sacrifice his own daughter. His daughter . . . and Mabh's. And he would have had Sonny help him do it, and put the blame on Mabh for awakening the Wild Hunt at the same time. Sick misery filled Sonny, only to be replaced by cold fury.

Mabh's eyes narrowed, and she watched him—watched him with green, glittering eyes that, were they not so filled with cruel malice, Sonny would have recognized immediately. Kelley had those very same eyes.

Mabh leaned forward slightly. "My Hag *did* convey the

bargain to you, did she not?"

"Cryptically," Sonny muttered, teeth and fists clenched. "And with exceedingly poor grammar—"

"But you agreed. Then and now."

"No."

"And instead of my daughter"—the Darkling Queen smiled dangerously—"you brought me. . . . a pony."

"I—"

"If you had any questions, Janus, the time to ask them is now long past." Her eyes flashed red for an instant.

"I assumed—"

"Ah, well. You know what they say about the dangers of 'assuming.'"

"My lady, the fault is mine. There must be something—"

"The bargain was for the girl."

"*No.*"

"Where is she?" Mabh hissed. "The bargain is broken. *You* broke it. You *must* tell me."

"N-n . . . no . . . " Sonny fell to his knees and felt his head jerk backward as though someone had yanked on his hair. His eyes flew wide, as much as he tried to keep them squeezed shut.

"Oh," Mabh purred as she gazed into his mind from high up on her perch. "Oh, this is marvelous. . . . All because of you, little Janus, my imprisonment is at an end! You know the rules. Your broken oath gives me the power to take what was not given to me as promised—and to do *that*, I'll need

283

freedom." She grinned wickedly as the manacle and delicate chain around her ankle shimmered and dimmed to an insubstantial wisp of silvery flame and the passageway in the sky behind her closed. "Thanks to your charming ineptitude, I can once more come and go as I please. I can enter Herne's precious Tavern. All so that I may take what was not freely given to me. And I can wreak a little havoc while I'm there!"

She laughed merrily.

To Sonny, it was the sound of the world ending.

"This worked out rather better even than I'd hoped. Thanks for your pains, fleshling. I will not forget." Mabh raised her hand, slicing through the sky to open another rift in front of her like a wound in the air.

In the moment before she stepped through, several of the Janus Guard came bursting out of the trees about ten yards behind Sonny.

"Chloe!" Maddox shouted. "Mabh, you bitch! Let her go!"

Chloe groaned, and the Darkling Queen seemed to suddenly remember that she held the Siren dangling by her hair—twenty feet above the earth.

She let her go.

Maddox was almost fast enough to catch her. Sonny winced as Chloe's head bounced off the ground. As Maddox got an arm around her and half lifted her, the Siren clutched at his sleeve, and Sonny heard her pained murmur: "I didn't want to tell him . . . but he threatened to take away my music."

"Tell who, Chloe?" Maddox asked gently. "What?"

"Auberon. About the girl." The Siren's lovely voice was reduced to a thready whisper. "Mabh was so angry when she found out that I told him. She thinks Auberon wants to do the girl harm. . . . "

"Shh . . . "

"Tell Sonny . . . I'm sorry. . . . " Chloe's hand fell limply to the ground.

With a snarl, Sonny launched himself in the direction of the statue. Mabh wanted a fight? She was about to get one. He could feel the rest of the Guard surging forward behind him. But Mabh stroked the horse statue beneath her and it suddenly snorted and reared, tossing its enormous bronze head. The ground heaved as though an earthquake struck, throwing the Janus Guard about like toys; there was a sound of shrieking metal. High above them, the figure of the long-dead king uncrossed its swords. The horse's huge, heavy hooves tore free of the statue's base, and the Janus Guard picked themselves up to join in battle against the bronze, red-eyed effigy.

"Happy Halloween, children!" Mabh vanished from sight, her voice howling back at them. "I'm off to go collect my daughter and do some trick-or-treating!"

The rift spiraled and collapsed in on itself, and a storm of flaming pumpkins rained down from the sky.

XXXIII

"Will you walk with me, lady?" Herne bowed his head to Kelley as they left the Isle of Avalon behind and returned to the Tavern proper.

She smiled up at him and slipped her hand around his muscle-corded forearm. They strolled through the Tavern's garden, past a gathering of what looked like living topiaries—one of them a horse prancing around the terrace, leafy mane and tail rustling as it kicked up its heels. It reminded her of Lucky, and Kelley felt a stab of anxiety. She was worried about him. And about Sonny, who had gone to deliver him to a fearsome being about whom she'd heard only unpleasant things so far. It was strange, because the man walking beside her had once loved the Darkling Queen. She'd seen it in the vision Sonny had given her.

"In the days before she was so very dark, yes," Herne murmured. "I did love her. As she did me. Sometimes love can be a terribly destructive thing, lady. I have spent lifetimes trying to make amends for what love once made me do."

"Can you read my thoughts?" Kelley asked warily.

"No." Herne laughed softly. "Just your face. You glanced at the pony, frowned, glanced up at me, and your expression became thoughtful. It was fairly easy to interpret."

"Oh. Right."

"But henceforward, around your own kind at least, you will probably want to learn to school your thoughts. Or at least keep them from showing so plainly in your visage. That is, if you intend to take up the legacy of your birth."

"You think it would be dangerous for me to do so."

"I think it is your blood right, and the decision is yours and yours alone," Herne said. "But be warned, lady. There are those who might not be so eager for you to embrace that right. The Unseelie king among them."

"My father? Why?"

"Only Auberon's direct heir is able to inherit the throne after him. And the thrones of the Faerie kingdoms must remain occupied."

"So without an heir, Auberon has no worries about having to ever give up his kingship," Kelley said. "But I thought that the Fae were immortal."

The Horned One held up a hand. "Yes, and no. Faerie are immortal *only* insofar as they do not age or sicken. They can still be killed."

Right, Kelley remembered, *that's what Sonny does.*

Her thoughts turned again to him and to what Auberon had said. . . .

Herne was speaking. "That is the way of it for all of the rulers of the Fair Folk. The kings and queens of Faerie are protected by the power of their thrones. Without heirs, they remain utterly inviolate, and without deadly enemies."

"So . . . I'm a threat to Auberon."

"You could be. But you could also be a powerful ally, doubling the strength of the Unseelie Court." Herne shrugged. "I do not know which way King Auberon perceives you. He is a deep thinker, and I would not presume to know his mind."

"He offered to make me human."

"That, in itself, says something. But again, whether he made such an offer for his own sake, or for yours . . . I do not know." The Hunter's gaze was warm, sympathetic. "Think hard on this choice, Kelley Winslow. As one who has lived a very long life tangled in the threads of Faerie webs, I would urge caution when dealing with their machinations. Friend and foe are sometimes indistinguishable. Or one and the same."

"Can he do it?" Kelley asked. "Can my father make me human?"

"After a fashion," Herne said. "As Lord of the Unseelie Court of Faerie, he can certainly take back the power of the Unseelie throne that you by blood right hold—but only if you give it willingly. He cannot force it from you."

"I see."

Herne stopped her. "Were you to ever do such a thing, lady, I would ask for something in return, if I were you. Such a gift should not be come by lightly. Even by a Faerie king."

"I'll try to remember that. Thank you."

Herne paced slowly beside her.

"You are handling all of this really very well, you know," he said, a smile in his voice, as if he'd sensed her thoughts once again.

"Oh, I am not," she said. "I'm in total denial and pretty sure I'm dreaming." She put her other hand on his arm and squeezed. "But it's kind of a nice drea—"

Suddenly Herne the Hunter grabbed her by the shoulders and flung her hard against a mirrored pillar—out of the way of a flaming pumpkin that roared out of the night. The fiery gourd exploded into an orange ball of fire as it hit the flagstones of the Tavern courtyard.

All around her, Faerie were screaming—some in panic, but most in rage. The Green was sanctuary, and someone had just violated it.

"Where is my daughter?" shrieked the terrifying specter that appeared in the sky above the courtyard, dressed in a raven-wing cloak, with wild red hair and a flashing, green-eyed gaze. Something clicked in Kelley's brain in the midst of the sudden, intense bedlam.

"*You have your mother's eyes,*" Auberon had said.

Mabh.

The Queen of Air and Darkness was her mother.

"To the princess!" Herne bellowed. "Protect the girl!"

All around her, the Lost Fae shimmered and shifted. With a rush of invocations, weapons of all kinds appeared, gripped tightly in graceful, fine-boned hands. Kelley saw things heaving themselves out of the depths of the fountains—creatures with claws and teeth, wielding cudgels and axes; and other creatures that didn't need weapons.

The place erupted into chaos, and it was all Kelley could do to get out of the way and avoid being trampled by those trying to protect her.

In the sky above Mabh's head, she saw cloaked and hooded wraiths, screeching curses and flinging lightning-lashed tempests at the Faerie warriors with devastating effect. She knew suddenly what these were.

Mabh's Storm Hags, Kelley thought, terrified. *They're here for me.*

Something must have gone terribly wrong with Sonny and Lucky.

She ducked and ran for the safety of the arbor that led to the shore of Avalon's lake. But there were so many twisting passageways in the Tavern that she quickly became hopelessly lost. Bursting through a set of double oak doors out into the cold night air, Kelley found herself suddenly standing in the car-filled parking lot of New York's Tavern on the Green, back in the mortal world.

A group of costumed revelers poured out through the doors of the tavern behind her. "Happy Halloween, missy!" one of them slurred, tipping a pointy wizard's hat in her direction.

Kelley watched, stunned and horrified, as something that resembled a bat-winged howler monkey leaped from the trees onto the unwitting reveler and tore the hat to shreds. Before its claws could rend flesh, Kelley screamed at the people to run for their lives and ripped the clover charm from her throat with one hand. She flung out her other hand without stopping to think, willing the horrible creature to be gone.

Brilliant light flashed in a corona all around her.

There was a *pop!* and the thing disappeared with an extremely surprised look on its face. Kelley fell to her knees, her brightness diminished, winded by the amount of effort it had taken to do whatever it was she had just done.

In the distance, she heard sirens and screaming.

She stuffed the charm into the tiny purse that dangled from her wrist and ran.

After falling on her face for the third time, Kelley finally kicked off Tyff's ridiculous heels, heedless of cold or the sharp gravel of the path. In the distance, she heard more screaming—terrified cries from human throats. She ran up the rise of a low hill and looked out over a panorama that could have come from a

Hieronymus Bosch painting—of demons torturing the souls of the damned in hell.

The Janus must have been overwhelmed, fending off Mabh and her minions, thought Kelley frantically, *and so the Samhain Gate had swung wide, undefended.* All manner of horrific creatures from the Otherworld poured out through rifts. Anyone unlucky enough to be caught in the park was being chased and tormented by beings that none of them could have imagined. Kelley saw spiny things and fiery things and pale, bony things with too-large eyes spreading out across the park with malicious intent.

All around her now, she could hear sirens in the air. Kelley knew that New York's Finest would be no match for the swarming Faerie monsters—the police would be nothing more than fodder against such creatures. She had to do something, and she had to do it fast. She had to find Sonny. Or, barring that, she had to find the one other person who she knew had the power to help her.

As her strength returned, the light started to flare from her skin once again. Kelley concentrated, and her brightness dimmed as she pulled every ounce of power she could grasp at into herself and stretched out with her awareness to try to find her father.

When his presence struck in her mind, it was like the impact of a hard-flung snowball. Suddenly she knew where he was—she just had to get there. Fast.

Half embarrassed to do so, Kelley turned and glanced at

the lacy, shining wings that floated out from either side of her spine. With an effort of sheer brute will, she made them flutter—then flutter faster. She could feel her feet lifting off the ground and felt a surge of triumph. But her concentration wavered. The wings crumpled, and Kelley fell forward onto her face in a drift of fallen leaves.

Cursing, she pushed herself up and started to run.

XXXIV

"Herne!" Sonny shouted above the din. "Where is she?"

All around him the Tavern was in shambles, shards of crystal and bits of broken tables littering the marble floors. Pockets of furious fighting between Lost Fae and Mabh's minions carried on with unabated ferocity. Blood pooled on the tiles, red and pale pinkish liquids mingling with green and yellow splatters.

Sonny reached the side of the embattled Hunter, who swung a huge ax in great space-clearing arcs. "Where is Kelley?" he asked again.

"We lost her in the fight!" Herne raised his voice so that Sonny could hear him. "She ran. Back into the park." He brought the ax down in a chopping blow that cleaved the head of something lumpy and angry looking in two. "Go! Find her before Mabh does. Or worse."

Sonny spun around and raced back out into the courtyard. All of the other Janus had been too occupied with the rampaging king statue to accompany him, except Maddox. Meeting up with him—and Lucky, for the kelpie, it seemed, would not let Sonny too far out of his sight—in the yard, Sonny burst out of the Tavern doors, his companions close behind. In the deserted parking lot, they paused just long enough for Sonny to orient his senses on Kelley's unique flame.

"That way," Sonny said, as soon as he could see her in his mind. The fuse on his Firecracker was sparking wildly now, and it would have been impossible for him to miss her.

Sonny turned to run south down the path leading from the parking lot, but before he and Maddox had taken a dozen long strides, an oak tree in front of them suddenly blew apart.

Sonny threw an arm over his face and tackled Maddox out of the way as thousands of needle-sharp splinters peppered them. The air rippled, and an overwhelming scent of decay washed over them. Lucky's eyes rolled white in his head and his nostrils flared.

A small army of stunted, troll-like fae circled the two Janus and the kelpie, slavering and swinging axes and pikes. Redcaps—named for their gruesome habit of soaking their long caps in the blood of those they'd slain.

"And you thought the piskies were a bitch," Maddox grunted, sinking into a defensive crouch beside Sonny. A redcap lunged, and Maddox lashed out in a judo kick, almost snapping the head off the creature. The spear it carried flew from its suddenly limp hands, and Maddox snatched it out of the air. Beside him, Sonny drew his bundle of oak, ash, and thorn and whispered his incantation, transforming it to sharp silver. Lucky struck out with his hooves, front and back.

A full-scale battle erupted, bloody minutes flying by. Then, quite unexpectedly, help dropped from the sky. The Fennrys Wolf leaped from out of nowhere into the center of the fray. Tearing two redcaps apart with his bare hands, his eyes black with battle madness, he turned to Sonny and grinned wildly. "Maddox and me will clear a path. Take the damned horse and ride, Sonny-boy. Ride fast."

Maddox nodded. "Go, Sonn. Go! Find her."

Sonny flung his leg over Lucky's back, and the kelpie bounded through the space that Maddox and the Wolf cleared free.

Thank the gods Tyffanwy had taken care to remove all the talismans. Without them, there could be no Roan Horse to call a Rider to, and Sonny could ride Lucky without fear of waking the Hunt. He needed the horse's speed to find Kelley in time—before Auberon or Mabh got to her first. Lucky pounded over the ground and crested a hill, and Sonny saw the Central Park Carousel silhouetted in the harsh light of the moon.

A single, piercing note shattered the still darkness.

A note from Mabh's war horn.

Beneath Sonny's thighs, Lucky bucked and reared, seemingly trying to throw the Janus from his back. Sonny would have been only too glad to oblige, but when he tried to fling himself off, he found that he could no longer move his legs. His knees gripped tight to the horse's flanks, and his hand was clenched in a frozen fist, grasping Lucky's mane.

The horn sounded a second note.

Sonny heard rather than saw the charms, then, rattling together just under the bow Tyffanwy had tied in Lucky's forelock. He reached forward and gave the ribbon a yank. It fell away, revealing three onyx gems concealed in the kelpie's mane, hidden by a glamour until that very moment. The veil was so sophisticated, so perfect, that it was no surprise both he and Tyff had missed them.

Sonny thrust his free hand into the pocket of his satchel and found the three stones from the path by the Lake. The ones he'd shown Auberon.

They were exactly that: stones. Common pebbles spell-cast to make them look like the onyx gems that had been tied throughout the kelpie's mane.

And the bastard sat there and playacted, implicating Mabh without ever actually saying it was her, Sonny thought bitterly as he threw the pebbles to the ground in a helpless rage. *I guess*

I know now where Kelley gets her acting talents—her father's a master at the art.

Beneath him, the kelpie tossed his head violently. Sonny felt the horse's muscles bunch and lengthen, his body mass increasing and growing heated, as if stoked from some great internal furnace roaring to life.

One last horrible note split the night air. Beneath Sonny, the kelpie leaped up, and the young Janus felt a second great heat bloom to life—in the place where, only a moment ago, his own broken heart had been.

He never should have taken the chance of climbing onto the kelpie's back.

He cursed himself bitterly. *Another grave mistake, Sonny.*

It was his last coherent thought.

A great emptiness spread through his chest in the wake of the blazing heat, and there no longer seemed to be any reason for him to fight the consuming fury that washed over him. The fiery stallion beneath him leaped into the air, and the only impulse left to Sonny was to hunt.

And kill.

XXXV

The notes of the war horn tore at Kelley. She put her hands over her ears as she ran and shut her eyes, which made her trip over what lay before her on the gravel pathway—a bloodied, wild-eyed apparition.

It was Bob.

He was gasping for breath and looked as though he might have run the entire way from the theater. He flung out an arm toward Kelley and tried to speak, but it was as if invisible hands clutched at his throat and covered his mouth. Kelley instinctively recognized his affliction for what it was: The boucca wasn't simply out of breath; he had been enchanted.

He struggled in vain to say something, but the words would not come out of his mouth. Flecks of pinkish foam appeared at the corners of his pale green lips.

Suddenly, as if the words of the Bard had a magic of their own, he began to quote his own lines from the play.

"Up and down, up and down," he chanted, keening with the effort to push the words past his pain-clenched teeth. *"I will lead them up and down."*

Bob pointed behind him with a shaking finger. *"I am feared in field and town. Goblin, lead them up and down."*

Kelley wanted to help the tortured boucca but found herself, instead, compelled to look past where Bob writhed in pain: up the road, to the top of the hill—and the carousel.

Dark glittering energy crackled and danced over the contours of the little building. The shuttered security doors, pulled down tight for the night, wavered like a mirage and faded from existence. Weird, eerie lights danced and played in the darkened shadows beneath the carousel roof, and thunderclouds boiled in the sky above. In the distance, Kelley could hear the baying of what sounded like a whole pack of Black Shuck.

All Kelley could think of in her panic was to hide. Become invisible.

Hadn't Sonny once said she could do that?

The howling grew louder.

Kelley wrapped her arms around Bob and wished with all of her desperate, terrified might that she could disappear. She looked down and saw Bob's pale green eyes go wide, and then he vanished from sight altogether. Both of them did.

She could still hear Bob's ragged breathing, feel his limbs trembling in her grasp. The effort of casting the veil almost caused her to black out. Darkness threatened to descend upon her, but she fought against it, holding tight to the wounded fae in her arms.

When she was able to see clearly again, she looked toward the carousel, and Bob's warning became suddenly, devastatingly clear.

The ride began to spin, wreathed in inky, glistening smoke.

In the air above the carousel, the magnificent fiery stallion that used to be Lucky galloped into view. He screamed and lashed out with teeth and hooves, long limbs coiled in flame. Astride his back, the Rider kept his seat effortlessly upon the bucking, plunging mount.

Kelley felt her strength falter as the tears streamed down her face and, briefly, the veil she had managed to call up wavered. The Rider's gaze shifted and for a moment they locked eyes. She cried out his name, but his expression remained remote.

Frozen and merciless.

Sonny . . .

The thin, cheerful music of the calliope twisted into a cacophony of skirling battle cries, and Kelley cringed at the howling rage. She watched in horror as the wooden horses of the carousel convulsed, shuddering into terrible life. Her nightmares were becoming real right before her eyes. Bloodthirsty

Faerie hunters shimmered into being astride the gaily painted saddles.

Sounds of the Black Shuck approaching grew closer.

Kelley pushed every ounce of strength she had into the protective veil she barely knew how to create. She looked down to see herself and Bob fade back into nothingness just as the Wild Hunt surged forth into the night.

Singing in their terrible joy, the hunters climbed into the sky to join their leader, the Rider on the Roan Horse. They were joined by a pack of thundering Black Shuck that burst through the trees and leaped into the air, snapping at the horses' heels.

Kelley turned her attention back to Sonny. A gust of wind whipped his dark hair madly around his beautiful, remote face as his silver gaze raked the space where he had seen her cowering with Bob only a moment before. Kelley whispered his name, but Sonny looked through her with unseeing eyes. Brow clouding with anger, he whirled his sword about his head and hauled savagely on the reins of his fiery steed.

Together they climbed a spiral path higher and higher into the storm, the Wild Hunt following in their wake.

This was all her fault. Even if she hadn't ever known who—what—she was, it was because of her that this was happening.

As the Hunt galloped off over the treetops and out of sight, Kelley let the veil drop. She was trembling in every limb with the effort of having maintained it for even that short time.

Huddled in her lap, Bob was still gulping for air, unable to speak. Fishing the clover charm from her purse, Kelley clasped it around his neck. His gasping cries stopped almost immediately as the protective aura of the talisman enveloped him, and he looked up at Kelley with gratitude.

"What happened to you?" she asked, her voice catching in her throat at the sight of him once again.

"Auberon . . . " Bob coughed—a sickly, broken sound. "He came to the theater looking for you. Took it badly when I wouldn't tell him where you were. . . . I came here to warn you. We were wrong. The Hunt . . . it wasn't Mabh. It was Auberon. Had to be. He doesn't want you back—he wants you gone. Dead."

"But he's my *father*," she whispered.

Bob attempted a sardonic grin that just came off as pained. "It's not like he sent you birthday presents, Kelley."

"Thanks to *you*, Goodfellow, I didn't have an address."

The sound of the Faerie king's voice made Kelley jump. She turned to see him stoop to retrieve something that lay in the grass beside the empty carousel house. When he straightened, Kelley saw that Auberon clutched a tall bronze war horn in his fist.

She rose to her feet and stood protectively over Bob. Without the shield of the charm she'd worn all her life, Kelley could feel her power humming in her veins, even drained as she was. The air seemed charged, electric, where it touched her skin.

"Impressive," he said as he walked down the hill toward

Kelley, his glance sweeping over her, lingering on her luminous silver wings. He stopped in front of her and smiled coldly. "Well—the apple does not fall far, it seems."

"I'm nothing like you," Kelley snarled. "I will *be* nothing like you."

"What will you be then? It is quite apparent, from where I stand, that you no longer belong to *this* world."

In the distance, they could hear the cries of humans in the park as the Wild Hunt—and all the other dangerous fae—rampaged through the night.

"Or what will be *left* of this world. After *they* are finished with it."

Kelley felt herself falter.

"Of course, all of this can be remedied. But only *I* can remedy it." Her father's voice softened. "Forsake your claim, girl. Give up the Unseelie power that resides within you. Do that, and I will grant you the means to stop the Wild Hunt. With my help, you can keep this world safe and rescue Sonny Flannery from the fate of the Rider." He pointed to the sky with the horn. "Save the man you love, Daughter."

"I'd *really* rather you didn't call me that," she ground out between clenched teeth. As strong as she was now that her Faerie gift was unleashed, Kelley knew she was still far too inexperienced. She didn't even know how to fly yet. There was no way she could even come anywhere close to stopping the Hunt. Not without help.

"Do we have a bargain?" her father asked.

304

"What the hell do you think?"

"I'm afraid I need to hear you say it," he murmured coldly.

"*Yes*, damn you." Kelley stifled a sob. "Give me what I need to stop the Wild Hunt. So that I can save Sonny." She looked up into her father's cold, dark eyes. "Do that, and I will let you take the Unseelie power from my blood," she whispered.

"Agreed," Auberon said as he stepped toward her.

"Wait." In the distance, Kelley could see one of Mabh's Storm Hags throwing thunderbolts at a careening carriage. She remembered what Herne had told her. "I also want something else in return."

"That is?"

"While I go take care of the Wild Hunt, *Dad*," she growled, "I want you to get 'Mom' and her psycho Bitch Brigade the hell out of my park. And this time make sure she never comes back."

"With pleasure, my dear." Auberon smiled magnanimously and spread his hands wide. "With very great pleasure."

Auberon placed a hand on her head and whispered a word. Suddenly it was like the song of Kelley's power went from a tune played on a pennywhistle to a full-blown orchestral score. She lit up the park.

Then, just as suddenly, there was silence. Darkness.

Kelley fell to her knees, hollow and empty. Too empty even to weep.

Her father stood before her, his icy skin glowing with *her* light and his eyes filled with a warmth that had been absent prior to that moment. She watched as he absorbed her gift fully into himself. The brightness faded; his eyes grew dark again.

"Okay," she said finally, her voice flat, muted. "How do I stop them?"

The king looked down on her, once more as distant as a marble statue. "I cannot tell you how. But I *have* given you the means by which you might accomplish the task. The rest, you'll just have to figure out for yourself."

"*What?*"

"Good luck, child." Auberon turned to go.

Kelley was seething. "You're a real son of a bitch. You know that?"

"I can be," Auberon said, as he looked at her with something like regret in his eyes. "Unfortunately, *you* are the daughter of one. Remember that."

He touched her cheek and then spun on his heel and stalked into the night, turning himself into a falcon as he went. Wings spread wide, the king flew away with Mabh's war horn clutched in his taloned grasp.

Not knowing what else to do, Kelley turned back to Bob, where he lay upon the ground, limp and unmoving. The charm may have kept the boucca from further hurt, but he was still desperately injured.

"Bob . . . " She shook him until he groaned. "Bob—Puck!

Wake up! The Hunt. They're awake and they're hunting humans."

Above her now, she could see the Hunt. They plunged and dipped crazily through the sky, howling with cruel laughter as one of the Faerie hunters chased down a woman dressed in a torn and bloodied Cleopatra costume, plucking her from the ground to drag her through the air by her feet. "They're hurting them!"

"Aye," Bob said, sounding a bit delirious. "Don't worry— they're just playing. They'll get around to killing them soon enough."

"I'd like to avoid that eventuality if at all possible, Bob. What do I do?"

"You must reach Sonny. You're the only one who can."

"He's two hundred feet in the air!"

Bob giggled a bit and his head lolled back. "You're a Faerie. Use your wings. . . . "

"Auberon took them!" Kelley almost screamed with frustration.

"Oh . . . " His voice was reduced to a whisper as his strength ebbed. "Then you must find another way. You have a *lot* of power. . . . "

"*Had*, Bob."

"Still . . . do. . . . "

"What are you talking about?" she pleaded desperately. "Auberon took it from me; I gave it back!"

"Thou marvell'st at my words?" the boucca gasped, his eyes closing.

"No—Bob!—no more Shakespeare!" Kelley shook him again, trying to jar him out of the poetic lapse. Now was not the time.

"But hold thee still," he murmured, those same cryptic lines he'd used to warn her in the dressing room. "Things bad begun make strong themselves by ill. . . . "

Then Bob the boucca passed out from pain.

Sonny, where are you when I need you?

It was a stupid question. All Kelley had to do was look into the sky and see him blazing across the treetops like a comet, the band of killer Fae hot on his heels as they pursued screaming humans about the park.

Kelley turned inward, searching for an answer. When she closed her eyes, she found herself once more in the vision she'd had in rehearsal so long ago, a place she now recognized as Herne's forest—the spring glade where Mabh had enchanted the kelpie. In her mind she looked across the clearing and saw Sonny standing once again in the shadows of the woods. He smiled at her, that sad curving of his beautiful lips, and lifted his hands, palms wide. The white branches of the birch trees at his back glowed dimly in the light that shone from Sonny's hands, arching over his head like the antlers of a stag.

The white King Stag . . .

That was it.

Kelley's eyes snapped open, and she gasped at the revelation. The Faerie king could take away *his* power from her blood . . . but Kelley was willing to bet that he couldn't take away *Mabh's*. Mabh, the Autumn Queen, who ruled the Borderlands. She, who had created the Wild Hunt in the first place, who'd twisted the Faerie hunters, stolen away and hidden their prey . . .

Mabh, Queen of Air and Darkness. Her mother.

Auberon had told her not to forget that, but she'd shied away from the fact.

Bob had told her too. *Things bad begun make strong themselves by ill.*

Fight fire with fire. That was what they had been trying to tell her.

Ignoring as best she could the chaos all around her, Kelley closed her eyes again and searched even deeper inside of herself—looking for the dark, dangerous spark of her mother's power.

There.

She touched something in her mind: twisting, serpentine energy. It was buried so deep that she never would have found it if Auberon hadn't taken away the blinding brilliance of her Unseelie gift. Kelley's mind recoiled from that initial touch, even though she knew she was going to have to use that dark gift. Draw upon it. Embrace it.

She clenched her fists and, concentrating fiercely, reached again. The power of Mabh's shadowy throne wrapped around her, suffocating, overwhelming. She was drowning again, just like the night she'd rescued Lucky. Until suddenly, like a key turning in a lock, something clicked. A door opened inside her, and Kelley was flooded with strength and fury. Mabh's power coursed through her veins like acid. She was deathly cold and on fire at the same time.

Stretching out her hands before her, Kelley tore through the veil between worlds as if it were flimsy silk, opening a rift right into the heart of Queen Mabh's realm.

Without giving herself a chance to think about it, she threw herself forward into the abyss.

The assault on her senses proved almost more than she could bear. The stench of the swampy terrain was overpowering, and the dank air clung to her bare arms like wet gauze. She had crossed over into some kind of nightmare. Above her, black, skeletal tree branches clawed at the gloomy air, and tiny insect-like sprites darted around her head, hissing and chittering at her in outrage. Kelley ignored them, fighting through the fetid ooze of a bog toward an outcropping of mossy high ground.

She reached the bank and her fingers dug into the spongy loam as she hauled herself up out of the brackish water. Something unseen slithered past her ankle, and Kelley squealed and snatched her feet clear of the muck, breathing heavily from exertion and fear.

She stood on shaking legs and surveyed her gloomy surroundings. Fog, thick and luminescent, carpeted the swampy ground. The forest seemed to be watching her with unseen, malevolent eyes, as if she was an intruder.

She wasn't.

As horrid as the place was, Kelley sensed a disturbing familiarity. It was almost a feeling of homecoming—if home was a haunted house. Part of her belonged here, and that frightened her more than anything.

In the near distance, she heard the baying of hounds. More Black Shuck—and they were coming toward her.

Mindless terror seized her, and Kelley ran for her life, heedless of the thorny branches that tore at her skin and the sinkholes that threatened to trip her with every step. The howling of the shuck grew louder and she could hear them crashing through the undergrowth, almost at her heels. Desperate, Kelley threw her arms up in front of her face and charged through a thicket of brambles, tumbling out into a clearing where a high, full moon dripped silver on the weedy grass.

The shuck were only moments behind her.

She tried to gather her mother's power, to call up another veil, to do something—*anything*—but fear made it impossible to concentrate. She closed her eyes and thought of Sonny. He was there, in her mind, under the trees. Over his shoulder, Kelley saw a flash of silvery white.

She seized upon that whiteness with her mind and drew it to her.

In that instant three enormous hellhounds burst into the clearing. Slavering and crimson eyed, they circled her, a quarry

311

run to ground. And Kelley knew that they wouldn't bother to wait for any hunter to come and finish her off. The lead shuck's massive black muscles bunched, and it leaped at her, snarling in rage.

Kelley shut her eyes tight and braced for death.

There was the sound of bone-crushing impact, and the snarl turned to a yowl of pain. Kelley's eyes flew wide-open—in time to see the magnificent white King Stag throw the limp body of the first shuck into a tree with its massive antlers. The other two hounds didn't hesitate but lunged for the stag's exposed flank. The stag bellowed and bucked, shaking loose one dog and goring it with its deadly antlers. But the last shuck clung to the stag's shoulders with its wicked claws, and blood flowed, silver, down the white hide as the stag's front legs buckled.

Kelley leaped to her feet and screamed defiance.

A flash of darkling energy exploded out from where she stood and lit up the grove with a burst of indigo light. The shuck recoiled and fell to the ground, where it died beneath the hammering hooves of the enraged King Stag.

The stag turned its head toward Kelley. Its gleaming silver hooves were sullied with the black blood of the shuck, but it was still the most regal creature Kelley had ever seen.

The great beast pawed the ground and snorted, eyes blazing with white fire.

Kelley reached out a hand and waited as it approached her, fear a tiny tight knot in her stomach. If the stag did not accept her, all it had to do was swing its head and the dagger-sharp points of its antler crown would gore her.

The stag nuzzled her hand, nostrils quivering. Then it dipped its great head and bowed to her, bending back one long, graceful foreleg so that Kelley could mount up on its back.

She almost wept.

Climbing up, Kelley wound her fists tightly in its thick, pale mane. She hung on for dear life as her noble steed leaped into the sky. It bucked and plunged, waiting impatiently as she reached out with her power and tore another rift between the realms, then galloped through the hole in the thin air, back toward the mortal realm and the Wild Hunt.

As they emerged in the skies over Central Park, Kelley heard the Faerie hunters roar with unbridled joy at the sight of the white King Stag.

Here was quarry. Here was prey worthy of the Hunt. As she'd hoped they would, the hunters abandoned the terrified mortals below and spun their mounts on their haunches, entering the chase. The Black Shuck accompanying them howled madly and shot after her in pursuit.

Higher and higher Kelley led them, away from the world of mortals, so far that when she looked down she could see ragged clouds below. As the muscles of the Faerie animal beneath her gathered and released and gathered again, hooves pounding through the pale air as though it were a mossy forest track, Kelley felt a thrill of exhilaration like nothing she had ever known, greater even than when she rode with Herne's hunters.

Close behind, the Roan Horse and its Rider were gaining on her. An arrow grazed her cheek, and Kelley knew she was running out of time. As Lucky and Sonny pulled almost parallel, Kelley drew her bare feet up underneath her, bracing them upon the stag's broad back and balancing in a precarious crouch. She took a deep breath.

This is going to hurt.

Kelley opened up a rift in the King Stag's path. She hauled on the stag's silver mane, momentarily sending the creature veering to the right, and threw herself at the Rider—knocking him flying off the back of the Roan Horse.

Arcing through the air, the last thing Kelley saw before she started to fall was Lucky gather and leap through the rift, still leading the Wild Hunt and their hounds as they charged madly after the stag. The hunting party plunged after the Roan Horse before he transformed back into a kelpie—right through the gaping hole in the sky, back into Queen Mabh's realm.

Good, she thought. *Mabh made them; Mabh can damn well deal with them.*

She sealed the rift with a thought and whispered, "Goodbye, Lucky."

Then Kelley and Sonny fell.

* * *

They dropped like a stone through the night, plummeting back to earth.

Tumbling end over end, Kelley searched desperately inside herself for the strength that would save them—for the power of her mother's magick. But the fearsome strength that had raged through her only moments earlier was gone, reduced to barely a trickle. Kelley was too new to this. Too tired. They were falling, and she knew there was nothing she could do to stop it. A sob of frustration stuck in her throat—it wasn't supposed to end this way.

She felt Sonny's arms and legs twisting about her and she realized that Sonny—mortal, human Sonny—was trying to turn them around in the air so that when they hit the ground, he would bear the brunt of the impact. With his arms wrapped tightly around her, Sonny cradled Kelley against his chest. She looked into his storm-gray eyes and saw that he stared serenely back at her, happy. Content to die if there was the smallest chance it could save her.

"No!" She struggled madly in the vise of his embrace. "Sonny—no . . ."

Behind Sonny's head, far below, she could see the blackness of the unforgiving ground rushing up to meet them.

She remembered when they had danced. He had called her his Firecracker.

Kelley squeezed her eyes shut, tears of effort freezing on

her cheeks, and called upon that image. At first, there was nothing—just a terrible emptiness—and then she felt her skin start to tingle. Electric sparks, drawn from the charged and stormy air around her, raced up and down her arms and legs. The wind screamed in her ears; bone-crushing impact with the earth was only moments away. Kelley gripped the front of Sonny's shirt and opened her eyes to see him smiling gently back at her.

"You dumb-ass," she muttered through clenched teeth. "You can't break my fall." She imagined her spine as if it were a lit fuse and—straining with an effort so intense it felt as though she would split her own muscles and flesh—she willed the firecracker to explode.

Her shoulder blades burned with sudden, dark fire, and Kelley's cry of triumph ripped through the sky.

"Not when I can fly!"

The ground beneath them—mere inches away—blazed with sudden purple fire as Kelley's wings unfurled, delicate as gossamer, yet strong enough to catch at the air and sweep her and Sonny back up into the sky.

She could see out of the corner of her eye as she flew that her wings were no longer silver. Those lacy, lustrous things were gone—taken by her father. *These* wings unfurled behind her as though she were an exotic butterfly, dark and sparkling, like an indigo starburst. The world around her shone amethyst, bathed in the deep violet light of her newfound wings.

Kelley was a Faerie princess.

In defiance of the Faerie king, she had taken up her destiny on *her* terms.

An expression of something that was almost awe suffused the features of Sonny's face, and Kelley kissed him quickly before he had time to say anything. She felt his arms tighten around her as they spiraled up, borne aloft on wings that were dark as the night, bright as a new star.

XXXVI

Sonny's boots touched lightly down on the solid
ground. They crunched in the frosty grass, and so
he knew he wasn't dreaming. But the nightmare, it
seemed, was over. He released Kelley from the crush of his
embrace and gazed down at her lovely face. She dimmed the
radiance that flowed from her, and the darkling wings flickered and faded from view. Putting a finger under her chin,
he raised her face to his, bestowing another lingering kiss on
her lips. Tyff's beautiful dress was tattered and stained, and
Kelley's legs and arms were covered in mud and scratches.
But her cheeks were flushed from the wind and her green

eyes sparkled. Sonny had never seen anything so beautiful in his life.

Over her shoulder he saw the wooden carousel horses back in their proper places, painted eyes empty of fury, saddles vacant.

The sound of languid applause reached their ears, and they turned sharply to see Auberon standing on the path.

"Well done, Daughter," he said. "I was not certain that you would find the strength necessary to defeat the Hunt."

Sonny put out a protective arm, but Kelley stepped in front of him and walked proudly over to meet her father halfway. She held out a hand for the war horn that the Faerie king still held.

"Of course." Auberon's lips twitched, and he handed it to her.

Grasping the long bronze horn in both hands, Kelley snapped it in two over her knee and threw the broken pieces to the ground. Then, wordlessly, she turned her back on her father and returned to where Sonny waited.

In the distance, they could still hear sirens.

Sonny opened his arms. Kelley walked into his embrace and looked up at him. Her gaze was still a little wild, and Sonny couldn't help but shiver at what he saw there now.

"Are you afraid of me?" she asked quietly.

"No," he said without hesitation. "Afraid *for* you, maybe."

Mabh's power was a fearsome thing to have to master, but Kelley didn't need to hear that just then. Tears rimmed her eyes, shining and unshed, and Sonny held her in his arms and kissed her. "My Firecracker . . . my heart."

"If you are quite finished here, my Janus, I require your presence in the realm."

He didn't need to turn to see that Auberon still stood behind them.

Kelley made a strangled sound of denial.

"You can require whatever you like," Sonny said coldly. "But I'm not going anywhere with you."

"Mabh has been driven back to the Faerie lands, but she won't stay hidden there long," Auberon said impatiently. "She will return to threaten not only my realm, but this one as well, unless she is contained again. You will help me accomplish that."

"No." Sonny gripped Kelley tightly. "I do not work for those who have betrayed my trust."

"Is that what you think I have done?" Auberon's voice was polite. Inquisitive.

"I know it." It hurt Sonny deeply to say such a thing. "You were as a father to me. . . . "

"And you were as a dutiful son. So you will be again," Auberon said, and his eyes went absolutely black. There was a sharp pain in Sonny's chest, right beneath his iron medallion, and he clutched at it, unable to breathe.

"Stop it!" Kelley screamed. "No! You can't take him with you!"

"Of course I can," Auberon said flatly.

"We had a *deal*!"

"Which in no way included Sonny remaining in this realm if you were successful in restoring him unto himself." The king lifted a shoulder in eloquent disdain. "He is a member of my Court. He must obey."

Sonny fell to his knees.

"Besides. I need him to undo his mistake." The lord of the Unseelie stepped toward him, holding Sonny's gaze with his own. "Is that not right, Sonny? It was, after all, your error that set Mabh free. So is it your obligation to help me mend that situation."

"No," Kelley said furiously.

"And it was *your* request of me, Daughter, that I see to it Mabh stays away from this place. You didn't specify how."

A neat trap, Sonny thought. Faerie tricks.

"No!" Kelley screamed at her father, but Sonny knew in his heart that Auberon was right. Mabh was free again because of *him*. And there was something else that Auberon hadn't said: Kelley remained in danger because of it. It was up to Sonny to put things right.

The fiery pain in his chest ceased abruptly as he made his decision.

"Kelley." He climbed to his feet and grabbed her by the shoulders to make her look at him. "Kelley . . . " He shook her a little, and the tears dashed down her cheeks. "I won't be gone forever. But he's right. I need to do this thing."

"But—"

"Shh . . . " He pulled her in tight to his chest and whispered into her hair. "Just like Pyramus and Thisbe in your play—I will find the hole in the wall. I will find a way back through."

"You know that story ends horribly, right?" she said, choking on a sob.

"Ah, my heart. What did Shakespeare know?" Sonny hugged her tighter. "He probably would have rewritten that bit if he'd thought about it. I *will* come back to you. I promise."

As Auberon stepped toward them, Sonny felt Kelley stiffen with cold rage. She pushed away from him and turned to her father, her green eyes flashing dangerously.

"Do I even need to tell you how unhappy I will be if anything bad happens to him?"

"No, Daughter," Auberon said softly. "You do not." The king gestured with one hand like a blade, and a crackling gateway opened into the Otherworld. "Come, Sonny. It is time to go."

Kelley met Sonny in one last embrace, and they kissed each other as if, in that moment, they were the only two people in all the worlds. Then he turned and stepped through the rift. Auberon lingered for another moment, looking back at Kelley, and Sonny heard him say, "You really do have your mother's eyes."

OPENING NIGHT

November 1

It was just over an hour to curtain, and Kelley should have been nervous. Instead she was numb.

Opening night. Magic time. The peak of her childhood dreams reached . . .

And none of it mattered.

Sonny wasn't there to see it. She sat in front of her makeup mirror, listlessly toying with a mascara wand, staring at the mess of powder she'd spilled earlier and hadn't bothered to clean up.

Outside her dressing room she could hear the bustle of the other actors—the boys tromping by, the whisper of crinolines as the dancers flitted past. She heard the almost constant murmuring of cast and crew still gossiping, exchanging theories over what had *really* happened in Central Park on Halloween—gangs, mass hallucinations, aliens. Speculation had been wild and endless.

At least all of the excitement had served to draw some of the fire away from Kelley's disappearance. Even so, it had taken forty-five minutes of solid apology and Quentin's grudging admittance of the fact that he really had no other options before he agreed to let her back onstage.

But now? Kelley couldn't care less. Even the sound of the quartet of musicians warming up in the wings did nothing to stir excitement in her.

She looked up at the sound of a knock on her door, which swung open. The glamour Bob had cast over himself nicely covered up the bruises he'd received at Auberon's hands, trying to keep her safe.

She smiled wanly at the boucca as he held out a hand, her four-leaf-clover necklace dangling from one long finger.

"Figured you might want this back."

Kelley held up her hair and turned so that he could slip the chain around her neck and fasten the catch.

"Can you make it so that this never comes off, Bob?" she asked quietly. "So that my power stays hidden forever?"

Behind her, she felt him hesitate. "I could. . . . Are you sure that's what you want?"

Kelley stared at her reflection in the mirror and thought

she saw her mother staring out from her own eyes. She imagined the surging, tantalizing energy singing through her veins silenced; the strength and power gone, and with it, the whispering malice that accompanied it. The simmering lust to do harm. The callous disregard for consequences . . .

"Power is power, Kelley. It's what you *do* with it that matters," Bob said. "I should know. And, if you want my advice, I'd keep all the power I have for the moment, if I were you. You just might need it. . . . "

"To get Sonny back," she finished the thought. "Maybe you're right."

"Come with me," he said. "I have something to show you."

He took her by the hand and led her out onto the stage, which lay dark and waiting for the curtain to lift. Kelley could hear the murmur of the audience in the house beyond. Bob led her to the center of the deck, where the two curtain halves met, and held one open a tiny crack for her to peer through.

Kelley gasped. Sitting in the center of the front row were Tyffanwy and Aunt Emma. And sitting on Emma's other side, holding her hand, was a smiling Sonny Flannery.

"It's just for the show," Puck whispered at her side. "He won't be able to stay to see you afterward, but he asked me to give you this."

It was an envelope, made of pale parchment with gilt edges. - *Firecracker* - was written on the outside; inside was a single wrinkled sheet of paper: page 26 of her script.

Sonny had circled three words in gold ink: *I love thee.*

Kelley hugged the piece of paper to her chest and turned gratefully to Bob. "How did you do it?"

"'Twasn't me—the Winter King gifted Sonny with enough of his own power to cross over."

"And how did *you* convince my father to do that?"

Bob ducked his head in mock modesty. "A little wheeling, a little dealing . . . "

"What did you have to give up in return?" she asked warily.

"Oh, I didn't really give up anything." He waved away her concerns.

"Nothing?"

"Nothing much." His eyes glinted. "In fact, I've found myself a bit of steady employment. After closing night, it's back to the Unseelie Court for me. Auberon's been lacking a decent henchman, it seems, ever since I left."

"*What?* He beat the crap out of you, Bob." Kelley eyed him in astonishment and gratitude. He'd done this for her. And for Sonny. "Are you sure about this?"

"You know what they say, Princess: Keep your friends close—enemies closer."

Bob winked and left her standing on the dim stage.

Kelley turned back and put her eye to the gap in the curtain, drinking in every line of Sonny's face, smiling with delight at the way he and Emma talked and laughed and couldn't seem to look away from each other even for a moment. She watched them until she heard the musicians start up the overture. Kelley blinked away happy tears.

Everything was going to be all right. She had her mother's power. But, more importantly, she had brains and guts, and now she knew enough about the Fair Folk to try to beat them at their own game. Tomorrow Kelley would start seriously planning how to get Sonny back for good. But not tonight.

Tonight was opening night.

Magic time.

ACKNOWLEDGMENTS

I owe a debt of heartfelt gratitude and affection to a lot of people. To Jessica Regel and Laura Arnold—my agent and my editor, two of the most awesome women I have ever met: They conspired brilliantly to get me to write this book in the first place and then went far above the call of duty to make sure they took care of me while I did! Thank you to Jean Naggar and the staff of JVNLA for welcoming me into the fold, and to the wonderful crew at HarperCollins: Editorial Director Barbara Lalicki for her keen insight and support; Maggie Herold, my terrific copyeditor, for making me look much smarter than I am; and Sasha Illingworth, my stellar designer, for making the whole thing look so damn good! Thanks to editor Lynne Missen and everyone at HarperCollins Canada for the warm welcome. Thank you, Mark and Danielle, for your friendship, your New York hospitality, and all the long walks through the Park—especially the ones at night! Thank you, Adrienne, for all the support. Thank you, Cec-monster, for keeping me going for all these many years. Huge love and gratitude to my family—especially my mom—for somehow understanding that I would wind up here, even if it was in spite of myself. And most of all . . . to John—for so many reasons, not the least of which is, without you, I never would have even made it past "what if?"

Follow Kelley and Sonny
to the Otherworld and beyond in

Turn the page for a sneak peek

"No!"

Kelley bolted upright in her bed, the blood-spattered images of her nightmare so vivid that they seemed to hang before her in the darkened air of her room. She took a deep breath, trying to slow the ragged pounding of her heart, and pulled her knees up to her chest.

Oh, Sonny, she thought bleakly, *not another one . . .*

The late April breeze sifting through the cracked-open window bared sharp, chilly teeth, but in spite of that, Kelley's sheets were soaked with sweat, and she felt almost feverish. According to the blue glow of the clock at her bedside, she'd been asleep for less than an hour, but it seemed that she'd dropped straight into the ravening maw of her dreams. Again. But these dreams were different.

Kelley still preferred to think of it as dreaming. It *wasn't*, of course—not in the conventional sense. When they had first started happening, Kelley had written them off as garden-variety nightmares. Vivid ones, sure—but just nightmares. Now, however, she knew the visions that tormented her from time to time were glimpses of actual events. She knew, for instance, that Sonny had managed to hunt down yet another of the dwindling numbers of the Wild Hunt. Hunt him down and . . . kill him.

Kelley knew it was real—she had seen the bright blood splashed across the hunter's cheek as he gasped for breath, and she had forced herself to wake before the terrible moment when she knew she would have to witness the light fading from his beautiful eyes.

She had her mother to thank for the disturbing visions, but that was hardly surprising. Her mother had a lot to answer for.

Kelley reached for the glass of water on her bedside table and knocked a stack of playscripts to the floor. With a sigh she bent to pick them up. In among the scattered pages was a postcard from her aunt Emma that she'd been using for a bookmark; it was from Ireland. Kelley turned it over and gazed at the glossy image of green, rolling hills. Though Emma had raised her, she wasn't really Kelley's aunt: in fact, she was

Sonny Flannery's mortal mother. Kelley was glad that Em had finally decided to return to the country of her birth and spend a few months there. Her departure had after all been a hurried one more than a century earlier, when in an attempt to replace her own stolen child, she'd taken Kelley from her cradle in the Unseelie Court of the Otherworld and tumbled ahead through time and space to find herself in modern-day New York City.

Kelley tucked the postcard back into its place and gathered up the rest of the fallen scripts. Sandwiched between copies of Shakespeare's *The Tempest* and a collection of Greek tragedies, she found a single folded sheet of paper. Her fingers trembling slightly, she unfolded it—page 26 from her old script for *A Midsummer Night's Dream*. She had told Sonny to keep the script as a good-luck charm, and he had sent that one page back to her on opening night with the words *I love thee* circled in gold ink.

Kelley swallowed the tiny sob that was building in her throat and, folding the page gently, pressed it to her heart for a moment, hugging herself in the darkness.

Shivering in the chill draft that seeped through cracks around the edges of the bathroom window, Kelley ran the tap and splashed water over her face and neck. She really didn't feel like going back to sleep.

When she looked up into the mirror, the green eyes that stared back at her from her own face seemed to smile sadly.

"So you saw, then."

Of course she had. Mabh sent her the visions like clock-work—every time Sonny was successful in one of his deadly pursuits. It was like supernatural spam, straight into Kelley's mental inbox.

"Another one down. Now only three of the Hunt are left . . ." As Kelley's reflection spoke, the features began to alter subtly to become those of a woman with Kelley's same eyes, but older. How much older was impossible to tell. She was ageless, effortlessly beautiful, and more dangerous than anyone Kelley had ever known. Mabh. Her mother. The Faerie Queen of the Autumn Court sighed mournfully and continued as if Kelley weren't glaring daggers at her. "He'll be coming after *me* soon enough, I daresay. . . ." She somehow managed to infuse an artful tremor of fear into the music of her voice. "They'll cage me again like an animal."

"You assume I care," Kelley said flatly as she pushed the damp hair from her forehead and turned her back on the mirror.

"Kelley!" The silky voice turned petulant as a pouty child's. "I'm your mother."

Wearily Kelley plucked a bath towel from the rack by the tub and hung it over the mirror.

"I'll wager you didn't know your boyfriend was such a bloodthirsty little thing when you promised your heart and soul to him," Queen Mabh continued, her voice only slightly muffled by the thick terrycloth. "How's that working for you, darling? Has he broken your heart yet? Men will do that, you know."

"Stow it, *Mom*." Kelley felt her jaw tightening.

"Has he called? Written? Sent a bouquet of ro—"

Behind the towel the glass shattered under the hammer of Kelley's fist, mercifully silencing the sound of her mother's voice in a rain of tinkling shards falling into the sink.

"Right. That's it."

Kelley jumped, startled. She turned to see her roommate, Lady Tyffanwy of the Mere—better known in the mortal realm as Tyff Meyers, model and party-girl supreme—lounging against the doorframe.

"Winslow," she declared, "you need to have some fun."

"Tyff, I—"

"Unh!" Tyff put up a hand. "We're going out."

"But—"

"Kell . . . no offense"—Tyff sighed—"but ever since Smiley hit the road back to the Otherworld, you've become a royal pain in the ass to live with."

"His name is Sonny. And I have not!" Kelley yelped in indignation.

"Have."

"I—"

"Look. Sure. You've been cheerful and chipper and patient and diligent and polite and on time for everything." Tyff turned on her heel and marched to her own room as she spoke, Kelley reluctantly following. "All of which tells me that you're wound tighter than a factory-fresh yo-yo string. Well—also the fact that you just broke our bathroom mirror with punching."

"Sorry abou—"

"Not the issue." Tyff threw open the doors to her vast wardrobe and began chucking bits of designer clubwear over her shoulders at Kelley. "In fact, *that* was the most interesting thing you've done in months. Now get dressed."

The River was an upscale boutique hotel in midtown, but most of the lower floors and lobby space were occupied by club-style lounges and an exotic-cuisine restaurant with, Tyff pointed out, a months-long waiting list. From the outside, it sure didn't look like much, Kelley thought. Inside the hotel, it was a whole different story.

The escalator was the only feature in an otherwise blank white lobby. Kelley stepped aboard the narrow moving stairs in the wake of her roommate, and together they were carried upward through a corridor lit by chartreuse fluorescent lights and into a hall that served as a reception area. It was vast and airy, dark with rich wood on all the walls. The ceiling seemed to disappear into leafy shadows overhead. A long concierge desk, carved with the shape of a twisted tree, was illuminated only by the flickering electric flames of an elaborate crystal chandelier that was festooned with hundreds of holographic images—like photographs, only they shifted and shimmered. As she passed, Kelley thought she saw a face in one of the portraits wink at her. But when she blinked and looked again, the grotesque face just seemed to be leering in general. She quickened her pace to catch up with Tyff, who was checking her jacket at a cloakroom off to one side of the hall. An impossibly thin, white-haired young girl staffed the desk—standing under a stuffed mountain-goat head that Kelley *also* could have sworn winked at her as she handed over her jacket.

Tyff grinned at the look on Kelley's face. "Come on!" she said, and tugged Kelley by the elbow down a long passageway lit, intermittently, at ankle level.

Kelley cast a nervous eye around at the River's patrons and extracted her elbow from Tyff's long-fingered grip. "I don't know about this. . . ."

"Stuff the nerves, Winslow. You said you'd come dancing tonight, and you are *not* backing out. I already told the big guy at the concierge desk not to let you leave without me. And he's really an ogre."

"You mean—"

"I mean a *real* ogre, yeah. He owes me a favor, and he's fairly enthusiastic about wanting to repay it. So he might accidentally break you if you try to go." She shrugged. "Ogres tend to have a little problem with fine motor skills."

"Nice."

"You said you wanted to have fun tonight."

"*You* said I wanted to have fun tonight! That is not the same thing!"

"I'm doing this for both our sakes."

"You're doing this because *you* like dancing. And torment-ing me, apparently."

Tyff ignored Kelley's protests and shoved her gently up a shallow staircase toward the main lounge. The level of illumi-nation in that area was almost blinding by comparison to the entrance—also a bit dizzying. The floor was composed of illu-minated square panels. From the corners garish green, gold, and purple spotlights swept the room, alternately obscuring and revealing an intricate mural on the ceiling—a swirl of leaves and flowers and snaking vines, surrounding a curled abstract female form at the center.

Mismatched furniture gave an eclectic air to the place; white leather settees and high-tech clear Lucite chairs molded into antique shapes stood scattered among several enormous felled tree trunks that lay diagonally across the floor and served as bench seating. Here and there the gilded walls shimmered with waterfall fountains.

Tyff grabbed them a couple of drinks from the long oak bar and led Kelley through a maze of bodies swaying to music. The club was packed, but in the corner Kelley saw a high-backed gilt chair sitting empty, as though reserved and wait-ing for some Hollywood starlet or New York celebutante. She followed Tyff through a set of soaring double doors that led out to a central courtyard overflowing with plants and flowers. April was early for such a profusion of blooms, but the River didn't seem bound by that particular law of nature. The whole place was like one giant, fantastical garden, and Kelley felt a bit like Alice down the rabbit hole—a rabbit hole full of Lost Fae.

Tyff led the way into the center of the courtyard, Kelley following in her wake, trying not to stare too much. The courtyard was lit only by dozens and dozens of candles scattered about in glass holders. The night air wrapped around them like a cashmere sweater—warm, soft, perfumed by flowers. Dancers swayed to the music that came from a band on a raised stage in the corner. A dark-haired Fae with an ethereally beautiful voice sang in a language that Kelley couldn't understand, her soaring tones somehow melding with an operatic score and an urban backbeat.

"I thought Herne's Tavern was where the Lost Fae went to party," Kelley said.

"The Tavern is where the Lost go if they want to get *away* from humanity. The River," Tyff waved a hand at the fantastical surroundings, "is where the Lost come if they want to get up close and personal with humanity!"

Kelley glanced about the place and realized that, in fact, the capacity crowd was equal measures of Fair Folk mixed in with unsuspecting New Yorkers looking to hang out in a hot clubbing spot with the beautiful people. Really beautiful people.

"C'mon!" Tyff shouted in her ear over the clamor. "Let's go see if we can find Titania—you gotta meet the queen!"

Kelley shook her head vigorously. "I really don't think I—I'm not—I'm not dressed to meet royalty, Tyff. . . ."

"You *are* royalty, Winslow."

"I'm still undecided on that point."

"It's not really optional, you know. You just are. And you look fine—obviously—you're wearing my stuff."

It was true. Even though Kelley felt bad from the last time she had borrowed from Tyff's huge wardrobe (they'd had to throw the Galliano dress in the trash, and Kelley still shuddered to think of it) she had to admit that the designer jeans and deep purple top that Tyff had thrust at her back in the apartment suited both her figure and her coloring, and the strappy sandals gave her some extra height that almost made her feel willowy.

"Anyway," Tyff continued, craning her neck to see over the crowd, "Titania's not like the other monarchs."

"What—scary and pathological?"

"You'll *like* her, Kell. She's really cool. Nice, even. And I've already told her all about you."

"She's not *here* here, is she? It's like the mirror thing my mother does, isn't it?" Kelley crossed her arms, determined to be obstinate. "Because I find that horribly creepy. It's like talking to a television set. And having it talk back."

"No, Kelley." Tyff sighed and blew a strand of shining, wheat-gold hair out of her ridiculously blue eyes. With her perfect skin, her hair and her eyes—not to mention the body—Tyff tended to stand out. Even in Manhattan. "She actually comes here. She owns this place."

"She owns the nightclub?"

"The whole hotel, actually. I think she won the land in a card game and then she built a women's residence on it in the

1920s—mostly that was a facade; it was really a sanctuary, a place to stay for all the Seelie girls who'd gotten caught in the mortal realm when your bad-ass dad, King Auberon, shut the Gate."

Kelley frowned. "So Titania still comes and goes as she pleases—even though Faerie like you were stuck here?"

"Yup." Tyff shrugged a sculpted shoulder. "The kings and queens of Faerie aren't exactly bound by closed doors."

"But Mabh was bound—"

"Only *after* she'd already poured most of her power into transforming Herne and his buddies into the unstoppable monstrosity that was the Wild Hunt. Even then it still took the two strongest monarchs to bind one lesser queen and—well, as we all discovered last fall, much to the detriment of a particularly expensive item of my wardrobe—even *that* wasn't anything close to permanent." Tyff's eyes restlessly scanned the crowd. "There she is!" she exclaimed suddenly, and, clamping a hand on Kelley's wrist, dragged her back into the main lounge and over to the thronelike chair that was now occupied by the most stunning creature Kelley had ever laid eyes on.

Titania, the Queen of Summer, was nothing like Kelley had expected. Perhaps it was all the Victorian fairy paintings she'd seen over the years, or the fact that Tyff, a Summer Fae, looked like the ultimate sun-kissed California beach babe. But, whatever she may or may not have expected, Kelley found herself staring. The queen's beauty was utterly exotic. Her flawless complexion was the color of honey and ripe peaches; and her hair, piled high in a cascade on her head, was a rich, dark shade of chocolate, shot through with ruby and bronze highlights. Her regal head was set upon a long, graceful neck, and she wore peacock-hued silks that showed tantalizing flashes of burnished skin when she moved.

With a start Kelley realized that she looked almost exactly like the famous bust of the ancient Egyptian queen Nefertiti. Kelley had only a fleeting moment to make that comparison, though, before Titania turned and her dark gold eyes caught and held Kelley in a stare that felt like standing in a beam of late summer sunlight.

"So *you're* Kelley," she said, her voice fluid and fair as birdsong. "It is such a pleasure to finally meet you—come with me, my dear girl." She gestured to the chair next to her. "Tyffanwy, love—your Queen is parched. Be a dear?"

Tyff smiled and inclined her head gracefully. Then she shot Kelley a wink and flitted off to fetch her queen refreshment.

"All this unpleasantness last Samhain." Titania shook her head. "Such a pity. Such drama. I'm so sorry for you that you had to discover your heritage in such an untidy fashion. I hear that you had something to do with thwarting the risen Hunt?"

"I . . . I was just in the right place at . . . uh . . . the right time, I guess," Kelley stammered.

"I'm sure it was much more than that." Titania smiled.

Kelley thought fleetingly that maybe hanging out with the

Fair Folk might not be so bad after all. Not if there were more Faerie like this. Tyff was right—she did like Titania.

The queen reached out and touched her cheek with real warmth. "You're too modest," she said.

"No. Really!" Kelley laughed. "It was kind of just dumb luck that I didn't wind up getting myself killed!"

"Terrible business." Titania's gaze roamed over the bobbing heads of the crowd. "Who was it, one wonders, who dared to wake the Wild Hunt?"

"You don't know?" Kelley didn't really feel like bad-mouthing Auberon just at that moment, but she wasn't sure what else to say. Her father had been the one to loose the Hunt. He had called the Roan Horse with Mabh's horn. Turned Sonny into a monster . . .